The Ticklemore
Tavern

LIZ DAVIES

CHAPTER 1

VIOLET

'Did you know that gin can be made from potatoes?' Violet asked.

The barman's eyebrows twitched. She thought he looked rather cute.

He said, 'I do know. Salt and vinegar, did you say?'

'Yes, please, and a packet of pork scratchings.'

The man put the snacks on the counter. 'You'd better watch your teeth on those.' He jerked his head at the pork scratchings. 'They're tougher than four-inch nails.'

'Oh, they're not for me; they're for my—' Violet wasn't sure what to refer to Sam as '—my potato man,' she continued.

'You seem to have potatoes on the brain.'

'Potatoes are useful things,' she pointed out.

'Vodka, crisps, men...?'

'Man, singular. And I happen to like potatoes – roast, boiled, chipped, mashed.'

'Gin-ned?'

'Is there such a word?'

'If there isn't, there should be,' the barman said.

She took a sip of her lemonade and lime. The ice rattled gently in the glass as she put it down and reached for the crisps. Munching, she glanced around, swivelling on her stool. Ticklemore wasn't a place she'd visited before. It seemed nice enough, but the Tavern wasn't exactly the sort of pub she was looking for – quaint and characterful, it was very different from the trendy places which typically sold artisan gins. However, it was fairly local and it boasted a surprising array of interesting ales, with curious names such as Wet Mallard and Dog's Backside. Honestly, who thought these names up? Their dark-brown bottled earthiness was a far cry from the clear clean simplicity of her gin.

'I'd have thought you'd have had a gin, considering…' the barman said. 'I'm Logan, by the way.'

'Violet. Pleased to meet you. I'm driving. Can you tell me if the manager is around?'

'I can and he is.'

'May I have a word, do you think?'

'You may.'

Violet waited expectantly for the barman to fetch his boss, but when he remained rooted to the spot, she sighed. '*You're* the manager, aren't you?'

'The licensee.'

'I take it you're a free house?'

'Nope. I expect people to pay for their drinks,' he quipped.

Violet wrinkled her nose at him. 'I haven't heard that one before.'

'Have you not?' He raised his eyebrows.

'I was joking.' She raised hers in response.

Logan wiped the already spotless counter with a cloth

and smiled at her. It made her tummy flutter.

'Do you like gin?' she asked.

'Ah, back to gin again, are we? I do, but I prefer ale.'

'I can tell.' Violet stared pointedly at the array of stubby brown bottles.

'Excuse me.' Logan moved away to serve a customer, giving her a chance to have a proper look at him. Early to mid-thirties, she guessed. Tall, broad shouldered, slim-hipped. Nice forearms. Nice bum. Attractive face – trim jaw, slightly wonky nose, dark floppy hair.

Violet liked eyes; they told you a lot about a person. Logan's were hazel and friendly, direct and crinkly-cornered. She had the impression he smiled often. He had a nice mouth, too, lips neither too fleshy nor too thin. The hint of stubble on his chin gave him a bit of an edgy look, and she wondered if it was deliberate or whether he couldn't be bothered to shave this morning. She guessed it would feel rough and deliciously scratchy.

'You were asking me about gin?' he continued, coming back to her.

'Will it get busy?' There were five people in the bar, counting herself, but it was only eleven-thirty in the morning, and she assumed he'd not long opened up.

'I hope so, it usually does.'

'You serve meals?'

'Yes. Would you like to see a menu?'

'Maybe another time.' She indicated her half-eaten packet of crisps. Eating crisps in pubs in lieu of proper meals had recently become an occupational hazard. Maybe she'd have a bite to eat at the next place. Or buy a sandwich on the way. A sandwich would be cheaper. 'I've got some samples in my car. Would you like to try a couple?'

'Samples of what?' He looked amused.

'Gin, of course.'

'*Of course*, silly me. Why do you have samples of gin in your car?'

'For publicans like yourself to try.'

'So, you're a gin salesperson?'

Violet didn't see herself as a salesperson, but needs must, and there was no one else to do the horrid job. 'More of a distiller,' she said, then her attention was caught by an older woman, possibly late sixties or early seventies, emerging from a door which she assumed led to a kitchen. It was one of those doors that swung both ways and she caught a glimpse of shiny stainless steel beyond.

Logan glanced up, following the direction of her gaze.

'Logan!' The woman's voice was sharp. 'Franklin needs some wine for the beef bourguignon.'

'Is that what's on the menu?' Violet asked.

'It's one of today's specials.' He raised his voice to say, 'He can have the cabernet instead, Mum.'

'Don't let the French hear you say that,' Violet joked. She was under the impression that bourguignon should be made exclusively with burgundy. A French chef would have a fit at the sacrilege of using a different wine.

'Burgundy is too expensive,' Logan said out of the side of his mouth.

The woman was still standing there, glaring. 'Can you take it to him?'

Logan sighed. 'I won't be a moment,' he said to Violet.

'Good. I want to tell you more about my gin.'

'I thought you might say that.'

Violet finished her crisps and licked her fingers. The bar was filling up, and Logan's mother gave her a final glare and went to serve a customer. Idly, Violet wondered what all that was about, then dismissed the woman from her mind as Logan returned.

He leant against the counter, his back nearly brushing the optics behind him, and folded his arms. 'So then, you distil gin?'

'I do. Wonderful gin, with amazing botanicals.'

His gaze was level and steady, holding hers. Then he pushed himself away from the counter. 'Mum, can you hold the fort for a few minutes?'

'Why, where are you going?'

'Outside. I won't be long. Hi, Scarlet.'

This last was said to a young woman who had swooped in, shedding her coat as she entered and draping it over the stand near the door. She and Logan swapped places, Scarlet stowing her bag underneath the bar, Logan coming out from behind it.

When Violet slid off her stool and stood up, she realised he was taller than her initial assessment, and she only came up to his shoulder. She liked tall men; all of her previous boyfriends had been tall. Violet acknowledged she had a type, and Logan was it.

Stepping smartly in front of her, he opened the door and gestured for her to go through. Although she was more than capable of opening her own doors (she was no shrinking violet, despite her name) she appreciated the gesture. Her dad always said good manners didn't cost anything, and she thought he might approve of the publican.

'This is me,' she said, coming to a halt beside a van.

'It's purple.' He was eyeing her lovely van with amazement.

'Violet, actually.'

'I used to like those Parma Violet sweets when I was a kid.'

'I didn't. I hated them. My Parma Violet gin is pretty good though. Want to try some?'

'Go on, then.'

Violet unlocked the van and opened the rear doors. As vans went, it was only a small one, but it suited her needs. 'I usually bring my samples to a pub landlord, not the other way round,' she told him, lifting a bottle out of a crate.

Violet loved the delicate purple shade of the liquid inside. It was the best thing about this particular gin, in her opinion. She hadn't been lying when she'd said she didn't like the taste of Parma Violets; however, it was one of her most popular flavours, and she was first and foremost a business person.

The bottle was half full and she unscrewed the top, poured a mouthful into a small plastic beaker hardly bigger than the ones that came free with cough medicine, and handed it to Logan.

He took it and swirled the liquid in the beaker, holding it up to the light. He had nice hands, she noticed; long-fingered with neatly trimmed nails. She had a disconcerting moment when she imagined those hands on her body, before she snapped back to what she was supposed to be doing – selling gin.

Logan sniffed, then took a sip. She liked that he didn't knock the whole lot back in one go, the way some people did. He was taking the time to taste it.

'Mmm. This is lovely. Delicate. It balances the juniper well.' He took another sip, then picked the bottle up and read the label. *'oriGINal Gin.'* he read. 'Clever.'

'I wanted *VirGIN*, but some famous guy had already

bagged it. I quite liked *imaGINe* too, but I did a survey and *oriGINal* won.'

'Who is your demographic?' Logan asked.

'Female, mostly. Young. Although as flavoured gins become more popular, the age is creeping up, and men are also discovering they like it.' She watched Logan studying the label. It was the same colour as the van, with a heart outlined in cream (although she preferred to call the colour stone) and her brand name emblazoned through it.

'Girly,' he said.

Violet lifted her chin. 'I happen to like girly.'

'So do I.' His eyes held a hint of mischief.

'Want to try another flavour?' she asked to cover the attraction she felt – she was here to sell gin, not to flirt.

'I think I should. I like to taste what I'm buying.'

As she opened a bottle of spiced pear and handed him a fresh beaker, she said, 'Does that mean you've sampled all those ales?'

'Of course, I have. How can I advise my customers if I haven't tried them myself? I expect you've tried your Parma Violet gin?'

'I had to, considering I made it.'

'Are all these flavours down to you?' He gestured at the crate which contained twelve distinctly separate gins.

'And more. I've just brought along the most popular flavours today.'

'Where are you based?'

'Near Hay-on-Wye.'

'That's not far. Why haven't I heard of you before now?'

'I'm only just starting out.'

'How many different flavours have you got?'

'Twenty-three.'

'That's a decent number.'

'It's decent gin.'

'It certainly is. Have you got a list?'

Violet handed him a sheet of A5 paper listing all the flavours and prices. He stared at it for a moment, and she guessed he was working out the approximate cost he'd charge for a shot, against the price of a bottle and deciding whether it was cost effective to stock her wares.

'Which ones are your most popular?' he asked.

'These twelve.' She patted the crate.

'What's the turnaround between placing an order and delivery?'

She pointed to another crate. 'Two minutes? I can be quicker if you're in a hurry. I carry a stock of all of them in the van.'

Logan burst out laughing, and Violet giggled.

'You've got yourself a deal,' he said, still chuckling, and held out his hand.

Violet wasn't at all prepared for the effect that touching him had on her. Oh my! Her heart stuttered and her mouth was suddenly drier than the driest vermouth as he clasped her hand. She hoped he'd felt it too, because for the first time in ages she found herself attracted to a man.

Let's just hope he's not already taken, she thought. But surely a guy this gorgeous must already have a woman in his life?

Before she left she intended to find out.

CHAPTER 2

LOGAN

Logan's eyes widened and he quickly released Violet's hand. Woah, the twinge in his gut at her touch had been totally unexpected, despite him being seriously attracted to her. He smiled rather nervously, his previous self-confidence knocked askew as his gaze caught hers and held it.

The seconds ticked by.

Oh boy, this was new. Nice, though. Different.

She was different. Sparky, lively, pretty. He couldn't tear himself away. Violet had held his attention from the moment she'd stepped inside the Tavern, alone and brimming with confidence.

A car pulling up next to her van shattered his mood, and he dropped his gaze to the crate of gin and cleared his throat. Before he could gather himself enough to make a move, Violet beat him to it. She hefted the crate, cradling it to her chest.

'Let me,' he offered.

'I can manage.'

'I dare say you can, but I'm stronger than you.'

'I dare say you are,' she shot back at him with a twinkling grin.

Her lively attitude fascinated him, almost as much as the purple hair bouncing around her shoulders, her large blue eyes, lightly tanned skin, and full pink lips.

Violet marched across the car park, heading for the pub's main entrance, and Logan hurried after her, admiring the view. Not only was she incredibly pretty, she also had a luscious figure. Captivated, he watched her hips sway.

'Do you mind getting the door?' she asked.

'What? Oh sorry. Of course.' Logan darted in front of her, holding it open to allow her through. A tantalising perfume reached him, and he almost gave in to the impulse to sniff her. She smelt wonderful.

With his heart beating faster than a brief walk across the car park warranted, he followed her inside. For once, he took no notice of his little empire – his attention was fully and utterly on the petite woman who was currently sliding the crate onto the bar.

As she turned to him, he was struck again by her gorgeousness.

'How old are you?' he blurted.

Violet raised her eyebrows. 'Twenty-nine.'

'I'm thirty-three.'

'Congratulations.'

'It's not my birthday.' It felt like it, though, and the best present he could imagine was standing in front of him with a bemused expression on her face.

'Were you thinking of asking me for ID?' she joked. 'There's no need: I'm not the one buying the alcohol – you are.'

Scarlet walked over to see what was going on. 'Is that

gin? Are we going to be selling it? She picked up one of the bottles. 'Ooh, salted caramel. Sounds divine. I can't wait to try it.'

'You've sold me *salted caramel flavoured* gin?' Logan made a face. It sounded awful.

'Don't knock it until you try it,' Violet told him. Turning her attention to Scarlet, she said, 'If you like that flavour, you'll love the toffee apple one.'

'Is there a bottle of that in here?' Scarlet picked up another one and read the label. 'Spiced pear?'

'That's part of my autumn collection. I've got a hazelnut flavour, too, and I'm experimenting with pumpkin.'

Scarlet looked thoughtful. 'Can you put anything you want in gin?'

'More or less. Whether it tastes good though is another matter.'

'What's gin made of?' Scarlet asked.

Violet's lips quirked into a wry smile, and she shot Logan a look that made his heart skip a beat.

'I make mine from potatoes,' she said.

Logan let out a groan. 'Don't get her started on potatoes. Sorry, I haven't introduced you. Violet, this is Scarlet Howells, one of my bar staff. Scarlet, this is Violet...?'

'Archer,' Violet supplied. 'I own a distillery. I'll have to give you a tour sometime.'

Logan was tempted to take her up on the offer, but before he could pin her down his mother hoved into view, and she didn't look happy.

'Are you going to spend all day chatting, or are you going to do some work? You've got a pub to run, you know! Scarlet, there's a man waiting to be served, and the couple on table six are ready to order.' His mother glared at them, including Violet in her admonishment.

'Sorry, Marie.' Scarlet hurried to the other end of the bar.

'I'd better be off,' Violet said. 'I've got a few more places to visit before I finish for the day.'

'Have you got a business card?' he asked.

'I certainly have.' She handed one to him. 'I'd wish you good luck with the gin, but you won't need it. Your customers will love it.'

He watched her leave, and the Tavern seemed dimmer without her in it.

'Who was *she*?' Marie demanded.

'Her name is Violet and she owns a gin distillery.'

'What? *Her*? She doesn't look old enough to vote. And she's got purple hair.'

'She's twenty-nine,' he said, his attention still on the door. He was half-hoping she'd walk through it again. 'And hair colour has nothing whatsoever to do with making gin.'

'Hmph. You looked cosy. What did she want and what's that?'

'Twelve bottles of different flavoured gins.'

His mother eyed the crate suspiciously. 'The punters won't like it.'

'You said that about the artisan ales.'

She jerked her head at the gin. 'It's a niche market.'

'Gin? Hardly. It's been around for centuries, in one form or another.'

'You know what I mean; the Tavern is a village pub not a trendy wine bar in London.'

Logan stifled a sigh. He'd had a similar conversation with her when he'd started stocking the artisan ales. He still did occasionally, despite the account book showing how popular those little brown bottles were.

'Mum, I know what I'm doing.'

The look she gave him told him she didn't think he did, and she followed it up with a snort.

The door opened and Logan glanced up from his pint-pulling. When he saw who it was, his heart skipped a beat.

'Do you want me to put this on your tab?' Logan asked the customer he was serving, placing the drink on the bar.

'Yes, please. We're sitting over there.'

He waited for the man to return to his table before speaking to Violet. 'Forgotten something?' he quipped to cover his sudden nervousness,

Violet smiled at him. It made his heart leap. 'I forgot to ask, are you married?'

Logan was vaguely aware of his mother's sharp intake of breath and Scarlet's snigger. 'No, I'm not.' Heat crept into his cheeks and he wondered if he looked as flustered as he felt.

'Do you have a significant other?' she continued.

He shook his head, dazed.

'Great! See ya!' she cried, then she was gone in a swirl of bouncing curls and tantalising perfume.

'The brazen madam.' Marie's mouth was set in a firm line and her hands were planted on her hips.

Logan ignored her. His mind was too full of Violet Archer.

'I think it's sweet,' Scarlet said, earning herself a sour look from Marie.

Logan, knowing how acerbic his mother could be, jumped in before she had a chance to say anything further. 'Scarlet, can you pop some optics on those bottles and find somewhere prominent to display them?' He indicated the crate of gin.

His mother made another dismissive noise, scowled at the crate, then stalked off.

Logan appreciated his mother's help and he knew she loved being in the Tavern, but sometimes she could be a little overbearing. She had a tendency to act as though she was the one whose name was above the door, not him. That was one of the problems with mixing business with family – lines often became blurred.

As Scarlet worked, rearranging bottles of spirits to make room for the gin, she asked, 'Is Violet a friend of yours?'

'Not at all. I only met her today. She came in to promote her distillery.'

'She seemed nice.'

She most certainly did, he thought. Pretty, too.

Scarlet gave him a sideways glance. 'I think she liked you.' She wiped a cloth over one of the bottles, and Logan poured a glass of cider for a customer. The bar was filling up and the lunchtime orders were coming in thick and fast. The Tavern might only be a village pub, but it was popular and had a reputation for good food. Ticklemore lay on the edge of the Brecon Beacons National Park and saw regular footfall from hikers and tourists travelling to and from the area, and increasing numbers of them popped into the Tavern for a drink or a bite to eat.

'Are you going to take Violet up on her offer?' Scarlet continued when there was a lull. 'I think you should.'

'What offer?' Marie demanded, dirty glasses in her hands. She put them down with a rattle.

Logan groaned inwardly. His mum had ears like a bat. 'Violet invited me to visit her distillery.'

'I don't expect that's all she's inviting you to do,' his mother sniped, coming to stand next to him.

Scarlet who was on the other side of the bar, collecting more dirty glasses, smirked, and Logan sent her a warning look. 'She's very pretty,' Scarlet continued, ignoring the hint.

Logan narrowed his eyes at her, but it was too late, the damage was done.

'Pretty is what pretty does,' his mother retorted cryptically. 'Besides, I didn't think she was anything special to look at.'

Logan thought Violet was very special indeed.

'You could do far better than her,' his mother was saying.

'I've only just met her,' Logan protested with a laugh. Crikey, his mum had already shoehorned him into a relationship when he'd only just met the girl. He put an arm around Marie and smiled fondly. 'No one has ever been good enough for me in your opinion, have they, Mum? That's probably why I'm still single – you scare them off.' He chuckled. 'Remember that girl who lived near Abergavenny? Charlotte? She was terrified of you.'

Thankfully he hadn't been too into her, otherwise he might have been annoyed that his mother had been so unfriendly. Poor Charlotte, she hadn't deserved his mother's treatment of her, and it was one of the reasons he'd ended the relationship. Besides, at the time he'd been working all hours to build the business up and hadn't had much time for romance.

But he had the time now, didn't he? With a full complement of bar staff, two damned good chefs, plus his mother on hand to make sure everything ran smoothly when he wasn't around, surely he could afford to have some time off now and again?

'I think I will take Violet up on her offer,' he said. 'I

haven't visited a brewery or a distillery in ages.'

Scarlet sniggered. 'I don't think it's her gin you want to sample.'

'Scarlet!' Marie snapped. 'That's enough.'

The barmaid bit her lip and Logan knew she was trying not to laugh. Scarlet wasn't in the least bit intimidated by his mother. There had been a bit of an atmosphere when she had first started working for him, Marie not seeing the need for any more bar staff.

Logan suspected part of her animosity was because his mother had thought he fancied Scarlet. She'd pointed out to him on Scarlet's first day, that fraternising with the staff was never a good idea. When he'd informed her he had no intention of fraternising with anyone, staff or otherwise, he didn't think his mum had believed him. Scarlet was young and attractive, and had a certain friendliness about her that his mum had mistaken for flirting. She was also in a steady relationship with a woman called Jemma, and Logan suspected that the little nugget of information might have had something to do with his mother finally accepting her, than her being a good worker, reliable, punctual, and friendly with the customers.

As soon as Marie realised Logan wasn't Scarlet's type, she'd mellowed and the two women got on well enough now – except for those times when Scarlet wound her up.

Today was one of those times, and all because of a lovely young woman called Violet Archer.

'I'll give her a call and arrange a date,' he said.

Scarlet grinned, mouthing 'date' at him and waggling her eyebrows behind his mother's back. He shook his head at her.

'You're needed here,' his mother pointed out. 'You

haven't got time to traipse about the country.'

'She's based near Hay-on-Wye. It's hardly traipsing.' It was less than half an hour away.

Marie let out a deep sigh, put a hand to her forehead and pulled a face. 'I think I'll go and have a lie down – I can feel a migraine coming on.'

Logan stared at her with concern. His mum was prone to debilitating headaches that could put her out of action for days. 'You haven't had one of those for ages. Can I get you anything? Do you have any of those tablets the doctor gave you?' He took her by the elbow to steady her. 'I'll pop you home in the van.'

'You've got enough to do here. I'll be fine. The walk might help, and even if it doesn't, it's not far.'

Logan collected her bag and coat from the office out the back, and accompanied her to the door. 'Are you sure you'll be OK walking home? It won't take me two minutes to drive you.'

'I'm sure.' She gave him a weak smile, and his heart went out to her. She could be incredibly stubborn when she wanted and he knew better than to insist.

Maybe it was time he bit the bullet and asked her to come and live with him at the Tavern? The pub was a three-storey building, with the top floor given over to his private quarters. The flat had three bedrooms so there'd be plenty of room. But – and this was the issue – he loved having his own space. He and his mum had lived in Ticklemore all their lives, just the two of them in the little terraced house his mum still lived in. When he'd bought the Tavern six years ago, it had been such a relief to move out (sorry, Mum) that he didn't think he could go back to living with her again.

He loved his mum to bits and would do anything for her,

but her whole world had revolved around him since his father had left when Logan was five years old, and sometimes the level of attention and care she lavished on her only child was stifling.

She'd been incredibly upset when he'd moved out but she'd got over it, especially since she saw him every day. Despite his protestations that she should be taking it easy, she insisted on helping him in the pub, and she seemed to enjoy it. Mostly; apart from her complaints about her bunions, her bad back, and the headaches that he'd thought had gone away but were now back with a vengeance. Once again he wondered if he should suggest she moved into the Tavern. At least he'd be able to keep an eye on her at times like this, because he knew he was going to worry about her for the rest of the day.

He'd call in to check on her after the lunchtime rush had died down. Hopefully she'd have taken some of the tablets the doctor had prescribed, and she'd be feeling better.

But, he found, as he waited on tables and bantered with the customers, it wasn't his mum who was taking centre stage in his mind – it was Violet Archer. He'd leave it a couple of days until his mother was back on her feet, then he'd give Violet a call.

He didn't think he'd ever looked forward to visiting a distillery as much as he was looking forward to visiting *oriGINal Gin*.

But his eagerness had nothing whatsoever to do with the gin.

CHAPTER 3

VIOLET

'How did you get on yesterday?' Rory checked one of the tanks, then straightened up to look at her.

'Pretty good.' Violet shrugged. 'Got seven pubs on board and that new restaurant I was telling you about in Hereford. One pub took a full crate of the autumn flavours.'

She couldn't be sure, but something in her voice must have alerted her brother, because when she met his gaze, he was studying her thoughtfully.

'Which pub was that?' he asked.

'The Tavern, in Ticklemore.'

'I've heard of it; Ticklemore, I mean, not the pub. It was in the news a while back – something about a painting being discovered in a shop there, and being sold for a fortune. It's supposed to be nice.'

'The painting?'

'The village. Has something happened, you look odd?'

'Odd? Thanks, Rory.' Something had happened, but she wasn't going to tell her brother that she hadn't been able to get Logan Cassidy out of her mind. He'd tease her mercilessly.

'Dreamy, like,' he added.

Oh, Violet had dreamt, all right. She'd dreamt of the publican's hazel eyes, his quick-to-smile lips, the way he'd looked at her. She was glad she'd gone back in and asked him whether he was spoken for. And she still couldn't believe she'd had the courage. After she'd fled back to her van, her cheeks blazing and her heart pounding, she'd collapsed into the driving seat and had given in to a fit of nervous giggling.

What must Logan have thought of her? Violet hoped she hadn't blown it with him. She had a habit of being blunt and it didn't always stand her in good stead.

'How's the pumpkin flavour coming along?' she asked, changing the subject.

'Just need to add the water, and it'll be ready for bottling.'

'Good, I'll get started on it later.'

Violet and Rory had distinct and separate roles, although they could, and did, stand in for each other when necessary. Both of them knew the distilling process intimately, from start to finish, but they each had their preferences and their different skill sets. Rory was ace at turning raw vegetable matter (in this case, potatoes) into ethanol; Violet's talents lay in infusing the ethanol with juniper first – to make it into gin – and then adding various botanicals to give the spirit a unique taste. Some botanicals worked brilliantly, others not so well, but she didn't know until she tried, and she kept meticulous notes. She'd recently been working hard on a range of autumn flavours, and pumpkin was the final one.

'I've, um, invited someone to have a look around the distillery,' she said, cautiously. She didn't want to share the information with Rory, but he was just as likely to answer the phone as she, and she felt he should be aware, just in case. Logan probably wouldn't call. He almost certainly wouldn't. Why would he? But just in case he did.

'Who?' Rory asked.

'The guy who owns the Tavern.'

'Why? Are we thinking of doing tours? That's a good idea.'

It certainly was, and she knew of several breweries and distilleries who opened their doors, showing the public what went on behind the scenes, and giving them taster sessions. She also knew of a few who allowed customers to infuse their own gins.

'Maybe,' she said, her thoughts more on the man she'd invited than on a new and possibly lucrative business opportunity.

'You fancy him, don't you?' Rory said. 'Is that what this is about?'

'I don't,' she protested. 'The invitation wasn't just for him, it was for his staff too. Scarlet was asking how gin is made and—'

'Scarlet? Violet? He's got a damned rainbow going on.' Rory chuckled. 'What's his name? Indigo? Jett? Red?' Her brother was positively chortling.

Violet frowned. 'Logan.'

'That's a colour – loganberries are red, aren't they?' He snorted with laughter.

'Shut up, Rory.'

He thought he was so funny, when in reality, her brother was a pain in the backside. 'If he calls, tell him I'll ring him back,' she instructed.

'I can show him around, if you like?'

'Don't you dare!'

'I was right – you do fancy him.'

'I'm going to see a man about some potatoes,' she said. 'I'll be back later to bottle the pumpkin.'

His laughter followed her as she strode out of the shed. That was the problem with working so closely with a member of your family; they often knew you as well as you knew yourself. Better. She and Logan were only eighteen months apart in age – Rory being the eldest, although you wouldn't believe it by the way he acted sometimes – and were very close. They had to be in order to run a business together. Occasionally though, she wished she'd set it up on her own. Today was one of those days.

Leaving her brother smirking, Violet made the short journey to Sam's farm. Sam provided the distillery with all the potatoes it needed and, as it was coming to the end of the summer and therefore the end of harvest time for the root crop, she wanted to ensure oriGINal Gin had enough stock to last them through the winter and early spring. With the business growing rapidly, although still very small scale, she felt she needed all the potatoes she could lay her hands on.

Making a mental note to speak to Rory about the possibility of taking someone on to help, she got out of the van and stretched. The air was warm, with a gentle breeze, and the fields and trees in the wide valley of the River Wye were green and lush – a brief hiatus before the first breath of winter.

Sam's farm was diverse, growing a range of organic fruit and vegetables, and they also kept some goats. One of them was in the farmyard looking at her.

'Are you supposed to be out here on your own?' she

asked it.

'No, she isn't,' Sam said, hurrying over to shoo the goat into a nearby barn. 'She's worse than Houdini. I had tethered her, but she chewed through the rope. It wouldn't be so bad if she wasn't the ringleader, but where she goes the others follow.'

'As long as it's not into my potatoes,' Violet joked.

'I hope not, too! Potatoes are part of the deadly nightshade group of plants and are poisonous to goats. Fancy a cuppa? I'm gasping.'

'I'd love one.'

She followed Sam into the house and was greeted by a Border terrier bitch and her five puppies in a cardboard box in the kitchen. 'Oh, how gorgeous.' Violet knelt and picked one up. 'How old are they?'

'Four weeks.'

'I want one,' she declared, cuddling the little scrap close to her and inhaling the wonderful smell of puppy. 'I want all of them.'

'They're spoken for,' Sam said, 'but if I ever breed from her again, you can have first dibs.'

Violet returned the puppy to its mother. 'Before I forget, I brought you something.' She took the packet of pork scratchings out of her bag and threw them towards him. Sam caught it deftly, then handed her a chipped mug of builder's tea. Violet sipped it.

'To what do I owe the pleasure?' he asked, watching her over the rim of his own mug. 'You're not here just to bring me pork scratchings.'

'This is business, I'm afraid.'

'Darn it, and I hoped it was a social call. All you want me for is my spuds.'

Violet laughed. 'I quite like your other veggies, too,' she told him. Sam's family had a regular stall in the Thursday market in Hay-on-Wye, where they sold a proportion of what they grew. Like oriGINal Gin, Ten Trees Farm was a family-run business, and his sisters and mother usually manned the stall.

'Where is everyone?' she asked. Apart from the bleating of the recaptured goat, the farm was quiet.

'In the poly tunnels,' Sam said, 'picking anything that's ripe for the market tomorrow.' He glanced at the old clock on the kitchen wall and Violet guessed he was probably needed.

'I'll be quick,' she said, getting a pen and a notepad out of her bag.

'You don't have to be.'

Something in his voice made her glance at him but before either of them could say anything further, his mum bustled in.

'Violet, how lovely to see you. Any more where that came from?' She pointed at her son's mug of tea.

'I'll make you one,' he said. 'You sit down. How's the picking going?'

'Another hour yet,' Gretchen said, sitting down with a groan. 'I'm getting too old for this.'

'Nonsense!' her son declared. 'What are you – sixty?'

'Cheeky so-and-so. I'm fifty-eight. Anyway, how are you, dear?' This last was aimed at Violet.

'Good, thanks, and you?'

'Can't complain. Thanks, love.' Gretchen accepted the mug from Sam with a grateful smile. 'Here about the potatoes, are you? How's business? Got any more gin for me to try?'

'As a matter of fact, I have.' Violet withdrew a bottle from her bag. 'Elderberry.'

'Mmm, sounds delicious. Remind me to give you a veg box before you go.'

Violet smiled. She loved Gretchen's veg boxes; they were packed full of whatever was in season, and Violet had fun coming up with different recipes depending on what was in the box.

The three of them had a chat whilst they drank their tea, then Gretchen went back to her harvesting, leaving Violet and Sam alone.

There was a rather odd silence for a moment, before Violet pulled herself together and reached for her pad and pen again.

They had just finished discussing the distillery's next delivery of potatoes, and Sam was saying, 'Do you fancy going—?' when his mum walked back into the kitchen with a wooden box in her hands.

'Here you go, love. You can bring the empty box back next time you come.' Gretchen put the box on the kitchen table, partly obscuring Sam's face.

Violet peered around some wavy carrot tops. 'You were saying?'

'Um, it doesn't matter.' Sam looked embarrassed.

'I'm sorry, love,' his mum said, placing a hand on his shoulder. 'Was I interrupting something?' Her expression was hopeful, but Sam shook his head.

'Pity, we could do with someone who makes gin in the family.'

'Mum!' Sam's cheeks turned crimson. 'Sorry,' he mouthed at Violet.

Violet grinned and got to her feet. You could always rely

on family to embarrass you, she thought – look at her and Rory. 'I'd better be off. I've got some pumpkin gin to bottle. Shall I bring you a sample, next time?'

Gretchen's face lit up. 'Yes, please!' She turned to Sam, nudging him with her arm. 'Why can't you find a nice girl like Violet? It's about time you settled down – I want some grandkids before I'm too old to enjoy them.'

'No sign of your girls getting married?' Violet asked, trying her best to deflect the conversation away from poor Sam, who looked mortified.

'Kirsty is talking about going to university – doesn't want to spend her life with her hands in the dirt, was the way she described it – and she ditched her last boyfriend. Nice lad, too…' The woman's sigh was wistful. 'And Libby says her and Walter are fine as they are. She says they're too young to settle down. As if! She's twenty-seven, hardly a teenager. How old are you, if you don't mind me asking?'

'Twenty-nine.'

'Any chance of you settling down?'

'Hardly! I don't even have a boyfriend.'

Gretchen sent Sam a meaningful look. Sam winced.

'Thanks for the tea, and the veggie box,' Violet said, putting her mug in the sink and reaching for the box.

'Sam will help you out to the car with it, won't you Sam?' Another meaningful look from Gretchen accompanied the suggestion.

When they were outside, Sam groaned. 'I'm sorry, I don't know what's got into her. As soon as I hit my thirtieth birthday, all she's talked about is me finding a "nice girl". You wouldn't believe how many times she's tried to set me up with one of her cronies' daughters. It's getting embarrassing.'

'That's OK. She makes me laugh.'

'She makes me want to cry,' Sam replied, mournfully. 'As I was about to say—'

'Violet, take these.' Gretchen dashed out of the door and across the yard, a bunch of flowers in her hand. 'Sam, you can give her these.' His mother thrust the flowers at him. 'Tell her they're out of the garden.'

'She's standing right here, Mum. She can hear you.' Sam rolled his eyes.

Violet took the flowers, trying not to giggle. It was a breath of fresh air coming to Ten Trees Farm, and she always went away with a warm glow in her heart and a smile on her lips.

As she drove back to the distillery, though, something Gretchen had said played on her mind.

It was true, she didn't have a boyfriend. But she wanted one. And she knew just who she would like it to be.

Watch out, Logan Cassidy…

CHAPTER 4

LOGAN

'You won't make any money if you keep giving drinks away,' Marie said in Logan's ear, making him jump.

'It's called a loss leader, Mum, and I'm only handing out thimble-sized amounts. Would you like to try some?' he asked two women who were passing. He was standing outside the Tavern a few days after he'd bought his first bottles of gin from Violet, giving free samples of variously flavoured alcohol to anyone who passed by and who looked interested and old enough. 'This is Purple Heather.' He showed the women the bottle, and they exchanged glances and nodded.

Logan poured a small amount into two tiny plastic tumblers and handed them to the ladies, then avidly awaited their verdict.

'That's lovely,' one of the women said. 'I don't normally drink gin, but I'd drink that.'

'If you'd prefer something a bit sweeter, how about this?' He held up a bottle of Dark Cherry. The liquid inside was the most glorious shade of deep red.

'I'll be blotto if we keep this up,' the second woman said, licking her lips after trying a sample. 'I'll take a bottle of that.'

'Sorry, I don't have a spare. You can pop into the Tavern for another drink, if you want, but I'm afraid I'll have to charge you for it.' He laughed, to soften the blow. 'You're not local, are you?'

'We're from Stroud. We've been hiking in the Black Mountains and thought we'd stop off in Ticklemore – such a cute name, by the way! – for a meal before we headed home. The pub doesn't happen to serve food, does it?'

'As a matter of fact, it does,' he said. 'We've just started serving for the evening, so if you'd like to find a table someone will be over shortly.'

'Who's on today?' his mother asked, after the ladies had gone inside.

'Me, of course, Scarlet, and Wayne.'

Marie let out a sigh. 'I'd better give you a hand.'

'How is your migraine?' he asked. She needn't help at all – they would manage perfectly well – but he knew she'd insist.

Marie hesitated. 'Oh, um, better, thanks.'

'Don't you think you should take it easy? You looked awful yesterday.' His mum's headaches had been known to last for several days, so he was surprised to see her up and about just twenty-four hours later. He'd wanted to pop in this morning, but when he'd phoned she'd said she was still in bed and for him not to bother. After checking that she had everything she needed, he'd set to work changing barrels and restocking shelves and fridges. Then he'd taken a trip to the market to pick up the things on the list that Franklin had left for him. Franklin was Logan's head chef, and he was the one who organised the menu and the kitchen. Logan felt honoured his chef trusted him to buy good quality ingredients; however, the man always chose the cuts of meat himself.

After Logan had been to the market it was nearly time to open up, and then what with lunches and wanting to promote the new selection of gin, he hadn't had a moment to himself. And he'd yet to phone Violet and arrange to visit her distillery. He hoped he hadn't imagined the spark between them the other day, and that she didn't make offers like that to the owner of every premises she went to.

His mother was staring at him with a pained expression on her face.

'Did you hear what I said, Mum? You need to take it easy.'

'How can I when you're rushed off your feet? Mind you, you wouldn't be so busy if you weren't messing about with this.' She glared at the trestle table and its contents.

'There has been loads of interest in it,' he replied, defensively.

'What have you got here, then?' a familiar voice asked, and Logan turned to see Hattie Jenkins peering at the bottles of gin.

'I'm thinking of stocking some flavoured gins,' he told the old lady. His mother made a dismissive noise behind him.

'Let's have a taste. What's this one?' Hattie jabbed a finger at the Parma Violet.

'That's Parma Violet flavour,' he said. 'Tastes exactly like the sweets but with an added kick.'

'It's a load of nonsense, if you ask me,' his mother snorted, as he poured Hattie a tot.

'Doesn't look like he's asking you at all,' Hattie replied. She knocked the contents of the tumbler back in one go and smacked her lips. 'Bloody lovely, that. I see what you mean about the kick. What about that one?'

'That's Plum and Pomegranate.'

Hattie held her tumbler out and Logan poured a small amount into it. Hattie continued to hold out the tumbler. 'That's not enough to wet a bee's whistle,' she said. 'Fill it up, there's a good boy.'

Logan did as he was told. There was no point arguing with Hattie, as he'd found out to his cost. She might be eighty but she had more get up and go than most women half her age. She certainly had more energy and zest for life than his mum. He'd never forget the time when she had persuaded him to break into Alfred Miller's shed and steal all the wooden toys he'd made. It was for a good reason and Alfred and Hattie were now a couple, but it could have gone very wrong indeed and it might have cost him his licence.

Hattie drank the Plum and Pomegranate in one mouthful, and grinned. 'I suppose I can't try them all?'

'You can if you pay for them,' Marie said, and Hattie pulled a face at her.

'Spoilsport.'

'The Tavern isn't a charity.'

'What do you know about charity, Marie Cassidy? You've not got a charitable bone in your body.' Hattie's chin jutted out and Logan could tell she was spoiling for an argument.

'If that's what two mouthfuls of gin does to you, you're going back on the sherry,' he warned Hattie, his tone joking. 'And it's called marketing, Mum.'

'It's called giving away your profits,' she retorted. 'It

won't sell anyway.'

Hattie smirked. 'You need to speculate to accumulate. And he will sell it, if the rest of the flavours are as good as these two. Does that say Raspberry Ripple?' She smiled hopefully as she pointed to the label on yet another bottle.

'It does, and yes, you can try it.' Logan unscrewed the top on the bottle and ignored his mother's sigh.

'I'd better get inside if you're going to waste your time out here. Someone has to wait on tables,' Marie grumbled.

'Mum, we can manage. Go home and rest.'

Too late; Marie was pushing the door open, her retreating back rigid.

'Stubborn woman,' Logan muttered under his breath.

'*Can* you manage?' Hattie asked.

'Yes, but my mother is adamant I can't – and before you ask, I'm not going to take on an apprentice.' A few months ago Hattie had got a bee in her bonnet about local business owners giving school leavers a chance by taking them on as apprentices. She'd persuaded a fair few, but not Logan. As he'd pointed out, anyone working behind his bar should be eighteen, otherwise the rules and regulations were too confusing.

'You can employ someone over eighteen, though, can't you?' Hattie suggested, gazing into her empty plastic tumbler as if wondering where the contents had gone.

'I suppose I could.' It was a good idea. It would mean his mum wouldn't feel obliged to help when she clearly wasn't well. 'It'll give me a bit more time, too,' he added. 'I haven't had a minute to myself today.' And he certainly hadn't found enough time to phone Violet.

'You could spend it doing more marketing,' Hattie chortled. She held out her tumbler for a top-up and pointed to the Apple and Cinnamon flavour. 'There's a theme here,' she said, drinking more slowly this time so Logan hoped there was a fair chance she might actually taste it.

Lucas said, 'Violet, the woman who makes the gin, said it was her autumn collection. She's right, I suppose, although I'm not entirely sure the Parma Violet one fits. She did say she was working on a pumpkin one.'

Hattie squinted at him, the folds around her eyes deepening. Logan hoped she'd be able to see straight to walk home, although he didn't think she'd had quite enough to drink to make her that squiffy.

'I've got an idea,' she said slowly, and Logan groaned. Hattie's ideas were legendary for being off the wall (although they usually tended to end up well) and creating work for other people.

'What?' he asked, a tad reluctantly.

'How about having an autumn theme in the pub, as a build up to Halloween and Bonfire Night? You could pimp your gin and have an autumn menu to go alongside.'

Did he just hear the words "pimp your gin" come out of an old woman's mouth?

'You can thank me by giving me a bottle of this.' Hattie held up the tumbler, which still had a tiny amount of gin left in it.

'That's genius,' he said, quickly considering her idea. 'I'd better get on to Violet and order some more gin.' It was also a brilliant excuse to phone her, and he could ask about visiting her at the distillery at the same time as placing his order.

CHAPTER 5

LOGAN

'Good morning, *oriGINal Gin*, how can I help?' The voice was male – not at all what Logan had been expecting when he'd phoned the distillery the next morning.

'Um, hi, er, this is Logan Cassidy from the Tavern in Ticklemore. Is, er, Violet around?'

'Sorry, she isn't. I'm Rory, can I help?'

'Um, I suppose. I'd like to place an order, please.'

'Hang on a sec, let me get a pen.'

Logan's disappointment was acute; he'd hoped to speak to Violet, and after he'd given the man his order, he said, 'Can you tell her I rang?'

'Of course. Did you want a tour of the distillery? Violet mentioned you might call.'

'Um, it's OK. Bit busy. You know how it is.' The tour was only an excuse to see Violet again – he didn't want to be shown around it by some big hairy bloke.

'No worries. When do you need this?'

'As soon as possible, please.' Maybe Violet would deliver it herself, but he highly doubted it.

'No problem, leave it with me. It'll be with you by Monday,' Rory said, and Logan had to be content with that.

But he wasn't content at all. He was downright *discontented*, and it wasn't until he'd come off the phone that he realised just how disappointed he was at not having spoken to Violet herself. Should he call back later?

He was tempted, even though he felt a little uncertain as to who this Rory fella was. The way that she'd asked whether he had a girlfriend had led Logan to believe she was single. Surely she wouldn't have come back into the Tavern to ask such a personal question if *she* wasn't?

He'd try again later. Maybe this evening, if he could grab a couple of minutes to himself, which reminded him...

It was early and the pub wasn't open yet, so he decided to take a stroll and call in to see a couple of people on the way. He'd start with his mum first, because although she'd seemed much better yesterday evening when she was helping out in the Tavern, she continued to have a headache. It had eased off a little but he wanted to check on her nevertheless. For all her gruff manner she was quite delicate when it came to her health, and the slightest thing could affect her nerves. He knew she couldn't help it, but sometimes it could be rather frustrating. Ever since he could remember he'd walked on eggshells around her, always mindful of her reaction, always considerate of her feelings, but the older she got, the worse she'd become.

When Logan pushed his mother's front door open and went inside he caught her balancing on the top rung of a set of step ladders, cleaning her living room window.

'What are you doing!' he exclaimed, hurrying to hold the ladder steady.

'I, er... it was dirty.'

'Why didn't you ask me to clean it? What if you'd fallen?' He helped her down. 'Your headache must be better, though.'

'It comes and goes,' she said vaguely.

Marie's migraines had always baffled Logan. Anything could bring one on, and they often went as quickly as they appeared. Sometimes they lasted for days, other times only a few hours. Sometimes it took her ages to recover, the headaches leaving her weak and wilting; other times, she was back to her normal self as soon as it had passed. It appeared to be the latter on this occasion.

'Promise me you won't do anything like this again?' Logan folded the step ladders and stowed them in her little garden shed.

When he emerged, his mother's expression was one of guilt and, not for the first time, he wondered what else she got up to when he wasn't around. What if she had fallen? She could have done herself a serious injury – broken a hip, even – and then how would she have coped? She'd have to move in with him, despite the stairs.

'You've got enough on your plate,' she said, putting the kettle on. 'Have you got time for a cup of tea? I didn't expect you to call in this morning.'

Obviously not, or else she wouldn't have gone up a ladder. 'Just a quick one.' He watched her make the tea. 'I didn't get a chance to talk to you yesterday, but I've been thinking about doing an autumn theme in the pub for September and October,' he said.

He was fibbing; he'd had enough chances, he just hadn't taken them, wanting to plan it out in his head and also speak to Franklin before he said anything to anyone, or placed any orders.

'How would that work?' she asked.

'In the same way we do Christmas. We'll run an autumn menu alongside the normal one. Franklin came up with a few ideas: pumpkin and bacon soup, bramble pie, pear and hazelnut dacoits, blackberry and bay pavlovas, pork and damson cassoulet, butternut squash tarte tartin, plum cheesecake, roasted autumn vegetables with Stilton, chicken with wild mushroom and pomegranate – to name a few. He hasn't finalised the menu yet, but these are some of the dishes he's been batting around. We'll have a push on bottled cider and the speciality ales. And the gin.'

Logan saw his mother's mouth tighten and he realised she wasn't keen on the idea.

'It's a lot of extra work,' she said.

'Not really. Franklin says he'll pare down the usual menu by a couple of dishes. He's fully on board with it.'

'Hmm.'

Logan pressed on. 'It'll culminate on Bonfire Night when we can have a pop-up bar on the field where the firework display is being held. I think the flavoured gin will go down a storm.'

'Ah.'

'What do you mean, *ah*?'

'That's what all this is about – gin.'

'It's part of it,' he admitted. 'The ones I bought from Violet are proving to be popular. I've ordered some more.'

His mother put a hand to her forehead, her expression pained, and he worried her migraine was back. It did that sometimes.

'Was it *her* idea, this autumn theme? Cause if it was, it's just an excuse to get other people to put in all the hard work to sell her gin.'

'No, it wasn't.' It was Hattie's, but he didn't think it wise to mention that. Hattie and his mother were chalk and cheese; to say they rubbed each other up the wrong way was an understatement. 'Anyway, Violet's not like that – she's really nice.'

Marie winced, putting her fingers to her temples and letting out a pained sigh.

Logan asked, 'Are you all right? Can I get you anything?' Thank God he'd arrived when he had, or else she might still have been up that blasted ladder when she became unwell again.

'I'm fine,' she snapped.

Logan wasn't so sure. 'Do you think you should have a word with the doctor again?'

'There's nothing they can do. He said as much last time I went.'

'I still think you should make an appointment. Maybe they can run some tests?' he suggested.

'We'll see. I'm usually as right as rain as long as I don't get too stressed.'

'Mum, I've told you a thousand times that you don't need to work in the Tavern. I appreciate your help, I honestly do, but your health is more important.' Logan was at a loss. His mother hadn't had one of her debilitating headaches for ages, yet she'd had one a few days ago and now she seemed to be developing another, and he tried to figure out what caused it.

He couldn't think of anything that might have stressed her out. Nothing had changed in her life, as far as he could tell. She wasn't spending any more time in the Tavern than she had previously. However, she wasn't getting any younger, so perhaps the hours she actually did do were finally proving too much for her.

Which brought him nicely to the other reason he'd decided to take a stroll this morning.

He gulped his tea and got to his feet. 'It's time I was off,' he said, kissing her on the cheek. 'Take it easy, yeah? Don't come into the Tavern today.'

'When is this autumn thing kicking off?' she asked, as she saw him out.

'I thought next Friday.'

'Aren't you rushing it?'

'Franklin assured me the menu change isn't a problem and, as I've said, I've already ordered more cider and a couple of the speciality ales; how does Nutty Squirrel grab you? Apparently, it's got undertones of hazelnut. Oh, and Pump It Up has got pumpkin notes in it.'

'You'd better hope it will be here in time.'

Logan knew she was referring to the gin. The orders from his regular ale supplier had a two-day turnaround.

'It will,' he said. 'I spoke to a bloke about it this morning.'

'A man? Not the woman with the purple hair who was in the Tavern?'

'Yes, a bloke, and he assured me it'll be delivered on Monday. Now, I really do have to get going. I'll ring you later. And take it easy. *Please.*' He gave her another kiss and dashed off, checking his watch.

The Ticklemore Tattler's office was only a short walk away, on the high street above the butchers shop, and he took the stairs leading up to it two at a time. The door at the top was open, so he knocked and went straight in.

'Hello, Logan, nice to see you.' Juliette, who owned the newspaper with her partner, Oliver, was sitting at her desk.

She got up to greet him, then indicated he should have a seat. 'What can I do for you?' she asked, sitting back down.

'Two things. First, I'm not sure if this is an advert or an article,' he said and he went on to tell her about the autumn theme in the Tavern.

'I think I can run that as a feature,' she said. 'What's the other?'

'I'd like to place a staff wanted advert, please. But don't mention it to my mum – I want it to be a nice surprise!'

CHAPTER 6

VIOLET

Violet couldn't stay mad with her brother for long, and her missing Logan's call on Friday hadn't been his fault. She should have given the Tavern's owner her personal mobile number, and not the distillery number on her business card. Although she was still a little cross because she had asked Rory to tell Logan she'd call him back there was no real harm done, however, because on this fine Monday morning she had a van full of gin and was on her way to deliver them to the man in question.

She'd made a bit of an effort with her appearance today – more than her usual quick shower and flash of mascara. Trust Rory to notice and he'd attempted to wind her up, but when he'd seen her expression he'd thought better of it.

'Good luck,' was all he'd said after she'd scowled at his initial teasing.

Violet hoped she wouldn't need it. She'd got the impression that Logan had been as into her as she was into him, but when he hadn't phoned for a few days, she had begun to think she might have got it wrong. She'd be able to tell today if she was barking up the wrong tree. She damned well hoped not. He was gorgeous – good-looking, witty, easy to talk to, and when they'd touched she had felt that all-important spark she so rarely experienced.

Logan, she saw when she strolled nonchalantly into the Tavern a short while later, was behind the bar. He had his back to her and she took a moment to admire the view. Perfect – Logan's broad shoulders, with her bottles of gin in the background. What more could a girl ask for?

'Where do you want it?' she called out, making him jump.

His face lit up when he turned and saw her. So there *was* hope…

'I've brought your gin. Where do you want me to put it?' she asked again.

'Violet…'

'That's me.' She smiled widely at him, unable to keep her delight in check. He seemed as pleased to see her as she was to see him.

'I thought Rory might have brought it, or you use a courier service.'

'My brother doesn't do deliveries and yes, we sometimes use a courier service. It depends.'

'On the quantity you're shipping and where to?'

'On who's asking for it.'

When her meaning sank in, he twinkled at her. His eyes crinkled at the corners and there was a definite gleam in them; his smile widened, too. Lordy, he was cute.

'Let me fetch Wayne and I'll give you a hand,' he said.

'I can carry it in myself. I just need to know where to put it.'

'My bar, my gin order, my rules. I'm not going to stand

here twiddling my thumbs while a lady humps crates of booze around.'

'If you put it like that…'

He held his hand out for her keys and she dropped them into his palm.

'I'm still going to help unload the van,' she told him. 'My van, my rules.'

'Why am I surrounded by stubborn women?' he muttered.

'I'm not stubborn.'

'Could have fooled me. Please, sit down, have a drink. Wayne and I will have it unloaded in a couple of minutes. Just show me which is my stuff, and we'll get it done.'

'It's *all* yours.' And so am I, she thought naughtily.

'Lemon and lime?'

'Yes, please.'

'When we're done, how about a spot of lunch? On the house?' He put her drink on the bar.

'I don't like eating on my own,' she lied. She was perfectly happy eating solitary meals, and she often did so. But not today.

'Who said you'd be on your own? I'd like to join you, if I may.'

'Won't you be needed?'

'Probably, but I don't care.'

'That's OK, then.'

'I won't be long. Don't go away.'

'I couldn't even if I wanted to – you've got my keys,' she retorted.

His chuckle drifted on the air as he went outside, and Violet hugged herself; this was going better than she'd expected. A little shiver travelled through her. It was going swimmingly. She'd never been all that good at flirting, but here she was flirting like a pro, and he was flirting back.

And he'd invited her to lunch!

Scarlet came in and Violet chatted to her for a few minutes about nothing much, the weather, gin... Thankfully the girl hadn't mentioned her boss, because Violet didn't think she could have hidden her interest in him.

'Let's go outside,' Logan suggested, when he'd finished unloading the van.

She slid off the stool and grabbed her bag. Then she noticed Scarlet's knowing look and she blushed. Scarlet gave her a thumbs-up, and Violet's blush deepened. So much for not showing an interest. Her attraction to him must be written all over her face.

'At least out here they won't be tempted to shout for me every thirty seconds,' Logan explained, choosing a table behind a tree where there was a smaller chance of them being seen. 'I'm hoping the old adage out of sight, out of mind will work for an hour. Until we get too busy, at least.'

'We'd better order then, so you can eat and go.' Violet knew what it was like to run a business and not have a minute to herself. Some days when she and Rory had a big order or two, they didn't even have time for a ten-minute breather, let alone a proper lunch.

'It'll be better next time,' he said. 'I've put an advert in the paper for more staff, and as soon as I appoint, I'm going to ask Scarlet if she wants a promotion.'

The only thing Violet registered was that there would be a next time. Swiftly followed by did he mean the next time he had lunch with someone, or the next time he had lunch with *her*. Usually outspoken, Violet was hesitant to ask in case she scared him off; she'd made a fool of herself once before when she'd dashed back into the Tavern to ask if he was married. She didn't want to make a fool of herself again.

There was a difference between showing an interest and being desperate. And Violet was definitely not desperate. She might fancy this man to bits (more than she'd fancied anyone in a very long time) but if he didn't reciprocate it wouldn't be the end of her world.

It would be a damned shame though, she thought.

He'd grabbed a couple of menus on the way out, and he handed one to her as they sat down. It wasn't quite noon yet and a little early for lunch, but she wasn't about to complain.

'Have whatever you fancy,' he said, which was unfortunate, because at the exact moment the words came out of his mouth, she'd glanced up at him.

The brief flare in his eyes told her he knew what had just flashed through her mind.

There was only one thing for it – she'd have to brazen it out. 'I didn't know you were on the menu?' she quipped.

His reply was a long time coming. 'I can be, if you want me to be.' He didn't sound jokey. He sounded as though he meant it.

'I do,' she said seriously. There was no point in beating around the bush, and she waited anxiously for his response.

'Thank goodness for that,' he said. 'I thought you were going to say you were joking.'

'I don't joke about matters of the heart,' she replied, deadpan.

Another pause, then he burst out laughing, attracting curious glances from a couple on a nearby table. Sobering, he said, 'I'd like to think this *might* be a matter of the heart at some point.' Then he grimaced. 'Too soon?'

'Not necessarily.' Her gaze was steady and open. She meant what she said.

A couple sat down at the next table and Logan said, 'We'd better order before we get too busy,' and the mood was broken. But his eyes held a promise, and Violet was looking forward to holding him to it.

'I'll have the chicken,' she said, her mouth watering at the thought of the aromatic sauce of wine, tomatoes and mushrooms the meat was cooked in. 'Do you know what would go well with this?' she asked.

'Peas?'

'Chardonnay.'

'Would you like a glass?'

'If I wasn't driving, I would.'

'I'm surprised you didn't suggest one of your gins.'

'Wine for food, gin for fun,' she said, firmly.

'Oh, well, that scuppers an idea I had, and it was going so well, too.'

'What idea was that?'

'Hang on, I'll just give our order to Wayne, then I'll explain.'

Logan was back in less than a minute and his expression was thoughtful. 'I was considering having an autumn theme for a couple of months, with the focus being on a menu suitable for the season. It was your autumn flavoured gins that gave me the idea.'

'Why do you think it's been scuppered?'

'You're right; people don't usually drink gin with their food. A gin and tonic beforehand maybe, but not *with*.'

'Some people do.'

'But most don't. I don't know what I was thinking.'

'Do people come here solely to eat?'

'No…'

'Well, then. You're appealing to those who want a meal and also those who just want a drink with friends, and those who do both. I'll quite happily have a glass of red with my meal, then drink gin for the rest of the evening.'

'You're biased.'

'I most certainly am. Besides, some gins do go well with food. It depends on the flavour of the gin and the dish you're trying to pair it with. Personally, I wouldn't, but it doesn't mean it can't be done. Is that why you ordered so many bottles of Toffee Apple?'

Logan nodded. 'It's a popular flavour with my customers. They all are.'

'Glad to hear it. You must come to the distillery – you could have a go at making your own flavour.'

'Can people do that?'

'Not in my distillery, not yet, but I've been thinking about it. A tour followed by a tasting session, or a tour followed by having a go at making some gin yourself. It means taking on more staff, though.' And that was something else she was considering.

'How many do you have?'

'It's just me and my brother at the moment, but I can't believe how the business has taken off. We only set it up eighteen months ago and we're already at the point where we need to expand. Thank you for taking a chance on me. My *gin*, I mean – thank you for taking a chance on my *gin*.'

'I'll take a chance on you any time,' he said seriously, and Violet's tummy did a slow roll.

'Who's having the chicken and who's having the fish?' Scarlet had appeared at the table and was holding two plates of food.

Violet said the chicken was for her and, as Scarlet popped the plate in front of her she could have sworn the woman winked at her.

'Enjoy,' Scarlet said, with a pointed look.

Violet got the impression she wasn't just referring to the food.

After Scarlet left, Violet and Logan tucked in, and Violet was delighted to discover that her meal was as delicious as she'd hoped it would be.

'Coming back to your autumn theme,' she said, in between mouthfuls, 'I think it's a great idea. Are you going to decorate, too?'

'I hadn't thought about it.'

'You should. You don't have to spend a fortune – some bunting, a couple of pumpkins, leaves threaded on string to make a garland…'

'You sound as though you know what you're doing. You wouldn't like to help me decorate, would you? You've got some great ideas.'

Logan might be joking, but Violet would be more than happy to help. 'If you like,' she said.

He smiled at her, and her tummy did that roll-thing again. 'I'd like that very much.' His voice was soft and his gaze locked on hers. 'I can't think of anything I'd like more.'

Violet could, but it didn't involve bunting. She turned her attention back to her food to push the image out of her head. Now was definitely not the time or the place for such thoughts.

'I think we'll make a great team,' he said. 'Not only are you going to help me decorate this place, you make gin and I serve it. It's a match made in heaven.'

Violet was sincerely beginning to hope it was.

CHAPTER 7

LOGAN

'When were you going to tell me you were planning on hiring more bar staff?' Marie's voice was strident as she strode into the Tavern's kitchen. It seemed she wasn't happy.

'When I'd taken someone on,' Logan said. 'It was meant to be a surprise.'

'It's a surprise, all right. There was some girl in the bar just now asking about the job. I told her she'd got it wrong, that we didn't have a job going, but she showed me the advert in the paper. I felt a right fool.'

'Where is she?'

'I sent her away with a flea in her ear.'

'Mum!' Logan shot out of the kitchen and into the bar, scanning it quickly. There was no obvious candidate, but he could see a young woman on the pavement outside, talking on her phone and giving the pub a confused look.

That must be her.

'Excuse me,' he said, going outside and hoping he wasn't about to make a huge mistake. 'Did you just ask about a job?'

'I've got to go. I'll speak to you later.' The woman ended her call and looked at him suspiciously. 'I did, but the lady inside said I'd got it wrong.'

'Sorry about that. She didn't know we are hiring. I wanted to surprise her. Look, come inside and we'll have a chat. I'm Logan – it's my name above the door.' He pointed to the plaque above the lintel.

'Yasmine. I suppose it wouldn't hurt.' She continued to look doubtful, and he didn't blame her.

Ignoring his mother who was glowering behind the bar, Logan led Yasmine into his office and closed the door.

'The woman is my mum and she's been helping out, but it's getting a bit much for her, so I decided to employ more staff,' Logan explained. 'I thought she'd be pleased.'

'She doesn't look it,' Yasmine pointed out.

'She'll come round.' He steepled his fingers. 'OK, tell me a bit about yourself. Do you have any bar work experience?'

'A bit. I had a job in a bar when I was in university. I know how to pull a pint.'

'That's a start. How about waiting tables? We serve food here.'

'I know. I live in Ticklemore.'

'You do?' Logan didn't recognise her, although he thought he should do if she lived in the village.

'I've only just moved here. Long story involving a disastrous relationship, a new baby and a fresh start,' she told him.

They chatted for a while, Logan trying to get a feel for whether she'd fit in. He wasn't overly concerned about whether Yasmin could change a barrel – things like that could easily be taught – he was more interested in her personality and how good she'd be with his customers.

Yasmine seemed personable and friendly, she was bright too, and she could do evenings which was a great help, freeing up either Wayne or Scarlet to cover the occasional day shift for him if he wanted to take some time off. Such as next Monday, for instance.

His breath caught in his throat at the thought of seeing Violet again. After she'd left yesterday, having arranged for her to come over early on Friday morning to decorate the Tavern and having extracted his promise to visit the distillery, he hadn't been able to stop thinking about her. Her smile, the way the sun gleamed in her hair, her curves…

Logan cleared his throat. 'I think I've heard enough. The job is yours, if you want it.'

'Really? That's great. Thank you.'

'When can you start?'

***

'You've taken her on, I see,' his mother said after Logan had shown Yasmine around and arranged for her to start work in a couple of days' time when she'd sorted out childcare.

'I thought you'd be pleased,' he repeated. 'You'll have more time for yourself.'

'*You* will, you mean.'

'I don't understand.'

'I heard about you and the gin woman.'

Logan blinked at her. 'She brought the delivery. It was lunchtime, so I suggested she ate here.'

'You've never eaten with any of the other delivery drivers.'

Marie seemed quite put out. She wasn't happy about him

hiring more staff, and now she was having a go at him for having lunch with Violet. He wondered what was going on. Was she ill? Did she have another migraine?

'I've never *wanted* to eat with any of the other delivery drivers,' he told her. 'I happen to like Violet. A lot.'

His mother heaved a deep sigh. 'Are you seeing her again?'

'I'm going to the distillery next Monday.' He didn't know why, but he didn't want to tell Marie about Violet coming to the pub on Friday morning. As long as his mother didn't pitch up early, she needn't ever know Violet had been there. And if she did find out, he'd tell her that Violet had only dropped by to deliver some pumpkins. It would be the truth – Violet was picking some up for him from the same bloke who supplied her with her potatoes.

'That's a pity. I'm going out on Monday, so you'll be short-staffed,' his mother declared. 'You'll have to rearrange.'

'It shouldn't make any difference to you. Yasmine will have started by then, and Mondays aren't usually busy. Where are you going?'

'Hereford. Shopping.'

'That's nice. You deserve a day out.'

'Who'll look after the pub while you're off gallivanting?'

'Scarlet. I'll see how she gets on with me not being here so much, and if it works out I'm thinking of asking her if she wants to be promoted to manager.'

'What!' Marie spluttered and reached for the bar to steady herself. 'You can't do that!'

'Why not?'

'She's not been here five minutes.'

'She's worked here for three years. She knows as much

about running the bar as I do.'

'What about the kitchen?'

'That's Franklin's area. I don't get involved, as you well know.' Logan ran a hand through his hair. He honestly didn't understand why his mum was behaving like this. He'd have thought she'd be pleased, if not for herself then for him. She often told him he was working too hard, which was why she felt she had to give him a hand in the pub. Now that he was doing something about it and making time for himself, she wasn't happy about that either.

Sometimes he didn't understand his mother at all.

CHAPTER 8

VIOLET

'Wow, a second visit in a week – to what do we owe the honour?' Sam grinned at her and Violet winced. He looked far more pleased to see her than she'd expected and she wondered why.

Actually, she did have an inkling why, but she was hoping if she didn't acknowledge the reason, it might go away.

'Pumpkins,' she said. 'I need quite a few.'

'You've not long had some – business must be booming.'

'They're not for making gin, they're for decoration.'

'How many do you want?'

'About thirty.' She'd counted one for each table, inside and out, and a couple to spare.

'What are you decorating? The distillery?'

'A pub.'

'The Duck and Dive?' Sam named the pub closest to where she lived.

'No, the Tavern in Ticklemore.'

He raised his eyebrows but didn't pursue it. 'Want to come and choose your own?' he offered, and Violet accompanied him to the pumpkin patch. Not only did the farm supply some of the local shops with pumpkins for Halloween, but they also offered a pick-your-own service, and there was a wooden sign at the entrance to the field with the words "Pumpkin Patch" engraved on it. Next to the sign was one of the larger pumpkins which had been elaborately carved.

'Did you do this?' Violet asked, stopping to admire it. It was a veritable work of art, and she made a note to try to be a bit more creative with the ones she intended to carve for the Tavern. She'd been planning on a simple jagged mouth and a couple of eyes, but maybe she should let her imagination run wild?

'Not me. Our Kirsty did it – good, isn't she?'

Violet had to agree.

'Do you want big ones, or aren't you bothered?' Sam asked, bending over to pick one up. The whole field was littered with orange orbs.

'Medium-sized, please, plus one larger one and a couple of smaller ones. She was thinking of combining several to make a feature on the bar. Logan said he'd ordered some lanterns, and the whole thing would make a lovely seasonal display. The only things lacking were the autumn leaves, because most of the trees still had a full cover of leaves, although give it a week or two and they'd soon begin to fall.

She pointed out some pumpkins she thought were suitable and stood back whilst Sam picked them for her. A hand-cart sat near the gate, and when he loaded them into it Violet was grateful they didn't have to carry them back to the yard. Thirty or so pumpkins weighed a fair bit, and not only that, they were bulky too. It would have taken them a couple of trips at least.

'Thanks for that,' Violet said, once they'd loaded the last one into the van. She closed the doors and walked around to the driver's side.

'Um, Violet?'

'Yes?'

Sam was looking at the ground and shuffling his feet, and with a sinking feeling she knew what he was about to say. The last time she was at the farm he hadn't managed to get round to it because of all the interruptions from his mother (where was Gretchen when you needed her? Violet thought) but today there wasn't another person in sight.

'Do you fancy going out some time? With me? For a drink. Or a meal. Or just a coffee? I don't mind which.' The poor man was blushing and couldn't look her in the eye.

Oh, dear, she'd guessed this was going to happen sooner or later. She liked Sam a lot, she really did, just not in the way he wanted her to like him. He'd make some lucky woman a wonderful husband, but not her. She'd never considered him boyfriend material – the spark wasn't there. And there had to be a spark, didn't there, otherwise what was the point?

She wanted a man who made her pulse race, who made her giddy every time he looked at her. A man whose voice sent shivers down her spine, whose touch made her long for more, whose company she craved.

Violet felt none of those things with Sam, the more's the pity, because he was a totally nice guy – any woman would be lucky to have him.

Just not her.

Anyway, there was another reason – Violet had her eye

on the owner of the Ticklemore Tavern. She simply couldn't get him out of her mind. Even just thinking about him gave her butterflies.

What would it be like to kiss him?

She hoped he'd be a good kisser. There was nothing as off-putting as a man who did a washing-machine impersonation with his mouth, or his lips were so wet a bib would come in handy. Then there were those kisses that felt their owners were being charged for lip-to-lip contact, and they wanted to keep the costs down as much as possible. And what about—

'What do you say?' Sam was peeping up at her from underneath his floppy fringe.

'Um, OK,' she replied, without thinking, and she only realised what she'd said when his eyes lit up.

Oh, dear, what a time to go off into a daydream. She could hardly admit that she'd been thinking about another man and had become distracted.

'Which would you like?' he asked eagerly.

'Which what? Oh, I see, er, coffee?' It was the safer of the three options.

'Great.' Sam seemed disappointed.

She didn't blame him; meeting for coffee was, by implication, a quick thing, fitted in around other tasks. A drink in a pub was longer, possibly a good couple of hours and involving several drinks; whilst a meal suggested spending yet longer again with a person.

'When?' His expression remained hopeful, and she winced.

'Um, I don't mind.'

'Tomorrow?'

Violet suppressed a groan. Why hadn't she said no? It

was too late to backtrack now – the damage was done, and it was only going to get worse. She would try to let him down gently, but after getting his hopes up it wasn't going to be easy, and right now Violet didn't like herself all that much. Being so dreamy wasn't like her at all – look how she'd landed herself in it, and now her conscience was guilting her into agreeing to go out with him.

'Sorry, I can't do tomorrow.' She tapped the van. 'I've got to deliver these.'

'How about the day after? Do you work on Saturdays?'

'I work seven days a week, but I can take an hour off.' She wasn't exaggerating – she could often be found in the potions room (that's how she referred to the room where all the botanicals were kept) experimenting with different combinations of flavours.

'How about we meet in the coffee shop on Castle Street in Hay?' he said.

'Would ten o'clock do you?' Violet leapt in before he could suggest a time, reasoning that ten was too early for lunch and there was little possibility that this non-date could be stretched out until lunchtime. Besides, ten in the morning was hardly a date time. It was more of a "let's meet a friend for a quick coffee whilst I'm in town time".

'Maybe we could have a walk by the river after?' he suggested.

'Maybe. Let's see how it goes, shall we? Thanks again for the pumpkins.'

Violet swiftly slid into the driver's seat before Sam got it into his head to give her a hug. Or worse.

Now look what she'd done, she thought as she drove off. It was so unlike her to get herself into sticky situations but she'd been thrown by the idea of kissing Logan. She just hoped that when she made it clear to Sam that she was only interested in him as a friend, he wouldn't go all huffy on her. They had a good business arrangement, one which was mutually beneficial, and she didn't want to spoil it.

Neither did she want to upset him, but she feared she was going to do so regardless. Because even if she *could* think of Sam as boyfriend material, there was something brewing between her and Logan Cassidy and she fully intended to find out what it was and where it might lead. Until she knew whether there was any chance of a relationship between them, no other man would get a look in.

Violet was becoming rather invested in the owner of the Ticklemore Tavern; more than she'd ever been invested in anyone before.

CHAPTER 9

VIOLET

Violet was an hour early. It wasn't deliberate – she'd woken early and hadn't been able to go back to sleep. So she decided she might as well get going. The thought of waking Logan and having him stumble out of bed, tousle-haired and sleepy-eyed had nothing whatsoever to do with the decision.

To her regret, he answered her knock fully dressed and alert, although his hair was still damp and she guessed he hadn't long had a shower. And thinking of that scenario made a whole load of other images pop into her mind.

'You're early,' he said. 'I was just brewing some coffee. Want some?'

'Please. Strong, no milk, no sugar. I've brought the pumpkins.'

'You're a star. Thank you.'

'I've carved them, too.'

'You have?'

Violet nodded. She should be exhausted as she hadn't finished the final one until gone eleven last night, and she'd been awake well before the first silver light of dawn had seeped into the sky. But she wasn't tired. She felt energised.

'I can't wait to see them,' he said, 'but first let's have some coffee. I need at least two shots to get me going in the morning.'

Logan could have fooled her – he looked as wide awake as it was possible for anyone to look.

'Me, too,' she said, and that was usually the case, but not today. Today there was an electric current fizzing along her veins that almost had her dancing on the spot.

'Here you go.' He placed a cup on the bar and Violet climbed onto a stool.

They stared at each other, neither of them speaking. She didn't know what was going through Logan's mind, but on her part all she could do was linger on his eyes and study his lips, and wonder yet again what it would be like to kiss him.

'What the hell,' she heard him mutter, and suddenly he was leaning across the bar, those lips coming closer, and she was leaning too, half rising from her seat, until their mouths met and she no longer had to wonder.

He tasted of mint, and his lips were soft, his breath warm on her cheek. Violet closed her eyes and surrendered to it, letting the sensations flow through her, raising her pulse until she could hear nothing but the thudding of her heart.

Hesitant at first, she became bolder, her mouth opening as his tongue teased her lips, gentle yet demanding, and she realised she was trembling as desire swept over her.

When they broke apart, Violet thumped back down on her stool, her legs unable to hold her up any longer and she gazed at him with wide eyes, her breath coming in little gasps.

To be fair, he looked as shocked as she felt. A kiss had been the last thing she'd expected this morning.

'OK?' he asked her.

Unable to speak because anything she said would probably come out as an unintelligible squeak, all Violet could do was nod.

'Are you sure?' His voice was rough, his gaze penetrating.

She nodded again and licked her lips nervously, the taste of him still lingering. The way his eyes zeroed in on her mouth sent a rush of heat to her face – and other regions.

At least she now knew he was a good kisser. Possibly the best she'd ever known. Not that she'd known all that many, but she'd had her fair share. And this was up there, at the top of the pile of best ever kisses.

She hoped it hadn't been a one-off. She'd have to kiss him again to make sure, but not right now, not with her on a barstool and the pair of them leaning across the bar. The next time they kissed, she wanted a full embrace, with his arms around her holding her close. She wanted to dig her fingers in his hair and—

'Do I need to apologise?' he asked softly.

'Most certainly not!'

'That's good; you had me worried for a moment.' His smile was almost shy.

'I might let you do it again, if you want,' she said. Her tone was prim and haughty, and he burst out laughing.

'Oh, I want,' he said, after he'd finished chuckling, his voice low.

'You'd better come round this side of the bar then, because, I'm not going to lie, my thighs are killing me from balancing on this stool.'

He didn't need telling twice, she was relieved to see. No sooner were the words out of her mouth than he was standing in front of her.

'Is this better?' he asked.

'Much…' She slid off the stool.

Tentatively, he put his arms around her and drew her into him. She stretched up, her head tilted, inviting him to capture her mouth. Her eyes were open, and Violet gazed deeply into his, but as his lips found hers her lids fluttered closed and she sank into his embrace with a soft sigh.

If she'd thought their first kiss was good, their second totally exceeded it. Her body was crushed against his chest, his arms holding her tight, one hand buried in her hair, his barely heard groan of desire turning her insides to mush.

Oh my, *oh my!*

'What are you doing to me, woman?' he growled when they came up for air.

Violet, her lips throbbing and her breath catching in her throat, replied croakily, 'I could ask the same thing.' Please don't let me go, she prayed silently, scared that if he did she might collapse in a heap at his feet.

Abruptly Logan's attention shifted and he lifted his head with a frown.

Violet was about to ask what was wrong when she became aware of the sound of an engine, and the unmistakable beep of a large vehicle reversing.

'Beer delivery,' he said. 'Sorry.' He kissed her on the nose, then released her.

It took Violet a second to regain her equilibrium, both physical and emotional, and she sagged against her stool for balance.

'And here was me thinking you were up and dressed because you couldn't wait to see me,' she teased, shakily.

'That, too,' he called over his shoulder as he went to deal

with the delivery, leaving Violet to return to her stool, drink her lukewarm coffee and mull over what had just happened.

Maybe strong black coffee wasn't the most advisable thing to drink after she'd been so soundly and thoroughly kissed, because every nerve in her body jingled and jangled. Her pulse had yet to return to normal and the trembling in her legs was still there.

Unable to sit still for a moment longer, Violet slipped off the stool again and went out to the van to fetch some pumpkins; she might as well make herself useful whilst she waited for him to emerge from the cellar.

She was outside, fetching the last of them, when Violet heard a noise behind and turned to see Logan hurrying towards her.

With her arms full of orange globes, she used an elbow to shut the van door as he came to a halt in front of her.

'I was worried you were leaving,' he said.

'Why would I do that?'

'Because of… the, um…'

Violet was tempted to let the pumpkins fall and show him how much she didn't want to leave, but she'd spent too long carving them to risk them being damaged.

'You can kiss me again in a minute,' she promised. 'Let me put these down first.' She dipped her head towards the pumpkins.

Logan blinked, then his face cleared. 'We're decorating the pub,' he said as though he'd only just remembered.

Yep, those kisses had made her forget things, too – her name, where she lived, the rest of the world…

'I didn't come here just to canoodle with you,' she told him with an arch smile.

'You didn't?' He looked disappointed and tried to relieve

her of the pumpkins. 'Let me have those.'

Violet shook her head. 'I can manage. You can lock the van for me, though. The keys are in my pocket.'

She found herself holding her breath as he slipped his hand into her jacket pocket, his touch, even through several layers of fabric, setting fire to her skin. To say that she was burning for him was an understatement.

This was all a bit fast. She'd only met him twice before, and now here she was snogging his face off and wanting more. And she wasn't just talking about ripping his clothes off, either. Yes, she wanted him physically – that was a given – but she wanted him *emotionally*, too. She was seriously falling for him.

It was too soon to say whether what she felt was purely lust, or whether it was the start of something deeper, so perhaps it was best if they took things a little slower? Violet may have had lots of first kisses in her life, and even several second ones; she may even have taken some of those kisses through to their natural conclusion. But she wasn't promiscuous, and she didn't believe in hopping into bed with every fella she kissed. She had to be emotionally invested in a man and in their relationship before she slept with him. Which was why she'd only had two lovers in her life.

Would Logan be the third?

She damned well hoped so.

'You've started without me,' Logan observed when he saw the inside of the bar.

Her original idea had been to place a pumpkin on each table, with the intention of having a lit candle inside each one. But alcohol, people, and naked flames weren't a good combination, so she'd invested in some battery operated lights instead.

They were all switched on and glowing cosily, and already the room looked autumnal. The pumpkins she had in her arms were destined for a display either on, or behind, the bar, so she popped them down on the counter and stood back, trying to decide where they might look their best.

She wondered whether Logan would kiss her again now she was free of her burden, but he had switched to pub-owner mode, moving beer mats out of the way and shuffling cocktail sticks, and she wasn't sure whether she was disappointed or not. Both, perhaps,

At least the not-kissing gave her some breathing space. Besides, she wanted to finish decorating the pub before it opened, and she suspected Logan felt the same way. They couldn't spend the biggest part of the morning snogging, no matter how enticing the thought.

A rattle at the door proved to be the deciding factor as the chef arrived, closely followed by a lad called Ivor, who Logan introduced as Franklin's assistant in the kitchen.

Logan let them in, then locked the door behind them.

With an unspoken agreement, she and Logan set about completing the decorating.

'Have you got any fairy lights?' she asked him. 'I'm going to pop these last few pumpkins outside, but don't forget to bring them in if it rains.'

Logan was balancing on a chair, hanging bunting from the ceiling. Violet had been most impressed that he hadn't gone down the Halloween route straight away. Although she loved All Hallows Eve as much as the next person, having cobwebs and skeletons on display at the beginning of September was a bit too much. The strings of bunting were triangles of variously patterned fabric in shades of brown, green, orange, and cream. He'd also managed to find some leaf-shaped ones and had hung those, too.

He climbed off the chair and took her hand. 'Come and see.'

His fingers were warm and her hand nestled happily in his. His touch sent a tremor through her and she took a deep breath, telling herself to behave.

'I haven't switched them on,' he said, 'because you won't be able to see them properly in daylight, but I spent a couple of hours last night after the Tavern closed, putting these up.' He pointed out the strings of delicate lights draped along the wall surrounding the garden and threaded through the trees and bushes. It must have taken him ages. 'You'll have to come back and see them in the dark,' he added.

'I will.'

'And can you help me collect those leaves you were on about?' he asked. 'For the garlands?'

'I'd love to.' Violet imagined walking in the woods, kicking through the leaves, holding hands and kissing. Every thought seemed to return to kissing... 'Not many leaves have started to turn yet,' she warned.

'I know. But it means I get to have a date with you in a few weeks' time.'

'You can have a date with me before then,' she told him shamelessly.

He stepped closer, until they were almost touching, and she simply knew he was going to kiss her again. And if he didn't, she'd kiss him.

'I'd like that,' he said, his eyes dark and intense.

So would Violet.

'Ahem! I'm not interrupting anything, am I?' a voice said.

Violet saw a flash of regret cross Logan's face, swiftly

followed by resignation, although his expression when he turned to his mother was bland.

'Hi, Mum. We were just putting up some decorations. You remember Violet?'

'How could I forget? It's a bit early for that, isn't it?'

Marie didn't say so, but Violet could take an educated guess that the woman had been referring to their canoodling and not the bunting.

'She brought us some pumpkins,' Logan informed her.

'Don't include me in this,' his mother said.

'I don't expect you to help, Mum.'

'You don't expect me to do anything. Has he told you he's making me redundant?' the woman said to her, giving her daggers, as though Violet was to blame.

Violet thought it prudent not to reply.

Logan rubbed the back of his neck. 'We've been over this. You're not being made redundant. You can work here as often and for as long as you want. I just thought having another member of staff would make things easier for you.'

'Easier for *you*, you mean.'

'What's wrong with that? I don't want to work all the hours God sends.'

'Clearly not.' Marie shot Violet another look.

'Can we discuss this later?' he asked, heaving a sigh. 'What did you want anyway?'

'That's charming, that is. Can't I pop in and see my son when I want to?'

'Of course you can! I'm not saying—'

'I came out for a copy of the Tattler,' his mother interrupted. 'Just in case you'd placed any more adverts in there that I needed to know about, and thought I'd come and see you.'

'I'd better be off,' Violet said, feeling distinctly uncomfortable. She took a final look around the garden. It would look magical after dark with the pumpkin lanterns lit and the fairy lights twinkling in the trees.

'Just a mo, I'll walk out with you,' Marie said, and Violet's heart sank. The less time she spent with Logan's mum the better.

Violet didn't know whether the woman was as caustic with everyone or whether Marie had taken a dislike to her, but whatever the reason, Violet would be happier if she had as little contact with his mum as possible. Which didn't bode well for her and Logan and any budding relationship, especially since he and his mother were close.

There was always something... Her last serious boyfriend had a best mate who he invited everywhere with them. Violet had ended it when he'd asked his mate to come with them on their holiday. Inviting him hadn't been the problem (although she hadn't been terribly pleased about it) – the three of them sharing the same room had...

Not that Violet was implying that she and Logan were serious. Not yet. A couple of kisses didn't mean they were dating. Although she'd like it if they were.

Marie turned around and walked away, without waiting to see if Violet and Logan followed.

'Sorry,' Logan whispered in Violet's ear. 'She's not normally here this early. She must have seen your van and wondered what was going on.'

Violet stroked his cheek. 'It's fine. I'll see you on Monday, yes?'

'Absolutely. I'm looking forward to it.'

'So am I. Here's my mobile number.' She drew a piece of paper out of her pocket and pressed it into his hand.

'Don't ring the distillery, unless you have a yearning to speak to my brother.'

'Hang on, I'll call you now, so you have mine.' He rang her number and she added him to her contact list.

'Are you going to stand there all day?' Marie had paused by the door and was watching them, her hands on her hips, and Logan put his phone away.

She looked like a veritable dragon and Violet tensed. It was a shame – she'd been having such a lovely time, too, and his mother had spoilt it.

As they walked from the beer garden and into the pub Marie stayed close, probably to make sure no more touching went on, Violet thought testily. What *was* the woman's problem?

Logan didn't take her back through the bar: instead he led them through a door marked "private" and opened another, this one leading to the outside. He was about to step through it when there was a loud crash from the depths of the building, followed by a shouted curse.

'You'd better see what's going on,' Marie said. 'I'll see her off.'

Her, indeed? Violet bristled – she had a name; it wouldn't hurt Logan's mum to use it.

Despite Marie's pinched mouth and marble-eyed glare of disapproval, Logan gave Violet a quick kiss on the lips. 'Monday,' he said. It wasn't a reminder, it was a promise.

'Monday,' she echoed with a smile, before bracing herself against the force of his mother's obvious annoyance.

Oh, well, Violet wasn't the shrinking kind; she'd dealt with worse than Mrs Cassidy in her time, and she wasn't going to let the woman intimidate her.

Marie yanked the door shut with a slam, and stalked

towards Violet's van.

'Nice to see you again, Mrs Cassidy,' Violet said politely, aiming her key fob at it and hearing the familiar beep.

'Likewise,' was the unsmiling reply. It was patently obvious to Violet that Marie wasn't at all pleased to see her again, and would be perfectly happy if she never clapped eyes on her in the future.

She opened the driver's door and was about to get in, but Marie said something which made her pause.

'If you hurt him, you'll have me to deal with,' the woman said.

'I've no intention of hurting him.' Violet was outwardly calm, but inside was a different matter. She let her breath out slowly, adrenalin making her twitchy. Was Marie hinting that Logan liked her enough to be hurt by her at this early stage in their relationship? It was a heady thought.

'It won't last, you know,' his mother continued.

'Excuse me?'

'You and him.'

'Why ever not?'

'He thinks more of the Tavern than any girl. Married to that pub, he is. And anyway, I won't let you come between me and my son.'

Violet gaped; surely she'd misheard? However, the hard expression on Marie's face seemed to suggest she hadn't.

'I would never do that,' she protested, but before she could say anything further the door behind them opened and Logan hurried out.

Marie's about-face was staggering. A smile appeared and her whole manner changed. 'I was just saying you can't miss that van, wasn't I, Violet? It's rather bright.' She flashed a look at Violet, daring her to contradict her.

Violet, still reeling from Marie's conviction that there was no future for her and Logan, was speechless. Which was most unlike her.

'Yeah, it's a great colour,' Logan agreed enthusiastically.

The twist of Marie's lips indicated that wasn't quite what she'd meant.

Logan slipped his arm around Violet's waist and gave her a squeeze. 'It suits Violet perfectly,' he added.

Marie's eyes narrowed. 'Just looking at it gives me a headache. In fact...' She rubbed her fingers across her forehead.

'Are you OK?' Logan asked his mother. He released Violet, his expression sombre.

'Not really. I think I will make an appointment with the doctor after all. I don't know what's the matter, but this headache won't shift and I feel so tired all the time.'

'Maybe you're coming down with something?' Logan said.

'No, that's not it. I've had it for too long for it to be a bug.'

'You should have said.'

'I didn't want to worry you.' Her voice was small and weak.

'Let me take you home.'

'What about the pub?'

'Leave the pub to me.' He sent Violet a regretful smile.

She smiled back. 'Go,' she mouthed, getting into her van and winding the window down.

'What was all the noise about?' Violet heard Marie say.

'Ivor dropped some empty baking trays, that's all.' His arm was around his mother, supporting her, his head bent in concern.

Violet felt for them both. No wonder Marie was defensive – she wasn't well. It explained a lot: her petulance, her dislike of Violet, her clinginess when it came to Logan… Violet had no idea of the woman's background, but if she was alone (there'd been no mention so far of a Mr Cassidy) and ill, then she was probably scared and needed Logan's support.

Logan was so attentive and concerned about Marie, it melted Violet's heart. A person could tell a lot about a man by the way he treated his mother, and Logan doted on his.

As she'd said, Violet had no intention of coming between a son and his mother. If anything, she wanted to add to their relationship not detract from it, and getting along with your boyfriend's mother was imperative, especially when the mother in question was so dependent on the man in question.

Violet did wonder if she was being rather premature in thinking of Logan as her boyfriend, but that's what he was about to become whether he was aware of it or not. After the kisses they'd shared earlier, there was no way she was letting this guy slip through her fingers. As far as she was concerned, he was perfect.

She'd just started the engine, her thoughts still very much on how Logan made her feel, when Marie glanced back over her shoulder.

Her expression turned Violet's assumption about the woman's health completely on its head.

Maybe she should re-evaluate the situation, because Marie had sent her such a look of satisfaction, smug triumph written all over her face, that Violet got the impression there was nothing wrong with Logan's mother at all.

Could Marie be putting it *on*, in order to put Violet *off*?

She hoped not, but if his mother was, then game on. Because what Violet wanted, Violet usually got. And she wanted Logan more than she'd ever wanted any other man in her life.

CHAPTER 10

LOGAN

Logan decided he and Violet had done a damned good job between them. The Tavern looked very autumnal this evening, which had kind of been the point. Not only were the pumpkins lit, so was the log burner, and the scent of wood smoke permeated the room giving the bar a bonfire atmosphere. Outside was even more magical, and he'd been on the receiving end of many positive comments.

'What can I get you?' he asked Alfred and Hattie. The elderly couple had been Friday night regulars ever since the pair became an item, and Logan loved the way they held hands and canoodled like teenagers.

His mother didn't. Seeing Hattie and Alfred loved up usually set Marie's teeth on edge. But she wasn't here this evening; she was at home with her feet up.

'Who's that?' Hattie asked, pointing to Yasmine.

'That's Yasmine. She's my newest member of staff.'

Hattie screwed up her eyes, scrutinising her. 'She's pretty. Young, too. About your age?'

'Stop matchmaking, Hattie,' Alfred warned, putting his

hand over hers. 'Logan doesn't need your help.'

Hattie didn't look convinced. 'He needs all the help he can get,' she replied, leaving Logan to wonder what she meant by that. Was he so unattractive that he needed help in getting a girlfriend? Did he smell (he resisted the urge to sniff his armpits). Was he lacking in personality?

'I'll have a Purple Heather gin, and Alfred says he wants to try a drop of that Nutty Squirrel ale. And you can give us a menu, too.' Her gaze darted around the bar, coming to rest on several of the decorations before moving on. 'The autumn theme was a good idea of mine,' she said. 'I ought to go into business.'

The bar was filling up nicely, with nearly all the tables taken. 'Can I pay you in kind? Tonight is on the house,' Logan said.

'I wouldn't dream of it! That's what friends are for. You helped me in the past – I am more than happy to help you.'

Logan vividly recalled the "help" he'd given, and was still surprised he hadn't been arrested for the part he'd played. Still, it would have been worth it, he thought, seeing how happy Hattie and Alfred were.

'At least if the Tavern folded, you could make a living out of carving pumpkins,' Hattie joked.

'I'd love to claim the credit, but I didn't carve them. A friend of mine did.' Heat stole into his face as he thought of Violet and the kisses they'd shared earlier today. He couldn't wait to see her again.

Hattie studied him. 'A *girl*friend?'

'Violet is female, yes. And she's a friend."

'By the soppy look on your face, she's more than just a friend,' Hattie observed. 'Good for you, Logan. It's about time you had a woman in your life who isn't your mother.

Talking about Marie, how does *she* feel about your female friend?'

'Um...' Logan didn't want to be disloyal.

'Not keen, I bet. She's going to have to untie the apron strings eventually, or else you'll end up being one of those middle-aged blokes who lives with his mother.'

Logan didn't know where to begin to unpick that little speech. But as he followed Hattie and Alfred to their table, carrying their drinks for them, he wondered whether Hattie was right about the apron strings. It wasn't that *he* couldn't let go of them, it was more the other way round. As far as his mother was concerned, Logan was still her little boy; but he suspected that could well be the case for most mums.

Was that so wrong?

He'd been her whole world for years, so he could understand why her focus was solely on him. He sometimes wondered if it was healthy for her, but it didn't seem to be doing either of them any harm, and if it made her happy then he was happy. Besides, there was her health to consider. She'd never been robust physically, despite outward appearances. For years she'd been plagued by debilitating headaches or other illnesses, and he did whatever he could to help her through them.

She'd had one of her headaches today – or was it a continuation of the one she'd had last week? They seemed to come in clusters and, he'd discovered the last time she'd suffered with them, cluster headaches were actually a thing.

Hopefully this latest one would soon go away. The last major attack had lasted several weeks, and it had been a few years ago. Although she'd had headaches since, they hadn't been nearly as bad as that one. He'd read that alcohol and strong smells could trigger a cluster headache, but Logan wondered if worry or stress could bring them on, too.

Over the years, he'd urged her to go to the doctor and she had been prescribed tablets, but she said she didn't like taking them because of the side effects.

The last time she'd had a severe attack, he'd been worried it might be something more sinister than a headache, so, without wanting to scare her, he'd tried to get her to ask her doctor to run some tests.

Thankfully though, the headaches had subsided soon after and she hadn't had many since, apart from the odd one now and again – and his worry had subsided along with them.

Logan ensured Hattie and Alfred were seated with their drinks in front of them and the new menu in their hands, and he was about to return to the bar and the customers who were waiting there, when Hattie asked, 'Where is Marie this evening?'

'She's not well,' he told her.

Hattie studied him keenly. 'She didn't like my autumn theme idea, did she?'

'I, er, didn't tell her it was you who'd suggested it. Sorry.'

Embarrassment surged through him. He hadn't deliberately set out to claim the idea as his own – he'd just known how his mum would react to any suggestion of Hattie's. He didn't understand why, but Marie held a certain amount of animosity towards Hattie. Hattie could be rather outspoken, extremely interfering and very determined, but her heart was in the right place and she genuinely cared for people.

'Ah, so it's not that then,' she said.

'What's not what?'

'The reason why she's not well. Is it because of this new

girlfriend of yours?'

'I don't follow.' Hattie could be rather cryptic at times. Logan put it down to her age.

'No, I don't suppose you do,' Hattie said.

'Hattie...' Alfred might be speaking softly but there was a warning note in his voice.

'It's all right,' she told him crossly. 'I'm not going to say anything. He probably won't believe me anyway.'

'What won't I believe?' By now Logan was thoroughly confused. He hoped the old lady wasn't starting to show early symptoms of dementia, and worry pricked at his mind. He'd always had a soft spot for Hattie.

'You're needed behind the bar,' she said, making shooing motions with her hand, and Logan looked around to see Silas and Nell gazing hopefully back at him.

Logan hurried over. 'Sorry about that. What can I get you?'

Silas and Nell were another couple Logan thought highly of. Silas was a local artist with a gallery in Ticklemore, and Nell owned a wonderfully quirky antique shop which was also in the heart of the village.

By the time he'd served them, plus the dozens of people who came into the Tavern throughout the course of the evening, Logan had pushed his concern about Hattie to the back of his mind.

A decent while later, he noticed the time and realised it was getting late. They'd stopped serving food two hours ago and the remaining clientele were enjoying their drinks. He'd better give his mum a call, but before he did that, there was someone else whose voice he wanted to hear.

'Violet, hi. I'm not disturbing you, am I?'

'Hi.' She sounded languid and he hoped he hadn't woken

her. It was eleven p.m.; not late, not for him, anyway. He had at least another hour to go before he could think about going to bed.

'You're not disturbing me,' she added, with a yawn. 'How did the first day of the autumn theme go?'

'Brilliantly. Thanks so much for helping me decorate the pub. Lots of people commented on it. But what they were more interested in was the food – which was awesome – and your gin. The flavours went down a storm.'

She yawned again. 'That's fantastic news. I'm pleased for you.' She paused. 'How's your mum? I hope she's OK. She didn't look too well earlier.'

Aw, bless her. It was so nice of Violet to ask after her.

'She gets these headaches; she's had them for years. They can last for hours or days; weeks even, on and off. I thought they'd gone because they seemed to have eased off, but unfortunately they've come back recently with a vengeance.'

'Oh, dear, that must be awful for her. Tell her I said hi, and that I hope she's better soon.'

'I will, thanks.' He took a second to compose his thoughts. 'I thoroughly enjoyed this morning,' he said cautiously.

'Me, too. Especially the kissing part.'

Logan let out a slow breath. He'd been scared to mention it in case she regretted it. 'Yeah, that was the bit I was referring to, although the decorating was fun, too.'

'I'd love to see how the garden looks in the dark.'

'You could come over now, if you like,' he said. 'We could sit outside and have a pumpkin latte.' Then he realised how it sounded. Oh God, he hoped she didn't think he was suggesting a bootie call.

'I'd love to, but it's a bit late.'

'Sorry, you're right. I wasn't thinking. Another night?'

'Definitely. Maybe I'll come and try something on your autumn menu?'

'I'll look forward to it.'

'I'm looking forward to Monday, too.'

'So am I.' There was a slightly awkward silence before Logan said, 'I'd better go – I've got to clear up before I go to bed.'

'I'm in bed, already.'

Crumbs: his imagination shot into overdrive. Perhaps it was a good thing he had the cleaning up to do as it would distract him from images of Violet. He was picturing her in *his* bed and although the details were a little fuzzy, it made him hot under the collar.

He heard her soft laughter, and surmised she'd guessed what was going through his mind. 'Good night, Violet,' he said, shaking his head. She was a right vixen.

'Goodnight, Logan. Sleep well.'

Yeah, as if that was going to happen now. He predicted he'd lie awake half the night thinking of her.

Thankfully he didn't, but her face *was* the last thing in his mind before sleep claimed him.

CHAPTER 11

VIOLET

Although she had been incredibly tempted to take Logan up on his offer to visit the Tavern last night, when she woke this morning Violet was glad she hadn't. There was always something that needed to be done in the distillery, and she was already cutting into her day by having to go into Hay-on-Wye – sleeping in this morning because of a too-late night yesterday wouldn't have helped.

Violet groaned as she considered the reason for going into town. She should have had the courage to tell Sam she wasn't interested in him in that way, and she felt like kicking herself. How could she have been so silly? And cruel, too. She wasn't so egotistical that she thought she was particularly special to Sam, but she knew he was hoping for more than she could give him.

In some ways it was a shame, because he was a lovely guy – kind, easy-going, not bad looking, and he'd make some lucky woman a wonderful partner. Just not her. Especially after yesterday. Violet still tingled from Logan's touch, and whenever she thought about his lips on hers her tummy fluttered in an alarmingly exciting way. Monday couldn't come quick enough. Or maybe she'd surprise him this evening and have a meal at the Tavern?

But what if he didn't have time to eat with her? Would she feel silly eating alone?

Maybe. Although it wouldn't be the first time she'd enjoyed a solitary meal, eating alone had always been done during the day as she'd hawked her gin from pub to restaurant trying to persuade people to stock it. Sitting at a table on her own this evening watching Logan work might be a step too far.

And for another thing, his mother would know why she was there, and the thought made her uncomfortable. Why couldn't Marie be more like Sam's mum? Gretchen was desperate to see Sam settle down. Perhaps too desperate. Whereas Marie appeared to be the total opposite. And Violet still had a suspicion that Logan's mother wasn't as unwell as she was making out.

Hoping she'd read the situation wrong, Violet hopped in her van and made her way to Hay-on-Wye, her thoughts very much on Logan and the Tavern, and not at all on Sam.

She found a space to park near the castle, and she smiled when she noticed the curious looks that her purple van attracted. Marie was right: it *was* bright, but it was meant to be. The van was a moving billboard advertising her distillery and the gin it created, and her ultimate goal was for everyone to think of *oriGINal Gin* whenever they saw that particular shade of purple. That day was a long way off but it didn't hurt to have dreams and aspirations.

The nearest town to the distillery, Hay nestled between the towering bluffs of the Black Mountains and the wide sweep of the River Wye. Famous for its literary festival, it had a ruined twelfth-century castle, numerous bookstores and loads of other quirky shops, not to mention a decent number of pubs, restaurants, and cafés. It attracted hikers, bibliophiles, and tourists in equal numbers, and was always busy.

Sam was already in the café, Violet saw as she approached. He'd bagged a window seat and was sitting in one of two squishy armchairs with a low table in between. When she entered and approached the table, she noticed an empty mug on it and she wondered whether it belonged to him, and if so how long he'd been sitting there.

Her already sunken heart sank even further. Oh, dear, this wasn't going to be easy.

Sam got up from his seat, which was a bit of an effort because it was reluctant to let him go, and attempted to kiss her. Violet, anticipating this when she saw him heaving himself out of the chair, turned her head. It was only when his kiss landed on her ear that she understood he'd been aiming for her cheek and not her lips.

She dropped into the chair opposite his, realised she needed to order at the counter, and tried to get back up. Crikey, if this was a marketing ploy to get customers to spend more because they couldn't leave, it was working brilliantly.

Sam, who was still standing, offered to get her a drink. 'What would you like? My treat, as I asked you out in the first place,' he added.

Violet would have preferred to buy her own coffee so this didn't feel so date-like, but she didn't want to come across as surly or churlish. 'A black coffee, please. Two shots.' She might need the extra boost in order to make a quick getaway after she'd let him down.

While he was at the counter, she stared out of the window, glum and uncomfortable, wishing she could simply tell him and be done with it. But she'd only just arrived and it wouldn't be polite; she could at least have a coffee with him, and when he suggested they see each other again, she would tell him then.

'This is nice,' he said, coming back with a tray containing two outsized cups on outsized saucers and a selection of small cakes. 'I didn't know what you liked but they do bite-sized cakes for those people who can't decide, and I couldn't decide.' He pushed the plate towards her. 'Help yourself.'

Violet had no appetite for cake, but she took one of the tiny morsels and popped it in her mouth. She was sure it was delicious but all she could taste was her shame in not being honest with him from the start.

'How did the pumpkin delivery go?' Sam asked, and Violet nearly choked as an image of being soundly and thoroughly kissed by Logan exploded in her mind.

'Good,' she replied after she'd taken a sip of scalding coffee to wash the cake down, and almost burned her mouth. So good, it brought heat to her cheeks and her heart missed a beat. She coughed to cover it, and hoped Sam would put her sudden blush down to her inability to eat a piece of cake properly.

'Who were they for?' he asked.

'Er, the Ticklemore Tavern.' She was blushing so much she thought her face might explode.

'I've heard they do decent food. Never been there myself.'

'They are stocking my gin. The autumn ones.'

'Hence the pumpkins?'

'Exactly.'

'For display, were they? Or soup?'

'Display.'

'That's kind of you.'

Violet winced. Kindness hadn't come into it – she'd wanted an excuse to see Logan again and when he'd jokingly asked whether she'd like to help him decorate she'd leapt at the chance. 'I was passing that way yesterday, so I said I'd collect them and drop them off.'

'I meant it was kind of you to think of me. Us. Ten Trees Farm.'

'Well… you know… us small businesses have to do our best to support each other.' Oh, my God, Sam thought she'd gone to Ten Trees Farm to collect some pumpkins solely as an excuse to see him.

Could this get any worse?

'This is nice,' Sam repeated. He looked uneasy and for a fleeting moment Violet thought he was getting the message without her having to say anything.

No such luck.

'Remember I suggested a walk along the river? How do you fancy a bit of lunch afterwards once we've worked up an appetite? I've booked us a table in the Scruffy Rooster, but I can always cancel if you're busy.'

Violet drew in a long slow breath, then let it out in a whoosh. 'Sam,' she began, hoping her tone of voice would give him an indication that what she was about to say wouldn't be good news.

His expectant and hopeful smile made her feel dreadful.

'It's like this… I really like you—'

'I really like you, too,' he said.

'—as a friend. A good friend, but just a friend.'

Sam slumped back in his seat and blew out his cheeks.

'A friend,' he repeated woodenly.

'I'm sorry—' she tried to say, but his shout of laughter made her jump.

'A *friend?*' he said again, chortling.

Violet wondered if he was having some kind of attack – hysteria, maybe? Or, God forbid, did he think she was joking?

'Yes, I'm sorry, Sam.' She studied his face and was mystified to see mirth written all over it.

'Don't be,' he spluttered. 'You honestly don't fancy me?'

'You're a good-looking guy, and you're sweet and kind, and lovely; but no, I don't fancy you.'

'Thank God for that!'

'Pardon?'

'At least I can tell her I tried.' He wiped his eyes, his face red.

Violet hoped he wasn't crying but she suspected he must be. 'Tell who, what?' she asked. This conversation was becoming downright bizarre.

'My mother.'

'What's she got to do with this?'

Sam shook his head slowly. 'The conniving madam.'

'You're referring to your mother, right?'

'I am. You know what she's like, always on at me to find a nice girl and settle down. She convinced me that you were madly in love with me, which was why you kept popping up to the farm, and that I should give you a chance.'

It was Violet's turn to sink back into her seat. The cushion let out a weird groan.

Or was it she who'd made the noise?

'I mean, I like you – what man wouldn't? And I quite fancy you. Again, what man wouldn't? But I honestly don't think of you as girlfriend material.'

Instead of being relieved that she hadn't broken his heart or bruised his ego, Violet found herself focusing on why Sam didn't think of her in that way? What was wrong with her? She'd make a good girlfriend, wouldn't she? What was it about her that was putting Sam off? And would whatever it was put Logan off, too? She began to wonder whether he would change his mind about her once he got to know her better. That the kisses they'd shared were only physical, and that she'd imagined the emotional connection between them.

'Why, what's wrong with me?' she demanded.

'Nothing. You're gorgeous.'

'That doesn't make sense,' she said.

'It makes perfect sense to me. You're beautiful, intelligent, ambitious, driven… Too much so, maybe.'

Violet stared at him.

'I need someone more like me; a homebody. The only way I'm driven is to make sure the veggies are harvested, or the fruit is picked.'

'That's being driven,' Violet said feebly.

'No, it's not. I don't want an empire, I just want to run the farm.'

'Who says I want an empire? I just want to sell gin.'

'You're too…' he paused, and she could tell he was trying to find a word that described what he meant but didn't upset her. 'Vivacious,' he said, followed by, 'Bubbly, spirited… bouncy.'

'Bouncy?'

'Lively. I meant *lively*.' Before she could leap in again, he said, 'Anyway, I could ask you the same thing – why don't you fancy me? And don't say you do, because I can tell you don't.' He was smiling as he said it, so she knew he wasn't offended.

'There's no spark.'

'Exactly!'

'That's that sorted, then,' she said, glad they'd cleared the air, even if the conversation had been one of the oddest she'd ever had. 'What are you going to tell your mum?'

'I'm going to tell her to butt out. She can't keep trying to set me up. Before you, she tried to get me to go on a date with the daughter of one of her friends from the market.'

'Why didn't you go? She might have been lovely.'

'I knew her from school. She was annoying. What about you? I bet you don't have someone trying to set you up on dates.'

Hardly, she thought; trying to stop me going on them was more accurate. Logan's mum, didn't like her, which made Violet sad. It was a pity Marie couldn't be more like Gretchen.

Thinking of Logan gave her an idea. 'There is someone I'm kind of seeing; the owner of the Ticklemore Tavern.'

'Good for you! More ammunition for me to fire at my mum – not only are you not in love with me, like she said you were, but you've also got a boyfriend.'

'I'm not sure if I can call him that yet,' Violet admitted, 'although we're getting there.'

'Is that what the pumpkins were about?'

'He had an idea of doing an autumn theme in the pub from now until Bonfire Night, and he asked me to help him decorate. I haven't seen it at night with all the fairy lights, but I'm going to pop in when it's dark.'

Violet grinned at Sam: she'd had a thought… 'I've got an idea,' she said. 'Are you doing anything tonight?'

CHAPTER 12

LOGAN

His mother sounded a little brighter on the phone this morning, Logan thought, but she still wasn't her normal self. She'd mentioned calling in the Tavern later, but he'd managed to talk her out of it, especially when he'd offered to pop in and take her a meal from the Tavern's kitchen. She was even happier when he'd told her he'd eat with her.

When he was growing up she'd always cooked hearty meals for them both, and sitting at the table to eat together every evening had been one of the things she'd insisted on. It had become more difficult as he got older because he'd inevitably wanted to be out with his friends and tended to eat on the fly, and it became even more difficult once he'd taken over the Tavern, but he tried to share a meal with her whenever he could.

He decided to walk the short distance to his mother's house rather than drive, and had packed their food into a bag to carry, because it was a glorious autumn evening: warm, sunny, with the drone of lazy bees in the air. Stretching his legs would do him good, even though he'd been on his feet all day.

Logan strode down the road, feeling chirpy and upbeat. He was rarely down, but this evening he felt happier than usual, his thoughts filled with how well the Autumn Theme had gone (he'd begun to think of the initiative in capital letters). The majority of food orders had come from the seasonal menu and even in broad daylight the unlit pumpkin lanterns looked pretty, as did the bunting and garlands. He'd lit the log burner lunchtime, and the crackle and glow of the flames, and the smell of the wood made the pub all the more inviting.

And then there was Violet. It was safe to say she was in his thoughts more than the Tavern was, which was unheard of, and he realised he was developing strong feelings for her – far stronger than a couple of kisses warranted. What he felt for her couldn't be explained by mere sexual attraction (although he felt that, too, in spades). He really liked her and he couldn't wait to see her again.

'It's only me,' Logan called to his mother as he knocked and walked into the house. He found her in the living room, sitting in her favourite chair, with the curtains closed.

'Headache still there?' he asked, and she put a shaking hand to her head.

'It's better than it was.'

'Is there anything you need? Anything I can get you?'

'No, I'm all right. I might be able to manage a bit of food, though,' she said, her attention on the bag in his hand.

'I'll warm it up then, shall I?' Logan was aware he sounded falsely bright, and was using the kind of voice people often reserved for the elderly, and he tried to tone it down. His mother wasn't old, but even if she had been she didn't deserve to be spoken to like a child. He wouldn't dream of speaking to Hattie in such a manner, and not solely because she'd send him away with a flea in his ear if he did.

'What are we having?' Marie asked.

'Chicken with wild mushroom and pomegranate, and bramble cheesecake to follow,' he said, going into the kitchen.

'Is that on your new-fangled menu?' His mother appeared in the doorway.

'It is, and it's proving to be very popular.' He lifted a large dish out of the bag and opened the microwave door.

'We'll see.' Marie stepped forward and turned the dial on the oven. 'I don't like my food microwaved, if I can help it,' she said. 'Warm it up in the oven.'

That was news to Logan. He suspected it had more to do with the oven method taking three times as long as the microwave, rather than any culinary preference on his mother's part. It meant he'd be away from the Tavern for longer than he'd intended, but he didn't begrudge spending more time with her. He had Yasmine now and she was working this evening, along with Scarlet and Wayne, so even though it was Saturday and the pub's busiest day, they should be able to cope for the time being.

As though thinking about Yasmine had conjured her up in his mother's mind, Marie asked, 'How is the new girl working out?'

'Fine, so far. She coped brilliantly yesterday. I've no doubt she'll continue to do so. She's working this evening, which is why I can spend a bit more time with you.'

Marie didn't look convinced. 'Are you still planning on taking Monday off?'

'I don't see why not. Mondays are always quiet, so it's the best day.'

'Is this going to be a regular thing?'

'Possibly. I'll have to see how it goes.'

His mother was silent for a moment, then she said, 'We could do something together?'

'Good idea, but not this Monday, eh? Anyway, you said you were off to Hereford shopping, but I do think your headache has got to ease before you should think about going shopping. Besides, I'm visiting Violet's distillery.'

Logan didn't miss the way his mother's mouth tightened or the way her eyes narrowed. He had no idea why she didn't like Violet, and he had no idea what to do about it. If he was going to see more of Violet – and he sincerely hoped he was – then his mother would have to learn to like her. Or at least be civil to her. He'd see how things progressed, and if it looked like he and Violet were an item and his mum continued to be disapproving, he'd have to have a word with her.

As they waited for their food to heat up, talk thankfully turned away from days off and distillery visits as Marie told him what she needed doing in the garden, how annoying her neighbours on the one side were, and various snippets of gossip about the villagers. Logan listened with half an ear, taking some of it with a pinch of salt. In a small place like Ticklemore it was impossible not to be aware of everything that went on when it came to its residents, but he tried to be impartial and non-judgemental. However, gossip was rife, and with little else to occupy her (apart from the Tavern), his mum took an active interest.

'Benny has been going around collecting people's garden waste in a hand cart,' Marie told him. 'He says he can make better use of it than the council. He's on about setting up a series of compost heaps in the allotment and then selling it back to people cheaper than they can buy it in the shops.'

'That's a great idea,' Logan said.

'And Marge is after people to make cakes for a bring-and-buy sale for the church,' she continued. 'I'd make one, but I don't feel up to it.' She rubbed her temple and pulled a face.

'I'm sure Marge will understand.'

'I'm not,' his mother retorted. 'You know what those WI types are like.'

He didn't, and he had no intention of asking. All he knew was that the Women's Institute was one of the driving forces in the Ticklemore community and Marge was an active and enthusiastic member in getting things done.

Logan checked the time. 'I'd better get back. The evening rush will be starting shortly.' He rose and began gathering the dirty dishes.

'Leave them. I'll wash them and pop them into the Tavern tomorrow.'

'Are you sure? It's no trouble.'

'I'm not so ill that I can't wash a couple of plates.'

Logan gave her a doubtful look. 'At least you ate a good dinner.' She'd polished off the lot.

'Franklin's a good chef.'

'He's the best. I love that he's embraced the new menu.'

His mother made a non-committal sound, and Logan realised she still wasn't entirely convinced, despite enthusiastically consuming the evidence. 'Shall I make you a nice cup of tea before I leave?' he asked.

Marie shook her head. 'You get going.' She got heavily to her feet, ignoring his protests, and saw him to the door.

Logan gave her a kiss on the cheek. 'Thank goodness your headaches don't affect your appetite,' he said. 'You've got to keep your strength up.' He stepped outside and zipped up his jacket. The day might have been warm and sunny but clear skies meant the temperature dropped quickly when the sun started to go down. 'Try and rest this evening, yeah? I'll call you later.'

His mother wasn't looking at him; she was looking beyond him, and her lips were compressed into a thin line of dislike. Logan turned to see what had annoyed her and was surprised (and disproportionately pleased) when a purple van trundled past. It was heading towards the Tavern. A man sat in the passenger seat and Logan wondered if it was Violet's brother.

'You didn't say you were seeing *her* tonight,' his mother snapped.

'That's because I didn't know I was. Besides, she mightn't be going to the Tavern.'

'She's got a bloke with her.'

'So I saw.'

'You want to watch that one. It's not right, leading you on if she's got a boyfriend. Or worse,' his mother added ominously.

'She hasn't got a boyfriend.' Logan was hoping he was about to step into that role. 'She's got a brother, though.'

'That sort don't go out with her *brother* on a Saturday night,' Marie retorted.

'She's probably still working – which is what I should be doing.' He gave her another quick peck and told her to go back inside and rest.

Marie ignored his advice, and Logan felt his mother's eyes on his back as he hurried along the road, eager to see whether Violet had stopped at the Tavern or whether she'd driven on by. He was also keen to know who the man in the passenger seat of her van was, because in a way, his mother was right: Saturday night wasn't the best time to try to persuade publicans to stock your wares. Any bar or restaurant worth their salt would be too busy to deal with cold callers. Besides, his was the only establishment with an alcohol licence in Ticklemore.

His heart leapt when he saw Violet's unmistakable van in the Tavern's car park, and he dashed inside, using the private entrance so he could nonchalantly appear in the bar, rather than scurrying through the pub's front door. He wanted to try to catch sight of Violet and her mysterious man before Violet spotted him.

Composing himself, Logan sauntered into the kitchen. 'How's it going?' he asked Franklin.

The chef was tossing something in a pan, and he jerked his head toward the line-up of pegged orders. 'Busy,' he said shortly.

'Good. That's what I like to hear.' Logan strolled to the door leading to the bar and narrowly avoided being smacked in the face as Yasmine barrelled through it.

'Sorry, Logan, I didn't see you.'

'It was a silly place to stand,' he said, trying to peer around her as the door swung back and forth before coming to rest.

Yasmine called out the order and added it to the others.

'Busy?' he asked.

'Definitely. I didn't realise the Tavern was so popular.'

Logan was grateful that it was. Unable to justify lingering in the kitchen – he was getting strange looks from Franklin – he took up his position behind the bar and began serving.

Ah, there she was, sitting at a table near the log burner, chatting. The man Violet was with looked to be around the same age, tall, well-built, wide-shouldered. Short blond hair, tanned face and forearms. Not bad looking, especially when he smiled, and he seemed to be doing that a lot. If the guy was Violet's brother, the two of them didn't look anything alike.

Jealousy unfurled in Logan's belly. Irritated, he stamped it down. Violet wasn't his – not yet – and she was free to see whoever she wanted.

However, if she *was* seeing this bloke, it was extremely bad taste for her to bring him here, and Logan wondered whether the poor chap realised that Violet had been free and easy with her kisses. He narrowed his eyes as she put a hand on the man's arm and laughed up at him. The pair of them looked very cosy.

Just then, Violet glanced around for someone to take their food order and caught his eye.

Her smile lit up her face and Logan hastily revised his assessment of the situation. Would she give him such a glorious smile if she was here with another man?

'I'll get this,' he said, as Wayne made to cross the room to go to her table.

Logan tried not to dash over, wanting to appear a little more sophisticated, so he stopped to say hello to a couple of people, and gave one or two a casual smile. Eventually though, he was standing in front of her and her gentleman friend (gosh, that was the sort of thing his mother would say) and he was lost for words.

'Are you here to take our order?' Violet was beaming up at him, the bloke she was with not quite so beamy.

'I didn't expect to see you here this evening,' Logan blurted.

'You suggested I should come and see the full effect of

our efforts at night, so here I am.' Violet glanced meaningfully around the room.

The bar looked wonderful, the flames in the log burner flickering, fairy lights twinkling, the bunting giving everything a festive air.

'I love that you thought to bring battery operated lights,' Logan said, patting the pumpkin in the middle of the table. He had trouble taking his eyes off her, but now and again his gaze shot to the man sitting opposite and he tried to gauge his reaction.

'Oh, I'm sorry, I should have introduced you,' Violet said. 'Logan, this is Sam, he's my potato man.' She chuckled. 'Sam, this is Logan, who you've probably gathered by now, owns the Tavern.'

'Pleased to meet you,' Logan said.

'Likewise.' The man, Sam, wasn't giving anything away. But at least Logan now knew the bloke wasn't her brother. But what was his relationship to Violet, and why was he here with her tonight?

'Should I take your order?' Logan was eager to scuttle back behind the bar, where he felt safest. It was also a place where he could have a quick think and try to work out what was going on. Although he was the epitome of a friendly publican, to Logan the banter with his customers was second nature and he could chat to them whilst his mind was on other things.

He scribbled down their starters and mains, and to him it felt that the pair were on a date. He noticed that Sam was drinking one of the speciality ales Logan had been touting for the autumn theme, and Violet had a soft drink in front of her, which figured, considering she was driving.

He gave their order to the kitchen, then dived behind the

bar and immersed himself in its comforting rhythm, all the while keeping one eye on the occupants of table 14, and wishing they were sitting a little closer so he could listen.

He couldn't help but notice the way she occasionally touched the man, resting her hand on his, stroking his arm once, reaching across the table to tweak his cheek. It was all quite intimate, and the jealousy that had unfurled in his stomach when he initially saw them together was now rampaging throughout his whole body. This was definitely not the behaviour of a friend. Was she flirting with the guy? Logan thought she might be. It was difficult to tell without hearing exactly what was being said, and she was sitting at an angle to the bar so he couldn't quite see her face fully. However, he could see the man's, and Sam had yet to take his eyes off her.

Logan could feel anger slowly building, his mother's words coming back to haunt him. It wasn't right that Violet had been leading him on if she already had a boyfriend, and he was beginning to suspect that she did.

He let Yasmin take the food to table 14 when it was ready, not trusting himself to say something he shouldn't.

When Violet looked up, twisting around slightly as Yasmine put the plates down, and she saw him looking at her, the expression on his face must have alerted her that all wasn't well, because she blinked and frowned at him.

Logan looked away, shaking his head, annoyed with himself as much as with her. He had a policy of never getting involved with either his staff or his clientele. It looked like he was going to have to add "and anyone else involved in the industry" to the list. She was a supplier of his, he was a customer of hers, and that's the way it should have stayed.

Needing to get out of there for a second, he slipped into the corridor leading to the private rooms beyond, and went into his office, closing the door behind him and sagging against it. A couple of kisses, that was all they'd shared, just a couple of kisses; so why was he so upset? It wasn't as though they'd declared their undying love or anything.

A knock on the door made him sigh. Couldn't he have five minutes peace? He knew it was Saturday evening, and he knew how busy the place could get, but five minutes was all he wanted – five measly minutes.

Taking a deep breath he yanked the door open and there she was, Violet, standing in front of him, a concerned expression on her face.

'What do you want?' He knew he was being abrupt, but he hadn't expected to see her there, and the sight of her unnerved him more than it should have done considering he hardly knew her.

She looked upset. 'What's wrong? Have I done something? I thought you'd be pleased to see me.'

'I was.'

'*Was?* What's changed your mind?'

'You're with someone.'

'Yes, I introduced you.'

'You certainly did.'

She squinted at him, worrying at her bottom lip. God, she was sexy—

'Do you think Sam and I are *together?* Are a couple? Like, boyfriend and girlfriend?' She squinted some more. 'You do, don't you?' The squint made her look slightly cross eyed; then he realised she wasn't *cross eyed*, she was *cross*.

'I don't believe it,' she cried. 'Is that what you think? That I'd snog you to death, then bring my boyfriend into your pub? What the hell do you take me for?' She shook her head slowly. 'If that's what you think of me...' she repeated.

He couldn't resist her any longer. With a groan, Logan realised how stupid he was being, and his arms shot around her to crush her to him, his mouth coming down on hers.

For an awful moment he thought he'd overstepped the mark and that she was going to push him away, but when she gave herself to his embrace, relief surged through him and he lost himself in her kiss.

'Ahem!'

Logan ignored the noise – he was having far too much fun. Whoever it was could go away. The bar could manage without him for a few more minutes.

'I said, *ahem*!'

Logan's enjoyment had a bucket of cold water thrown over it as he realised the voice belonged to his mother. Refusing to leap away from Violet like a teenager caught necking behind the bike sheds, he gently withdrew his lips, but kept his arms around her. She gave him a squeeze and he held her even tighter.

'Am I interrupting something?' His mother looked positively mutinous.

'You know you are.'

'Well! I thought you'd be busy, so I'd save you a trip.' She held up the bag that the containers of food had been in.

'I *am* busy,' he said, a smile threatening. Now wouldn't be a good time to grin from ear to ear, because his mum was clearly in a mood, and if he upset her any further her headache might come back. He knew the reason she was here and it had nothing to do with saving him a trip, and everything to do with being nosey.

'I'm glad to see you're feeling better,' he said.

'I thought a bit of fresh air would do me good.' Her tone implied it hadn't.

'And I thought you were going to take it easy this evening?' he countered.

'Clearly.'

What was that supposed to mean, he wondered? Sometimes what went on in his mother's head was a total mystery. 'I could have picked that up in the morning,' he said, indicating the bag.

'I thought I'd save you the bother. I know how busy you are.'

Why did she keep harping on about him being busy? He was always busy – you were if you ran a pub. There was always something that needed doing, but that was also the reason he'd taken Yasmine on – so he could be a bit *less* busy.

'I'd better get back,' Violet said, slipping out of his arms, but not before she'd given him a tender kiss on the lips. 'Sam will be wondering where I am and my food is going cold.'

'I'll warm it up for you.'

The look she gave him made him go weak at the knees as she skirted around Marie and headed back to the bar. It spoke of promises and unfinished business.

Whereas his mother's expression shouted disgust and ire.

'I'd better…' He jerked his head at the door leading to the bar.

Marie raised her eyebrows.

What was wrong with her? His mother was making him feel like a naughty kid, and there was no reason for it – he was single and so was Violet. They weren't hurting anyone and what they did behind closed doors was no one else's business. OK, he conceded they had been kissing in his office with the door open, but no one had seen apart from his mother, and although it probably wasn't nice to witness your grown-up son in a clinch, her reaction had been excessive and unwarranted. Besides, he reckoned, if any of Ticklemore's regulars had caught him kissing someone, they probably would have cheered him on.

Returning to the bar and carrying on working was Logan's penance, because if he hadn't leapt to the wrong conclusion regarding Violet's relationship with Sam, then he wouldn't have kissed her and he wouldn't now be wishing he could spend the rest of the evening with her. And the night. And maybe all day tomorrow, too.

Oh, dear, he'd got it bad, hadn't he? All it had taken was a pair of blue eyes, and several kisses, to realise he was well and truly smitten.

CHAPTER 13

VIOLET

'All sorted?' Sam asked as Violet took her seat.

She noticed he hadn't touched his meal, and she also noticed, as she'd walked back into the bar, a certain barmaid standing by their table, chatting. It didn't take a genius to work out the two were connected.

'The daft idiot thought we were an item,' she said. Violet picked up her fork and checked the temperature of her butternut squash tartin. To her surprise it was still warm enough to be palatable. It seemed as though she'd been gone ages, but it probably hadn't been as long as she'd thought.

'I can see where he's coming from,' Sam said, diving into his own meal. His attention wasn't on it though. It was on the member of staff who'd been talking to him.

Violet followed his gaze. The woman was younger than her and awfully pretty. Violet could most definitely see the attraction, and it seemed Sam was very attracted indeed. His colour was up and there was a twinkle in his eye she hadn't seen before.

'Who's your new friend?' she asked.

'Huh? Oh, Yasmine. She works here.'

'I thought she might,' Violet replied dryly.

'She's new.'

'I wouldn't have guessed.' Yasmine appeared confident and quite at ease. 'Why don't you ask her out?'

'Me?' Sam gaped at her, open-mouthed.

'Well *I'm* hardly going to, am I? She's not my type.'

'Er...' Sam blushed and Violet giggled at him.

'You like her a lot, don't you?' she teased.

'I've only just met her.'

'So? There's no rule that says you have to know someone for so many weeks or months before you're allowed to fancy them.'

'I don't know anything about her.'

'That's why you should ask her out – to *get* to know her.'

'She might be married.' He paused. 'She's not wearing a ring, though.'

'If you don't ask, you'll never know. Or do you want me to ask her for you? *My friend wants to know if you'll go out with him,*' she chimed in a high pitched voice.

'Stop it,' Sam hissed. 'You sound like a school kid.'

She giggled again, looking up at the bar and catching Logan's eye. Her giggle became a cheeky smile. Logan smiled back, setting her heart thumping. Damn it, but the guy was handsome. Sexy, too.

'Do you think I should?' Sam asked.

'If you like her as much as your face is saying you do, then you definitely should.'

He beckoned Yasmine over. 'Shh, here she comes.'

Violet concentrated on her meal as Sam stood up, and she tried not to listen.

'Can I get you anything else?' Yasmine asked.

'Erm, no...' Sam looked terrified.

'Is there a problem?'

'Not at all.'

Violet sneaked a glance from under her lashes. The poor girl seemed confused.

Sam was blushing. 'I was, um, wondering, er, if you'd like to go out sometime. If you've not got a boyfriend. Or a partner. For a drink, or a coffee. With me.'

Don't invite her for a coffee, Violet groaned inwardly. Wine and dine her, she wanted to shout at him. She had a sip of her drink instead, wishing it was gin, not lemonade.

The silence between Sam and Yasmine stretched out, awkward and cringing. Eventually Violet heard Sam's sharp intake of breath, but before he could say anything further Yasmine blurted, 'I've got a daughter. She's one and a half.'

Violet risked another look. Sam was blinking owlishly.

'You can bring her, too, if you want,' he said.

Another silence, this one not as long, then Yasmine broke it by saying, 'OK. As long as you don't mind.'

'Of course I don't mind. She could have juice, or something. We'll just have to pick somewhere child friendly.'

'I'm not going to bring Trinity on a date. I meant, I'll go out with you as long as you don't mind me having a daughter.'

Sam sounded surprised. 'Why would I mind?'

'Some men do.'

'I'm not some men.'

By now Violet was openly staring.

Yasmine's expression was thoughtful. 'I can see that.'

'Give me your number, and I'll call you after you finish

work,' Sam said.

'It'll be late.'

'Doesn't matter.'

They swapped phone numbers, then Yasmine hurried away, and Sam dropped into his seat.

'Phew. I thought she was going to turn me down. She was a bit defensive, don't you think? About her daughter.'

'She's probably had a few knock-backs when men find out she's got a child.'

'That doesn't bother me. You don't get to thirty without having a past.'

'I don't think she's as old as us.'

'I was talking about me.'

'You've got a past?'

'Don't look so shocked,' he said, around a mouthful of food.

Violet had finished hers. She was sure it must have been lovely, but she'd hardly tasted any of it. 'Do you want to tell me about it?'

'Not really, but now I've mentioned it, you're going to keep on until I do.'

Violet smiled sweetly at him. 'You make me sound like a right dragon.'

'That's because you are—'

'Cheeky. Go on, spill.'

'I was engaged once. Her name was Elise. We got as far as naming the date, booking the church and the reception, and even sending the invites out.' He stopped.

'You can't leave it there. What happened?'

'I called it off.' His head was down and Violet couldn't see his expression. 'I shouldn't have let it get so far. I knew it wasn't right. I didn't love her the way I should have done, the way she deserved. Elise was a wonderful girl: loving, caring, thoughtful, pretty, and great fun to be with. But...' He sighed heavily. 'She wasn't the one for me.'

'Why did you ask her to marry you?' Violet wasn't being judgemental; she genuinely wanted to know.

'I didn't. She asked me, one Christmas in front of everyone, the whole family, and I was so shocked I said yes. My mother was over the moon, of course. You've seen how she is. Before I knew it, the pair of them had set a date. When I called it off she was horribly disappointed.'

'I expect she was, the poor girl. But it's better to end it before the wedding, and not after.'

'I was talking about my mother. Elise wasn't as upset as I thought she'd be. She confessed she didn't think my heart was in it.' He shook his head sadly. 'I still hurt her, though. I didn't intend to, but I did. But I couldn't marry her. I loved her, just not as much as I should have.' He finally met Violet's gaze. 'She's engaged to a farmer over Hereford way, and my mother has been setting me up with dates ever since.'

'I think my problem is the polar opposite,' Violet said, checking that neither Logan nor his mother – who she hadn't seen since the woman had caught them kissing – were in earshot. 'Logan's mother hates me.'

'How could anyone hate *you*?'

'I know, right?' Violet joked. 'Seriously, she does. I've no idea why, but she's taken a total dislike to me. She keeps shooting me daggers, and she even told me it wouldn't last because she wouldn't let me come between her and her son.'

'You wouldn't do that, would you?'

'Of course not! I love that Logan is so attentive and caring to her. But she seems to think I'd try to take him away or something. I wish she was more like your mum.'

'And I wish we could swap places.' Sam looked wistful. 'My mum drives me barmy. She even tried to set me up with the sister of the guy who empties our septic tank. And she's never met her. I didn't even know the fella *had* a sister.'

Violet grimaced, wishing he hadn't put the image of a septic tank in her head. 'I bet she'd make a lovely mother-in-law, and at least *she* likes me. You don't know how lucky you are!'

'I feel like a baby-making machine,' he said indignantly. 'She only wants me for my ability to give her grandchildren. I suppose I am lucky, though. And I suspect Logan is, too. My mother and his might have very different outlooks, but they both come from a place of love.'

'Soppy sod.'

'I am, aren't I? But it's true. My mum is desperate to see me settled and happy, and I bet Logan's mum feels the same. But whereas my mother is trying to throw any woman at me and hope someone will stick, I suspect Logan's mother thinks that no woman will be good enough for him.' He caught sight of Violet's face which was saying what her lips were struggling to form. 'I'm not for one second suggesting you're not good enough for him,' Sam added hastily.

'Good. I'm pleased you cleared that up. I thought I might have to take you outside and beat some sense into you.'

'You know how some mothers get…'

'It's a pity Logan has to have one of them for his mother. It makes me thankful mine is normal. She sits slap bang in the middle of the pair of them. I think she'd be shocked though, if I took a guy home to meet her. My dad, on the other hand, might try the "I hope your intentions are honourable" stuff. He can be over-protective at times.'

'Better than not giving a hoot. And you can't accuse either my mum or Logan's of that.'

She supposed Sam was right, but it didn't alleviate the feeling that she was in for a tough time with Marie, and she might never win her round. If, that is, what was happening between her and Logan carried on. She hoped it would.

Violet and Sam ordered dessert, followed by coffee, and when that was consumed she led her friend outside to look at the garden.

'It's lovely,' he said. 'Almost Christmassy but not quite. There's a difference.'

'Yeah, it's September, not December,' she retorted.

'You know what I mean. With all these fairy lights and whatnot, it could so easily have gone the other way. Maybe I'll suggest to Yasmine that we come here for a meal.'

Violet was incredulous. 'Not on your first date! She won't appreciate being taken to the place she works. Please tell me you won't.'

'Do you think?'

'I most certainly do. Now, speaking of dates, I've got to see a man about a distillery.' She fished her keys out of her pocket. 'Go wait in the van; I won't be long.'

She watched him make his way through the bar, then Violet sought Logan out. 'I'm just checking we're still on for Monday?' she said.

'I'm looking forward to it.'

'So am I. Oh, and if Mr Potato Head tries to book a table for two in the next week or so, tell him you're full.'

'Why is that?'

'There might be a growing romance between a certain

farmer and one of your bar staff. He's plucked up the courage to ask her out, but he mentioned coming here for a date. The silly idiot!'

'Why is that silly? The Tavern is a perfect place for a first date.'

'Not if you work here, it isn't. Men! Good grief.'

'*You* came here for a date – kind of – and I work here.'

'I repeat – men!'

After giving him a swift kiss on the lips, Violet danced out of the pub, singing *Love is in the Air*, one of her mum's favourite tunes.

It was only when she was outside and walking across the car park that she wondered if she was including herself in that.

Maybe she was…

CHAPTER 14

LOGAN

Logan swilled the razor under the tap and put it on the side of the wash hand basin before he rinsed his face and patted it dry. Checking his cheeks and chin in the bathroom mirror after wiping the steam away for the umpteenth time that Monday morning, he was satisfied with the result.

He'd been up since the crack of dawn making sure everything was done that could be done, anxious that the Tavern ran smoothly on this rare day off of his. Normally his mother would be on hand if he had to be away from the pub, but the whole idea of him taking on another member of staff was that she needn't be. Scarlet was perfectly capable of managing the pub, and it was about time he let her, especially if he wanted to ease some of the ties binding him to it.

Of course, it was still his business and he was ultimately responsible for it, and he wouldn't have it any other way. But, and this was the point, he had to start living a life outside of the Tavern. He had to take time off; he had to take a holiday now and again. Today would hopefully be the first of many days off, and the fact that he was going to spend it with a woman he was falling for was an added bonus.

Satisfied that he was looking as good as he could, he almost danced into his bedroom to pick out what he was going to wear. Normally he just threw on a pair of jeans and a T-shirt, or a shirt, or sometimes a sweater, never paying much attention to what he wore, but not today. Today he wanted to make an impression. The problem was, he only owned jeans, or the suit he'd bought when he'd gone to the bank, cap in one hand, business plan in the other, to beg for a mortgage on the Tavern.

He didn't think wearing a suit today would be appropriate, so he had no choice other than to dig out his newest pair of jeans, and try to find a shirt to go with it. He decided to keep it simple and went for a white button-down one, but even then he couldn't resist rolling the sleeves up to just below his elbows.

He checked himself in the mirror again, and decided he'd have to do. It wasn't like this was a blind date (he wasn't even sure if it *was* a date) and she was a total stranger who didn't know what he looked like. She'd seen him up close and very personal, and she hadn't run away screaming yet, so he had to assume she didn't mind what she saw. At least he'd smell nice, he thought, as he squirted some cologne in the general direction of his chest.

It was early but he was ready, and he wondered what to do with himself for the next hour. If he set off now he'd only have to park up somewhere along the way and twiddle his thumbs, because it wouldn't do to arrive too early. But on the other hand, what if there was traffic? He could get stuck behind a tractor, or there might be an accident, or horrendous roadworks. Perhaps he should set off now, just in case?

Crikey, he hadn't felt this nervous in a very long time indeed.

Maybe he'd have a cup of coffee, then go?

He patted his pockets, checking he had his keys, his wallet, and his phone, then he headed downstairs into the bar. The Tavern wasn't open yet, but his staff had started to trickle in, and as usual he'd already switched on the stainless steel coffee machine that sat on one side of the bar, and which produced far nicer coffee than the jar of instant he had in his kitchen cupboard.

He was halfway to making himself a cup when his phone rang.

It was his mother.

Rolling his eyes and sighing, for a moment he seriously debated not answering but then he thought he better had. She'd only keep ringing if he didn't. He'd spoken to her earlier and asked her if she needed anything, so he wondered why she was ringing him now.

'Hi, Mum.'

'Can you pop in? I need to see you.'

'Is later OK? I'm just going out.'

'Oh, yes, your distillery visit. I'd forgotten. It doesn't matter, I'll just have to manage.' Her voice sounded strange.

'What is it?'

'I don't feel at all well.'

'Is it your head?'

'Yes.'

'Have you taken anything for it?' he asked.

'The tablets the doctor prescribed, but they haven't touched it.'

'How long ago did you take them?'

'An hour or so.'

Damn, the painkillers should have kicked in by now. 'Do you think you should give the surgery a call and see if they've got any appointments for this morning?'

'I suppose I could. But even if they can fit me in, I don't think I'm in any fit state to walk there. Oh, dear.' She sounded quite upset.

'Give the surgery a call and let me know. If they can give you an appointment, I'll take you.' The surgery wasn't far, easily walkable from his mum's house, but he couldn't allow her to walk if she was in pain.

She said in a small voice, 'You're a good son.'

Logan wasn't so sure about that: his first thought hadn't been about his mother's health, but about being late for his distillery visit.

He paced up and down the hallway, waiting for his mum to phone back, and when she eventually did the news wasn't what he'd been hoping for.

'I've got an appointment at one-thirty,' she told him, which didn't leave enough time beforehand to make it to *oriGINal Gin*, and perhaps not afterwards either, because he'd planned on being back in plenty of time for the evening rush. He was just about OK with leaving Scarlet in charge during the day, but not for the evening as well.

'I'll pick you up ten minutes before,' he told his mother, and she let out a whimper. It scared him. 'Can you wait until your appointment? Or should we just hop in the car now and I'll take you to A&E?' She sounded as though she was in some considerable pain.

'Let's see what the doctor says first,' she moaned.

'I'll be there in five minutes,' he said, heading out of the door and getting into his van. He didn't want her to be on her own. But before he started the engine, he gave Violet a call.

'I'm not going to make it today,' he said without preamble, regret sweeping over him.

'That's a shame. I was looking forward to it.

'Me, too. I'm sorry, but my mum's not well. I'm going with her to the doctors later.'

'I hope she'll be better soon.'

So did Logan. 'Can I take a rain check? I really want to have that tour.'

'Of course. Another time is fine.'

'I'm not sure when. I'll have to see how Mum is, and sort the staff rota out.'

'No worries. Just let me know when you want to come over.'

'Violet?'

'Yes?'

'I really am sorry.'

'So am I.' Her tone was soft and warm, and he was left in no doubt that she meant it. And, despite his concern over his mum, his heart soared.

***

'I'll come in with you,' Logan offered when his mother's name was called.

Marie frowned at him. 'I'm perfectly capable of speaking to the doctor on my own,' she snapped. His mum had been short with him ever since he'd arrived at her house.

Tell a lie, she'd been a bit tearful for the first few minutes, apologising for upsetting his plans for the day.

He'd assured her his visit to the distillery could be postponed and he could go again another time, then he'd fussed around her, making her a cup of tea and trying to get her to eat something. But all he'd succeeded in doing was to make her grumpy.

On the bright side, the tablets she'd taken earlier seemed to have worked because her headache appeared to have abated somewhat. Which was good, because if it hadn't he had told her in no uncertain terms, he was taking her to the hospital whether she wanted to go or not.

He was sure there was nothing to worry about – people had headaches all the time – but in the back of his mind there was the worry that it might be something more sinister than a migraine.

Despite his better judgement, he remained in the waiting room while his mum saw the doctor, and he tried to read an article on his phone about the latest brewery trends, but he couldn't concentrate. All he could think of was that the doctor might be hinting that something might be drastically wrong and she was on her own. He didn't think it was likely, but nevertheless…

'What did he say?' Logan asked, jumping to his feet when his mum sailed through the waiting area heading towards the exit.

'Stress,' she replied shortly.

'That's good, isn't it? At least it's nothing more serious.'

'Hmm.'

'How is your headache now?'

'Still there,' she snapped.

'Did he give you anything?'

Marie waved a piece of paper. 'More painkillers and a muscle relaxant. He reckons it will help with the tension in my shoulders and neck.'

'I wonder what's causing it?'

'I wonder.' Her reply was terse. She stiffly clambered into the passenger seat of the van, huffing and puffing her displeasure.

Yet again, Logan pondered whether he should invest in a car as he helped her up into it, but he'd bought the van shortly after he'd bought the Tavern (it had been a lifesaver when he'd been renovating the place) and it still came in handy now, so he was reluctant to trade it in.

'It's not like you've got a great deal of stress in your life,' he pointed out.

'What would you know about it?'

Logan blinked. He thought he knew quite a lot about his mother's life, but from her reply he guessed he didn't. 'Sorry, I assumed—'

'Don't.'

'OK.' Suitably chastised, he drove her home in silence via the chemist, to get her prescription filled.

She didn't speak again until he pulled up outside her house. 'Are you going back to the pub?' she asked before she got out.

He shrugged. 'I might as well.'

Marie said, 'I suppose it's too late to go out and about now. Sorry I ruined your day.'

'You didn't ruin it.' He twisted in his seat to look her in the face. 'I'm glad you told me you weren't feeling well. I'd hate to think of you in pain while I was out enjoying myself.'

Marie's mouth tightened into a thin line. 'I thought the trip to the distillery was business, not pleasure.'

Logan refused to be drawn. 'I can always rearrange – Violet didn't mind when I told her I couldn't make it today.'

His mother reached for the door handle, and Logan hurried out of the driver's seat and around to her side to help her down.

She took a deep breath. 'I'm worried,' she said. 'I think it might be more than just a headache.'

'What makes you think that?'

'I can't put my finger on it.'

'See how it goes with these new tablets, eh? If they work, great; if not, you'll have to go back and see him. Shall I come in with you for a bit? I could make you a bite to eat, or run the vacuum cleaner around?' Anything to be of help or to make her life easier.

'I'll be fine. Stop fussing. Sorry to spoil your day off,' she repeated.

'If you're sure?' he replied, doubtfully, not wanting to leave her alone.

She flapped her hands at him. 'Go back to the pub; you're needed there. I can manage.'

Having no choice, he did precisely that, but when he got to the Tavern his staff had other ideas.

CHAPTER 15

VIOLET

Violet stared at her phone in dismay. Poor Marie. She hoped the woman would be OK. How awful for her, and for Logan too, and she felt guilty about the thoughts she'd been having regarding Marie's health. Logan's mother was patently unwell, but hopefully the doctor could prescribe something.

At a loose end and unable to settle in her potions room, she decided she needed to get out and about, to restock some of her jars of botanicals. Beth, her best friend, was the ideal person to do that with, and she happened to be free Violet discovered, when she phoned her. So half an hour later saw the pair of them traipsing across some fields and heading for a patch of woodland not too far from the distillery.

It was Violet's favourite place to forage. She liked to use as many natural ingredients in her gin as possible, the wilder the better, and Beth was an expert forager; she even ran courses and she often pointed out things Violet missed. Whether those things could be used to flavour gin was another matter, but Violet was always grateful for her help and enthusiasm.

'You like this new chap of yours, then?' Beth asked casually, flicking her long dark hair away from her face as she bent to pick the last of the season's blackberries.

'I might do.' Violet had already brought her up to speed on what had been happening in her life since she'd seen her last.

'What's he like?'

'Good-looking, kind, sexy, fun.'

You've just described my ideal man. Has he got a brother?'

'Not that I know of,' Violet laughed. Then she sobered. 'He does have a mother, though.'

'Most people do. But I honestly don't think I'd want to date anyone's mother.'

'I'm serious. She seems to be a big part of his life.'

'Are you saying he's a mummy's boy?'

Violet considered the question carefully. 'I don't think so. He cares for her, obviously, but I think she's the one having trouble letting go, not him. But there may be a good reason for that,' she added and went on to tell Beth about the phone call from Logan earlier.

'Oh, dear, I hope she'll be better soon,' Beth said, echoing Violet's reaction. 'Look, rose hips.' She pointed out a bush bearing a mass of red fruit. 'We'll come back in a month or so to pick these; they'll be softer after a frost or two, and you'll get more juice out of them. Do they know what's causing her headaches?'

Violet shrugged. 'I don't think so – that's why he was going with her to see the doctor. What do they taste like?'

'Slightly sweet with a tart aftertaste. They were used in

World War Two as a replacement for citrus fruit because of their high vitamin C content. When are you seeing him again?'

'Sounds like an ideal flavour for gin,' Violet remarked. 'I don't know. It depends on his mum, I expect.'

When Violet was out with Beth, their conversation was often sporadic like this. It was one of the things she loved about her friend.

'How about some hazelnuts?' Beth walked over to a tree whose branches were covered in green, unripe nut casings.

Violet had picked these in previous years, and the nut was the main ingredient in her hazelnut flavoured gin. Eagerly, she gathered several handfuls, careful not to take too many. She'd leave the nuts to ripen in her airing cupboard.

'Yum, hazelnut butter,' Beth said, moving to another tree and taking her selection from there.

Both women carried wicker baskets to put their finds in, and Beth's was already half full as she tended to eat anything she foraged. Violet had fewer options as she preferred to drink hers. Or at least make the gin other people would drink. For a distiller, she didn't drink very much at all.

'Fancy popping back to mine for a spot of late lunch?' Violet asked, suddenly feeling hungry. 'I could do us a Ploughman's. Mum gave me a jar of pear chutney that would go down a treat with it.'

'You've twisted my arm,' Beth said. 'I love your mum's preserves.'

Violet and Rory's parents owned a smallholding near Hereford. They'd both taken early retirement, and were thoroughly enjoying growing their own fruit and veg, collecting the eggs from their five chickens, and arguing with the two enormous pigs that had originally been bought as piglets to fatten for the table, and who now lorded it over Violet's parents because neither of them had been able to send Grunt and Squeak to their doom. Instead, her mum bought her bacon and pork chops from the butcher, and made the most delicious chutneys to accompany it.

Violet and Beth, happy with their mornings' haul, were just about to walk back, when Beth spotted something.

She tapped Violet on the arm and pointed.

Violet looked. 'Are those blackberries? If so, they're not quite ripe.'

'These, if I'm not mistaken, are loganberries. But they don't usually grow wild. Birds must have dropped the seeds, I expect,' Beth added.

Violet continued to gaze at the dark red berries, which looked like a cross between a blackberry and a raspberry; which was exactly what the fruit was, Beth explained, as she picked one and tasted it. She handed another to Violet who popped it in her mouth.

The flavour exploded on her tongue, sweet, but not too sweet; tart, but not too much. It was perfect. And the name...!

An idea forming, she harvested some, and she knew exactly what she was going to do with them.

Violet was going to make loganberry gin.

***

Violet had always hoped Rory and Beth would get together, but no such luck. It would be marvellous to have her brother and best friend fall in love, but although they got on extremely well, the attraction had never been there.

Every time the pair of them were in the same room together Violet hunted for it, but it wasn't to be, and today was no exception.

Rory had been in the distillery when Violet and Beth returned from their foraging trip, and was more than happy to join them for lunch. Rory never said no to food, especially when he didn't have to make it himself.

Violet sent Beth out to fetch him (always the optimist) and she was slicing a quiche when the two of them entered the kitchen, Beth giggling at something Rory must have said.

'You've never made *me* my own gin,' were the first words out of her brother's mouth.

'I don't think there's such a thing as a *rory*berry,' she retorted briskly.

'You've got it bad,' he sing-songed back to her. 'Violet's in luurve.'

'So what if I am?' she demanded, which stopped Rory in his tracks and even had Beth raising her eyebrows.

'*Are* you?' he asked.

Violet hesitated. 'To be honest, I'm not sure. Here, make yourself useful and slice the bread.' The loaf was from an artisan bakery in Hay, and Rory bought a fresh one every morning when he was coming to the distillery. Which, to be fair, was most days.

He might not live on-site, having his own place in Hay, thank God, but the business was half his and he had an equal desire to see it succeed. Occasionally he took a day off, as did she, but it was rare.

Violet had opted to live in the old farmhouse. Most of the land had been sold off years ago, leaving a rundown house, a huge barn and several dilapidated outbuildings – perfect for a small distillery like theirs. Once they'd all been done up, of course. The house still had some way to go, but it was hers and Violet loved it.

'You really like him, don't you?' Rory repeated, his tone serious.

Violet blushed. 'I've not known him long.'

'Being in love suits you.' Rory nudged her with his elbow.

'I'm not—' she began, then stopped. Was she? She honestly didn't know. As she'd pointed out to the gruesome twosome a few minutes ago, she'd not known Logan for very long. But that didn't prevent her from thinking about him far more frequently than she'd thought about any other man in the past. Even when she had been with a guy, half of her mind had always been on other things.

But when she was with Logan all of her had lived in the moment. Especially when he'd kissed her. Heck, she was still living it now, and she touched her lips as the memory of his mouth on hers leapt into her mind.

'If you are, great; I'm pleased for you,' Rory said. 'But don't go jumping into anything. Take your time, yeah? I don't want to see you hurt.'

'And neither do I,' Beth added.

'Me, three,' Violet said jokingly, trying to lighten the mood. 'Anyway, it probably won't go any further. He's got too much on his plate.'

'Because of his mother?' Beth guessed.

Rory slapped a hand to his forehead. 'Wasn't he supposed to be having a tour today?' Her brother looked around the kitchen as though he expected Logan to be hiding in the pantry.

'He was, but he had to take his mum to the doctors – she's not well.'

'I'm sorry, Violet. I expect you'll rearrange?'

'He said he would.'

'His mother's ill health shouldn't prevent you from having a relationship with him,' Beth pointed out.

'It's not just that – she seriously doesn't like me. I'm beginning to wonder if dating Logan mightn't be more trouble than it's worth, all things considered.' It wasn't too late to back out. They'd hardly got off the ground in terms of a relationship. But the thought of not seeing him again did funny things to her insides, which wasn't at all pleasant.

'You don't mean it?' Beth asked, taking a seat as Violet placed three full plates on the table. 'This looks yummy. Thank you for inviting me.'

'You're welcome, any time; you know that.'

'Just not when Logan is here, eh?' Rory teased. He turned to Beth and said, 'She's been suggesting I go look at some new tanks today – anything to get me out of the place while she showed lover-boy around.'

Rory was right: Violet had hinted very strongly that he might want to make himself scarce today, but only because she didn't trust him not to say something he shouldn't. Normally he never got to meet any of her boyfriends, and when he did she hadn't given two hoots whether her brother said anything out of turn.

That she now cared what Rory might say to Logan, wasn't lost on her. She wanted to keep Logan to herself for a while longer and be more certain of her footing with him before she allowed her brother anywhere near him.

'Do you blame me?' she demanded. 'I haven't forgotten the time when you told Mason Harvey that I was wearing knickers with the days of the week on them. I was mortified.'

'We were kids.'

'I was *seventeen* and I still haven't forgiven you.' It was no wonder she wanted to keep the two men apart as long as possible.

Beth was staring at her, her expression unreadable.

'What?' Violet asked.

'Did you know your eyes light up when you talk about Logan?'

Violet didn't know. Although she was fully aware that her heart sped up whenever she thought about him – which appeared to be all the time. She'd have to make an appointment at the doctor's surgery herself if it kept on doing that.

'So what if his mother doesn't like you? The only thing that matters is whether *Logan* likes you,' Beth stated.

'True…' Up to a point, she admitted silently. But Beth hadn't seen the look Marie had given her or heard the woman say she wasn't going to let Violet come between her and her son. She'd sounded rather venomous.

In one way it gave her hope, because if Marie saw her as a potential threat it must mean Logan was seriously interested in her. On the other, it was going to be hard to win the woman around. If she ever did.

Rory swallowed a mouthful of food and said, 'You've never backed down from a challenge in your life. This isn't like you.' His eyes were full of concern.

That was also true. If anyone ever said to her she couldn't do something because she was too young, too old, too inexperienced, not skilled enough or, the real no-no, because she was *female*, Violet had always seen it as a personal challenge and would then set out to prove them wrong.

'Let's look at this logically—' she began.

'Let's not,' Beth interrupted. 'The heart wants what the heart wants.'

Violet shot her a look. 'As I was saying, not only is his mum unwell, we live a half an hour drive away from each other, and we also both have demanding businesses to run – his more than mine, because at least I can more or less choose when I work. As long as the gin is bottled and ready to go, I can do it at midnight if I want. Oh, and did I mention his mother doesn't like me? I wish she was more like Gretchen.'

Beth snorted. 'Seriously, you don't. Gretchen is a lovely, lovely lady, but you wouldn't get a minute's peace with her. Did I tell you she tried to set me and Sam up once?'

'*No!* She didn't?'

'She did.'

'She did the same to me last week. I think she bullied Sam into asking me out.'

'Did you go?'

'I did. We had coffee and I tried to let him down gently. I needn't have bothered – he doesn't fancy me in the slightest. However, he does fancy a barmaid at the Tavern.'

'Good for him. But I mean it when I say Gretchen might be as trying as Logan's mum, just in different ways.'

'That's what Sam says.'

'Well, then, we can't both be spouting nonsense. What you've got to decide is whether all the negative things you've mentioned outweigh how you feel about Logan.'

Violet thought.

They didn't.

They might make things a little more difficult but, as Rory said, she'd never run away from a challenge in her life.

Saying that, she didn't think of Logan as a challenge. He felt more like her destiny.

'Hurry up and finish your lunch,' she said to Rory and Beth. 'I've got a new flavour of gin to make.'

CHAPTER 16

LOGAN

'You're back early. How was the distillery visit?' Scarlet asked when Logan walked into the tavern after making sure his mum was settled and that she'd taken one of her tablets.

'I didn't go.'

'Why ever not?'

'Mum rang – she had a terrible headache, so I took her to the doctors.'

'Is she all right?'

Logan blew out a breath. 'I think so. He's given her some different tablets, so I'm keeping my fingers crossed they'll work.'

'Let's hope so. It's a shame about not going to the distillery, though; I know how much you were looking forward to it.' She raised her eyebrows at him and he looked away.

Was his interest in Violet so obvious? 'I've spoken to Violet and she understands. We'll arrange it for another day.'

'When?'

'I don't know – whenever I can sort out another day off, I suppose.'

'Give her a call now,' Scarlet urged. 'I can work around you and your plans.'

'I suppose I could.' He dug his phone out of his pocket, his body flooding with pleasure when he heard Violet's voice.

'How is your mum?' she asked, before he could say anything.

'She's OK, I think. The doctor gave her some tablets. Look, sorry about today, I was looking forward to it.' He'd already told Violet that, but he was keen to stress how disappointed he was. 'Can we sort out another day?' He was looking at Scarlet as he said it, and she nodded vigorously.

'How about right now? If you've already planned to have today off you may as well come over.'

'Now?' It was already late afternoon, and there was the early evening rush that he'd originally intended to be back for because he hadn't organised cover. The pub's busiest time was between six p.m. and eight, when people ate out. 'I need to be in the Tavern this evening.'

Scarlet snatched the phone out of his hand. 'How late can he make it before it's too late? Sorry, this is Scarlet speaking.'

Logan made a grab for his mobile but his interfering barmaid darted out of reach.

'OK, cool, he'll be there. Nice talking to you,' she said.

Scarlet handed him his phone, but when Logan tried to speak to Violet, he realised he was talking to thin air. 'What did you do that for?' he demanded.

'Because you need a break from this place, and if you help with the teatime crowd we can manage after that. She's expecting you at eight. Besides, Mondays are never particularly busy.'

'But—'

'But nothing. Violet is happy to give you a *tour* this evening—' Scarlet smirked '—so you should take her up on it.'

***

Violet's distillery was on the outskirts of Hay-on-Wye, along several small lanes which terminated in what appeared to be a farmyard. It was dark by the time Logan pulled up outside the house, and all he could see were the shadowy outlines of several large buildings.

Violet must have heard him arrive because as he switched off the engine a floodlight illuminated the yard. She was standing in the doorway of the old farmhouse and smiling. Logan smiled back. Boy, was she a sight for sore eyes.

'Better late than never,' he said, getting out of his van and walking towards her.

'I don't usually do tours in the evening. Actually, I don't usually give tours to the general public at all. You're my first.'

'Am I the general public?' He was disappointed, hoping he was more to her than that.

'Do you want to be?'

'No.'

'A friend, then?' She was gazing at him quizzically.

'More than that.'

'Are you sure?'

'I am.' And he was. Totally and utterly sure.

Tentatively, he kissed her, hoping it was the right thing to do, but he kept it light, and didn't go in for the passionate clinch he secretly wanted. He was here to visit the distillery, not for anything else (although that would be welcome), so the kiss was a brief brush of the lips before he stepped back.

'Tour first?' she said, licking her lips as though she wanted to capture the taste of him. Her pupils were huge, her eyes a deeper, darker colour than usual.

'OK.' *First?* What was going to happen after that? A coil of excitement tightened in his stomach. He couldn't wait to find out.

'This way.' Violet led him across the yard towards one of the outbuildings, and flipped a bank of switches as soon as she unlocked the door. 'What do you know about distilling?' she asked.

Logan blinked in the bright lights. Wow! The space was big, but it wasn't the size which caught his attention – it was the array of gleaming copper and steel stills and tanks, and the myriad of pipes running to and from them.

'Probably not enough,' he admitted. He'd not been expecting this. Although he had visited a whisky distillery before, it had been a commercial operation run by a famous producer. He'd almost expected *oriGINal Gin* to be a kitchen-table operation, but what he was seeing here was on a professional scale.

Violet grinned at his reaction. 'The gin might be artisan in that I select and combine the botanicals by hand, but making the actual base alcohol isn't.'

'I can see that.' He was taking everything in, impressed.

Violet continued. 'There are two basic steps when it comes to unaged spirits: fermentation and distillation. You can ferment almost anything, but I use potatoes.'

'I never would have guessed,' he teased, remembering their very first encounter and how fascinated by her he'd been.

'Potatoes, plus yeast, plus heat, and voila! Alcohol is the result. We aim for roughly 12% proof at this stage. However, it's not drinkable yet; it's more like sweet gloopy soup, and is fairly horrid.'

She guided him around the room as she talked, pointing to various pieces of equipment, and explaining the process, Logan asking loads of questions, utterly fascinated. There was that word again. It described Violet perfectly.

'Then we come to the stills,' she explained. 'The mixture is transferred to these, and this is where distillation takes place, where the raw alcohol is made. I suppose we could bypass all this,' she gestured to the huge tanks, 'and buy it in, but I want to know where my plant materials come from.'

'Sam's farm?'

'Exactly! All organic, all local, so, we make our own base spirit. In order to get from the yucky soupy stuff to clean, pure alcohol, we distil it several times, and each time more of the ethanol is separated from the other compounds, until what we're left with is neutral flavourless alcohol. It's only at this point that we infuse it with juniper berries to make gin.'

Logan was taking it all in, admiring her knowledge and skill. When she showed him into what she called her potions room, he was even more impressed. Shelf upon shelf was stocked with jars, all neatly labelled, and containing things as diverse as peppercorns and rose petals.

'This is where the magic happens,' she said, her eyes shining. 'I play around with different botanicals until I find a combination that works, and a new flavour of gin is born.'

'There's a bit more to it than that,' Logan surmised.

'Of course, another round of distillation for the sturdier botanicals, or vapour infusion for the more delicate ones. But in essence, that's it. Do you want to try a few flavours?'

Logan nibbled at his bottom lip. 'I'd better not, I'm driving.'

'You could always stay?'

His eyes widened.

'I've got a spare room.'

'Oh. OK.' That wasn't what he'd been hoping for…

'Come with me. I keep a stack of bottles purely for taking to potential suppliers so they can try before they buy.'

'I remember.'

She ushered him into another room where the bottling and labelling took place. 'I'm up to my behind in Christmas flavours at the moment. Care to try some?'

'Absolutely!'

She unscrewed the top of a bottle, the liquid inside a burgundy colour. Pouring out a small measure, she handed him a tiny tumbler. 'Christmas cake.'

He tasted it. 'That's rather moreish.' There was a rich full fruity flavour with a hint of marzipan.

'Isn't it just? What about this one?' She opened another bottle. 'Gingerbread.'

He tried it. 'Oh my goodness, it tastes *exactly* like gingerbread.'

'That's the intention. Another?'

The next was cranberry and pomegranate, followed by marshmallows and chocolate, praline, roast chestnut, and, surprisingly, eggnog.

Logan was beginning to feel a little tipsy. Violet, he

noticed, hadn't touched a drop.

'Lastly, there's the peppermint one, and the orange and dark chocolate flavour. Of course, I always carry other flavours with me, but I find seasonal gins go down a treat.'

These were going down very well indeed and Logan wished he'd eaten something which would have helped soak up all the alcohol he was busily consuming.

'Shall we leave it there? Or do you want to know more?' she asked.

'I'd love to see how you come up with a new flavour, but we can do that another time?' he asked, hoping he wasn't overstepping the mark by suggesting there would *be* another time.

'That's something else I was thinking about – not just offering tours of the distillery but giving people an opportunity to make their own flavour gins. It would mean an initial outlay to buy small infusers, but I think the business could cope with that. I'll have to play with some figures and see what's feasible. Did I tell you we're considering taking on someone to help?'

'How's that going?'

'Rory and I are in discussion, shall we say… We're squabbling about what we want the new person to do. He wants help with the fermenting and distilling side – I want help with all the damned paperwork.'

'It's a nightmare, isn't it? Not only do I feel I need to be in the bar whenever it's open, which is nearly twelve hours a day, but there's all the other stuff that goes on behind the scenes that also needs doing.'

Violet asked, 'Do you fancy a drink?'

'I think I've just had one.' More than one. It was going to his head. Or was it her perfume that was making him dizzy?

'I was thinking of having it in the house, sitting on the sofa. It doesn't have to be gin.'

'In that case…'

She carefully locked up, then she showed him into the house, told him to take a seat, and disappeared through a door that led to the kitchen. He caught a glimpse of dark pine units and a large fridge.

The sofa looked very inviting; soft, squishy, and well-used.

'Wine?' she called.

'Please.'

'Red or white?'

'Red, please.' He wanted something to cleanse his palette after the many flavours that had passed over his tongue in the last half hour. He also felt he needed a more substantial drink than white wine, after the lightness of the gin.

She came into the living room, carrying a couple of glasses in one hand and an open bottle of red in the other. Handing him a glass, she poured them both a decent amount, then she joined him on the sofa and sat back, swirling the liquid around in her glass before inhaling it. Finally, she took a mouthful and he watched her throat move as she swallowed. She had a lovely throat, soft and white. He wanted to kiss it. The rest of her, too.

'Don't tell me you're a wine aficionado as well as gin?' he asked.

She looked surprised, then realised what he was referring to. 'No,' she laughed. 'I just like the smell. I wouldn't know one wine from another. All I know is whether it tastes good or not.' She let out a long breath. 'It's been quite a day for you.'

'I suppose.'

'I hope your mum gets better soon.'

'So do I.'

'Sorry, I'm being selfish,' Violet said.

'In what way?' He took another sip of wine, the liquid slipping easily down his throat, warming his insides.

'Because I want to see more of you,' she said.

Ah.

'If you want to?' she added, sounding uncertain.

'I most definitely want to,' he whispered.

'Good.' She put her drink down on the little table by the side of the sofa, then reached for his, took it out of his hand, and placed it next to hers. 'I wouldn't want to spill any,' she said, moving closer.

Logan froze, anticipation surging through him.

Her lips were parted and her eyes were luminous in the lamplight. He could feel the stir of her soft breath on his face and he closed his eyes.

Gently, oh so gently, she kissed him, their mouths the only point of contact between them for several wonderful seconds before he was unable to resist any longer and he put his arms around her, desperate to hold her.

Lord, she felt good. She smelt good too, and he gave himself up to the sensations sweeping through him. It wasn't the gin making him giddy at all, he realised– it was her. She made his head spin, filling his senses completely and utterly until he could think of nothing but her.

He dragged his mouth away, trailing kisses along her jaw and down her neck, to nibble at that sweet spot just below her ear. Her muted whimpers sent a stab of desire right through him.

'Wait.' She pushed him away, and he realised he was

lying half on top of her.

He stopped nibbling and his hands ceased their roving, as he eased off her. Her hair fanned across a cushion, her face flushed, her expression resolute.

'Not yet,' she said.

What a pity...

'Too soon?' he guessed.

'Much.'

'I agree. I'll have you know I don't jump into bed with just anyone,' he said primly, with a hint of teasing in his voice,

'Neither do I.' Her tone was equally as light.

'Seriously, I'd like nothing more than to make love to you. Just so you know.'

'I can tell.'

He tried not to blush. His desire for her had been rather obvious.

'Drink your wine,' she told him. 'Let's chat. I want to get to know you better.'

'Such as, what's my favourite food, and whether I like rom coms?' he laughed.

'Do you?'

'No.'

'Neither do I. I like Star Wars.'

'I prefer old black and white thrillers, like Rear Window.'

'We're doomed. We've not got a thing in common.'

'We do have something,' he said.

'What?'

'My favourite colour is violet. Actually, it's not,' he amended. 'It's blue.'

'Make your mind up.'

'Blue is the colour of your eyes.'

'Charmer. Is that your pick up line?'

'No, it's the truth. Can I kiss you again?'

'As long as that's all you do.'

'I promise. You can even tie my hands behind my back.' Damn, that came out wrong.

'We need to get to know each other better first,' she said, a wicked gleam in her eye.

With a sharp intake of breath, Logan reached for her, and for the rest of the evening he lost himself in the softness of her lips.

CHAPTER 17

VIOLET

'How's your head?' Violet asked.

Logan groaned as he sloped into her kitchen the following morning. 'It's been better.'

'Coffee?'

'Please.'

'Painkillers?' She handed him two tablets and he took them.

After watching him swallow with a great deal of wincing and nearly burning his mouth on the hot drink he tried to wash them down with, she thought she'd better address the elephant in the room.

'About last night… Do you regret it?'

'Yes,' he said. 'Do you?'

'I see.' Her face tightened, and her stomach turned over. That'll teach her, she thought – she shouldn't have asked.

'I regret not making love to you,' he clarified, with a sexy smile.

The tension slowly seeped from her. 'I see,' she repeated, her tone gentle. 'That's good. Breakfast?'

'Ugh. No thanks.'

'Shower?'

'Are you suggesting I join you in one?' he asked, looking decidedly perkier.

'No.' She grinned at him. 'I've had one already.' Although the idea was certainly appealing. She'd been hard pushed to control herself last night, but she'd meant it when she'd told him she wanted to get to know him better first.

'How long have you been up?' He peered at the digital display on the cooker.

'Since six.' It was now half-past seven.

'Do you always get up this early? Because if you do, I can categorically say we're not compatible.'

'Only when there's a strange man staying in my house.'

'Hey, who are you calling strange?'

'If the cap fits,' she smirked. 'You wanted me to tie you up last night.'

Logan blushed and she giggled. He was cute when he was on the back foot. And he was exceptionally sexy with his hair sticking up and the stubble on his face. She remembered the roughness of it on the skin of her neck as he kissed his way to her collarbone, and she shivered. One of the hardest things she'd ever done had been to push him away. But her invitation to stay over hadn't been an invitation to sleep with her, no matter how tempted she'd been.

'There are fresh towels in the bathroom. Help yourself. When you're finished we'll have another coffee in the sunroom.'

A short while later she heard the shower running and she tried not to think of him in it, naked, water cascading over his shoulders and down his… Nope, she definitely wouldn't think of that.

Instead, she busied herself by making a fresh pot of coffee. It was a pity she hadn't known in advance he was going to visit last night, because she'd have bought some bacon and sausages, and would have cooked him a full English. Mind you, he looked a little too green around the gills to manage anything fried.

She was just about to pour their drinks, when he returned to the kitchen.

Without preamble, he walked up behind her, slipped his arms around her waist, and kissed the back of her neck.

Gosh, that felt good, and she snuggled back into him for a moment, coffee forgotten. He smelt of her shower gel and when she twisted around in his arms to kiss him properly, she ran a hand through his damp hair and it took all her willpower not to drag him off to bed. Instead, she dragged herself out of his embrace and indicated a door on the far side of the kitchen.

'Go into the sunroom, and I'll bring the coffee.' She needed a second alone to compose herself. Oh, dear, she had it bad, didn't she, and the more time she spent with him, the more she realised how much she was falling for him.

'Feeling better?' she asked as she joined him. The shower and the painkillers seemed to have done him the world of good.

'Yes, thanks. I can't believe how much I drank last night, considering I was only having tiny glasses of gin.'

'The tiny glasses aren't the problem, it's the number of them. Then there was the wine…'

'Why don't you have a hangover?' he moaned. 'It's not fair.'

'I didn't drink much – I only had two glasses of wine,

and I didn't drink any gin. I often don't, to be honest.' She had to taste it when she was making it, obviously, but the sips were teeny-tiny ones, else she'd be permanently blotto. 'I don't think you're OK to drive,' she observed.

'You don't?'

She shook her head. 'You wouldn't want to risk it, so how about I drive you to Ticklemore this morning? I'll bring your van over later. We'll finish our coffee then I'll drop you home.'

'I wish I could stay, but…'

'So do I. We could have gone for a walk, then had a spot of lunch.' She didn't tell him what she fancied doing after that, otherwise she might throw her inhibitions to the wind and do it right now.

It was still quite early when they arrived in Ticklemore so when Logan, who now looked considerably less green-around-the-gills, said, 'Fancy some breakfast? The pub's not due to open for a couple of hours yet,' Violet readily agreed. She was ravenous.

To her surprise, he didn't head towards the Tavern. Instead he took her hand and led her down the main street.

'Where are we going?' she asked.

'I thought we'd pop into Bookylicious, the coffee-cum-book shop just down the road. I know if I go to the Tavern I'll start work and I'm not ready for that just yet. Besides, they do a mean bacon butty.' He smiled down at her.

They were still holding hands, and it felt nice as they strolled along the pavement. She felt as though they were a proper couple, and perhaps they were. Violet didn't like uncertainty – she never had – so she decided to ask him outright.

'Are we dating?'

'*I* thought we were,' he said.

'We are then,' she replied firmly.

'Glad we cleared that up.' Logan looked slightly confused.

'I didn't want to take anything for granted,' she explained.

'We're hardly friends with benefits, are we?'

'That's because we haven't got to the benefit stage yet,' she retorted.

'Oh, I think I had plenty of benefits last night,' he teased.

Violet felt heat steal into her cheeks.

'You're blushing,' he said, grinning.

'I'm not.'

'You are; it's cute. It's as sexy as hell, too,' he added, making her blush even more. 'Here we are.'

He came to a halt outside a building with double bay windows and a door in the middle. Through one of the bay windows she could see a café: the other window was stacked with books. He opened the door and gestured for her to go ahead of him.

The cafe was fairly busy, but she wasn't surprised, considering the delicious waft of coffee, and the aroma of bacon filling the air. Violet's mouth watered.

'Sit down and I'll bring it over,' a rather elderly lady said, after they'd given her their order. She had long white hair piled on top of her head in a bun with tendrils framing her face and Violet estimated her to be in her late seventies at least.

'Thanks, Hattie,' Logan said.

He was about to walk away, when Hattie said, 'It's nice to see you with a girl. And about time, too.'

Logan shot Violet a sideways glance. 'Hattie, meet

Violet, Violet, this lovely lady is Hattie.'

'So *this* is Violet, is it? Nice to meet you.' Hattie was studying her intently and Violet tried not to squirm.

Logan was saying, 'She owns the company whose gin you were drinking on Friday night. In fact, she makes it.'

'She does?' Hattie's face was wreathed in smiles. 'It's bloody good stuff,' she said. She licked her lips, as though she could still taste it.

Violet was always thrilled to receive a compliment, especially when it was about her gin. 'I'm so pleased you liked it,' she said. 'Which one did you try?'

'All of them, I think,' Hattie replied, and Logan nodded.

'Not all on Friday, I hasten to add,' Logan said. 'She tasted some of them before that. It was her idea to have an autumn theme in the Tavern.'

'And a very good idea it was,' Violet said.

Hattie simpered. 'I get one of those now and again.'

'I'll have to tell you about her sometime,' Logan said, when he steered Violet away from the counter and towards a free table. 'She's a real character, so full of beans and constantly meddling in people's lives.'

'You sound like you don't mind?'

'I don't. Ticklemore wouldn't be the same without her in it.'

Hattie appeared with a tray a short while later and proceeded to place its contents on the table. 'How's your mum? I heard she had another one of her headaches.'

'She's OK, I think. I'll give her a call later,' Logan said, biting into his bacon roll.

'Best make it a fair bit later,' Hattie said, glancing meaningfully at Violet, who tried to keep her expression neutral. 'So, tell me…' The old lady pulled out a chair and plonked her bottom down on it and Violet hoped she didn't intend to sit with them for the duration. No matter how nice Hattie seemed, Violet wanted Logan all to herself.

'What are you doing in Bookylicious at this time in the morning with the lovely Violet? Did she spend the night at the Tavern?'

Violet gasped at the woman's nosiness.

'No, Hattie, she didn't,' Logan said. 'She dropped me off this morning.'

Hattie looked thoughtful. 'You must have stayed at hers, then. Good for you! It's about time you got a bit of—'

'*Hattie!*' Logan sounded shocked.

'Wise decision. You know what your mum is like. If you'd been at yours, she'd have been interrupting you every five minutes.' She waggled her eyebrows.

'*Hattie!*' Logan's face was red. 'I drank too much to drive, OK?' He sent Violet an apologetic glance.

'If you say so.'

Violet struggled not to laugh. The woman was a total hoot, and Violet didn't care one jot if Hattie thought she and Logan had spent the night together.

'It wasn't like that,' he protested.

Hattie tapped Violet on the arm. 'You do know he's besotted with you, don't you? You can tell by the way he looks at you. Any fool can see that. Even Marie! Bet she's not best pleased about it, though.'

Logan gestured to his breakfast. 'Do you mind if we eat this in peace?'

'Not at all. Go ahead, I'm not stopping you. In fact, I think I'll have something myself.' She swivelled in her chair. 'Oi, Maddison, fetch us a brew and a slice of cherry Bakewell; I'm going to take my break early. These two need sorting out.'

Violet pursed her lips. She'd gone from wishing Hattie would leave them alone to wanting her to stay so she could hear more about Logan being besotted.

Logan groaned and shook his head. 'We don't need sorting out.'

'She likes you, too,' Hattie informed him, inspecting Violet so thoroughly it made her squirm.

Maybe she *would* prefer it if Hattie sat at another table after all.

'You've got to go for it,' Hattie said. 'There's no point in hanging about. I found that out where my Alfred was concerned. There's no time to lose – life's too short.'

'We're not old yet,' Logan pointed out.

'You soon will be. One minute you're thirty and you've got your whole life ahead of you, then poof!' She snapped her fingers. 'You're wondering where the last fifty years went. Make the most of it, I say. You've got to seize the day, make hay while the sun shines, strike while the iron's hot. If you don't grab life with both hands and shake the bejeezus out of it, you'll only regret it, mark my words. And don't let anyone talk you out of doing what you want to do. It's your life to live, and you don't want to have any regrets. You've got to think of your future, my boy.'

Crikey, what was all that about, Violet wondered.

Logan appeared dazed and Violet guessed that she, herself, was probably wearing a similar expression.

He got to his feet. 'I'll just go and pay. Finish your coffee,' he said, popping the rest of his breakfast into his mouth.

Violet picked up the oversized cup and tried to hide behind it. The woman was off her trolley.

'Quick, now that I've got you own your own, there's something I need to tell you.' Hattie leant closer to Violet. 'Watch out for Marie. She might not be as ill as she seems.' The old lady glanced around swiftly, then continued, her voice hushed. 'Logan's mother has had her headaches for a long time, but they get worse when something happens that she doesn't like, and I bet she's not too keen on you.' Hattie's eyes bored into her. 'I thought not,' she continued without waiting for an answer.

Violet vowed to try to control her facial expressions more – it wouldn't do for her to be read so easily.

'Thanks for the company,' Logan said, appearing by Hattie's side and stuffing his wallet in his back pocket. 'I'd better get back to the Tavern.'

'And I've got gin to make. Nice to meet you, Hattie.' Violet got to her feet.

'Think about what I said,' Hattie replied. 'Logan, this one's a keeper. Don't let her go, whatever happens.'

'That was cryptic,' Logan said, as soon as they were outside. 'I'm not sure if she's eccentric, meddling, or has a crystal ball. Her heart's in the right place, though, and I love her to bits.'

'She seems to think a lot of you.'

He smiled. 'She's like a grandmother to me. But to be fair, I believe she thinks she's everyone's grandmother. It's a pity she and my mum don't get on.'

'They don't?'

He pulled a face. 'I've no idea why, but I suppose they're chalk and cheese, so maybe that's the reason.' He paused. 'I enjoyed last night.'

'So did I.' She stood on tiptoe and gave him a kiss.

It lasted rather longer than she'd intended and it was a

good fifteen minutes later before she was on her way home after telling him she'd be back shortly with his van.

Finally alone, Violet had a chance to ponder what Hattie had said. The old lady was *almost* right when she'd said that Violet liked Logan, because Violet didn't just *like* him, she *more than* liked him. Which made her hope that Hattie had also been correct when she'd said Logan was besotted with her.

But what about the other stuff, the Marie stuff? Surely Hattie couldn't be right about that?

Hattie had more or less accused Marie of feigning being ill…

The accusation rang a bell with Violet as she recalled the smug look Marie had given her the other day. She'd claimed she'd had a nasty headache then, too, and said she wasn't feeling well, so Logan had taken her home. Violet had originally thought she'd imagined it. But what if she hadn't?

Violet wasn't sure what to think.

However, there *was* one thing she was increasingly sure about, and that was how she was beginning to feel about Logan.

CHAPTER 18

LOGAN

A shriek made Logan almost drop the glass he was polishing and he let out a yell of his own.

'I didn't expect to see you here,' Scarlet said, her hand on her chest. 'You gave me the fright of my life.'

'You and me both. Where else would I be, and why are you in so early?' Logan's own pulse was racing and he felt he needed to sit down. He'd been having such wonderful thoughts about Violet, and suddenly hearing a scream like that hadn't done his blood pressure any good.

'Your van's not here, so I didn't think you were either,' she said.

Logan could feel himself reddening: he was doing that a lot lately. Ever since he'd met Violet, in fact. 'It's um… it'll be here later. How did last night go? Did you cope all right?' He knew they had — the bar and kitchen had been immaculate when he'd arrived and everything had been in order — but he wanted to change the subject.

'Totally.'

'How was Yasmine?'

'Great! We could do with another one like her.'

'Seriously?'

'Yeah, she's fab: good with the customers, quick on her feet, doesn't need constant supervision—'

'I thought you meant we should take another person on.'

'We could do with it,' Scarlet said thoughtfully. 'Where did you say the van was?' She grinned as the penny dropped and wagged a finger at him. 'You left it at the distillery, didn't you? Is that why you don't have it?'

'Yes.' He exhaled sharply.

'Good for you.'

'I was tasting gin. I drank too much.'

'I bet that's not all you were tasting.'

'Haven't you got work to do? The pipes need cleaning.'

'Wayne cleaned them yesterday morning.'

'Were you that quiet?' Logan had checked the takings and they were up on the usual Monday, so they couldn't have been.

'Not at all. We were efficient.'

'Are you saying I'm not?'

'I wanted to prove to you that the Tavern doesn't need you in it 24/7. If something *had* gone wrong yesterday you probably wouldn't take another day off for the next decade.'

'True. OK, I agree, we do need to hire more staff.' His decision had everything to do with wanting to spend more time with a certain distiller, which wouldn't be easy if she was in Hay and he was in Ticklemore all the time.

He recalled Hattie's words and smiled. Perhaps the old lady wasn't losing her marbles after all. Besides, he didn't know how much time he'd have to spend away from the pub, depending on his mother's health.

The Tavern was running skinny as it was, and without

his mum popping in to help on an almost daily basis he'd need the flexibility of having another member of staff to call on. And with him going AWOL, it wouldn't leave Scarlet with a lot of support. As far as he was concerned Scarlet could hire as many staff as she wanted, as long as he could spend some time with the woman who he was falling in love with.

***

'What's this I hear about you having breakfast with that gin woman in Bookylicious this morning?' The words had left his mother's lips before she was fully inside the door of the Tavern.

'Hello, Mum.' Logan sighed. He might have known someone would tell her – you couldn't keep a secret in Ticklemore for love nor money. The surprise was that it had taken his mother until lunchtime to find out.

'I heard it from Barbara in the post office. When she realised I knew nothing about it, she couldn't wait to tell me.'

Marie's tone was accusing and Logan felt he should apologise, but he pushed the impulse away; he had absolutely nothing to apologise for.

'So?' He knew he sounded belligerent, but sometimes...

'You could have told me you were seeing her. And for breakfast no less. The shameless hussy.'

Had his mother just called Violet a shameless hussy? He didn't think people used phrases like that anymore.

'Why is having breakfast shameless?' he asked.

'She stayed the night, didn't she?'

'She didn't.'

'Oh.'

That took the wind out of her indignant sails, Logan thought.

But not for long.

His mother said, 'She must have been out early then, because Barbara said she saw the pair of you as bold as brass and it wasn't even nine o'clock.'

'We were eating breakfast at a table in a café. How can that be construed as being as "bold as brass"?'

'Everyone thinks you slept with her.'

'I didn't. And even if I had, it would be no one else's business but mine and Violet's.'

'And mine, if you make a show of me.'

'Mum, no one is making a show of you.'

'I still want to know why she was in Ticklemore before the cock crows.'

'Violet's here with your van,' Scarlet announced, waltzing into the bar with a big grin on her face. She'd been outside watering the pots and hanging baskets, which were starting to look a little jaded. When she spotted Marie's face, her grin faded.

Logan glanced out of one of the windows to see Violet jumping down from the driver's seat and slamming the door. She aimed the key fob at the vehicle and the lights flashed. Her own van pulled in just behind, the engine idling.

'Why is she driving your van?' his mother demanded.

Logan ignored her and waited for Violet, his heart giving a small lurch.

'I can't stop,' Violet said, hurrying through the door in a whirl of bright hair and sparkling eyes. 'We've just had a large order come in.' Her cheeks were flushed with excitement. Her smile dimmed slightly when she noticed his mother. 'Oh, hello, Mrs Cassidy. Is your headache any better?''

'Well done!' Logan cried. He was delighted for her.

His mother pulled her lips into a semblance of a smile but didn't reply to Violet.

'It's the biggest yet,' Violet said. 'I've been schmoozing a buyer who works for one of the better-known trendy bar chains, and she's finally cracked and placed an order.' She clapped her hands together and did a little hop.

Logan thought how cute she looked. 'I'll walk out to the van with you. Thanks for bringing mine back.' He deliberately didn't glance in his mum's direction, but he could feel her stare digging into the back of his head.

As soon as they were outside he paused, his hand on Violet's arm bringing her to a halt. 'When can I see you again?'

'When are you free next?' she countered.

'I'm not sure. I'll have to sort the staff rotas out.' He would like to see her this evening but he couldn't take any more time off so soon.

Violet didn't look certain and he suddenly felt awkward. 'I completely understand if you don't want to see me,' he added. 'Running a pub isn't conducive to having a social life.'

'What if I come to you?'

Logan raised his eyebrows. 'When?' His heart leapt.

'How about tomorrow? What time do you stop serving food?'

He could feel the smile spreading across his face. 'Nine o'clock.'

'I'll see you at eight-thirty. It'll save me cooking.'

You only want me for my hazelnut cassoulet,' he joked.

'Let's be honest, here. It's *Franklin's* cassoulet, not yours.'

'Maybe you should date him instead?' Logan stepped towards her and wrapped his arms around her waist.

'Maybe I should,' she murmured, her lips on his.

The kiss was disappointingly brief.

'See you later,' she said.

He couldn't wait. She hadn't left yet and he was already missing her.

Violet's brother gave him a brief wave and a nod, and Logan waved back. He watched the van pull out of the car park and drive down the road before he ventured back inside.

'She's lovely,' Scarlet muttered to him from behind the bar. 'If I wasn't taken, you'd have a fight on your hands.'

'She is, isn't she?' he agreed, studiously avoiding looking at his mother as he laid out some fresh beer mats.

Scarlet bumped him with her hip as she walked past, and he thought he could hear her humming *Here Comes the Bride* under her breath. He'd only just started dating Violet, and Scarlet was marrying him off already. But even as the thought entered his head he wondered if that would be such a bad thing?

Marie broke into his daydream. 'You still haven't told me why that woman was driving your van. Is she insured? Did you lend it to her?'

'I'd had too much to drink, so she kindly drove it back. And yes, she is insured.'

'Too much to drink? When?'

'Last night.'

'Where?'

Logan pursed his lips. This was like being interrogated by the police, without the benefit of a solicitor. 'I went to the distillery, OK?' He noticed that Scarlet had made herself scarce. He didn't blame her. He wished he could do the same.

'Last night? After the pub closed?' his mother asked.

'Before.'

'After you left my house?' Marie was incredulous.

'Yes.'

'Well! I never!'

'I wasn't needed here—' He broke off, wondering why he was explaining himself to her.

'I thought you'd come back here to work. Instead you spent the night with a floozie.'

'Violet is no floozie and we *did not* spend the night together. Not that it would be any of your business if we did.' Logan was finding it difficult to keep a lid on his temper. How dare his mother refer to Violet as a floozie.

Mindful of Marie's headaches and stress levels, he decided not to tell her that Violet would be having dinner here tomorrow evening. One piece of upsetting news a day was enough.

Logan was beginning to wonder whether his mother's tension wasn't helped by her fear that he wouldn't have time for her in his life if there was another woman in it. The thought had crossed his mind once or twice in the past, but he'd always dismissed it; probably because he hadn't felt about any of his previous girlfriends the way he felt about Violet.

Taking a deep breath and not wanting to quarrel with his mother any more than he'd done already, he moved closer and put his arm around her shoulders. She was stiff and unyielding, irritation radiating from her like heat from an oven.

'It's nothing to be worried about,' he told her. 'No matter what, you'll always be my mum, girlfriend or no girlfriend.'

'I didn't realise things had gone that far. So she's your *girlfriend* now, is she?' She shrugged his arm away, her lips a thin line. 'You don't know her.'

'Isn't that what going out with someone is all about – so you can get to know them?'

'I only popped out for a pint of milk and to see if a bit of fresh air would help.' She put a hand to her head. 'I can do without all this upset.'

'Why didn't you phone me? I could have fetched some milk for you, and anything else you might need.'

'I didn't want to bother you. I was enough of a nuisance yesterday.'

'You're not a nuisance. Whatever gave you that idea?'

'You don't want me around – you've made that perfectly clear.'

'What are you talking about?'

'You've hired that girl, Yasmine, so you don't need me any more. And now you're chasing after that Violet woman.'

'Mum—' Logan ran a hand through his hair, frustration making him irritable. How many times did he have to tell her that employing Yasmine had nothing to do with his mother. It was to do with him, and what he wanted out of life. 'It's a good job I *did* take someone else on, considering the doctor told you these headaches are caused by stress. Working in a pub isn't exactly restful.'

'See, that's what I'm talking about. You don't want me here.'

'If it affects your health, then no, I don't,' he insisted. 'You should listen to the doctor.'

'He doesn't know what he's talking about. It's not stress that's causing my headaches.'

'What is it, then?'

His mother put a hand on the bar as if to steady herself. Her voice was small as she said, 'I'm not sure.'

'In that case, maybe you should go back to the surgery and demand they send you for some tests. Do you want me to come with you?'

'I know what he'll say – give the tablets a chance to work.'

Logan sighed in exasperation. He didn't know what to do for the best. She seemed determined to be cantankerous; but he put it down to the fact that being in constant pain was bound to make anyone cranky.

'I'll leave it a bit,' she decided. 'See how I get on with them. Can you drive me back? I thought I'd be able to manage a little walk but I'm not feeling too good.' She screwed up her face.

'Of course I can. Come on.' He took her arm and she leant heavily on it as he guided her out to the van.

He had to help her climb into it yet again, and once more he considered whether he should swap it for something more practical. His mum mightn't be able to get in and out of this for much longer, especially if her fears had substance and her health deteriorated further. He'd never known her to be this bad.

What if there *was* something sinister behind her headaches?

But then again, she'd been having them for as long as he could remember, on and off, and he had to admit they tended to be more prevalent when she wasn't happy about something. They'd started when she'd discovered his father had been having an affair and had left them for another woman, and they had continued to plague her over the years during times of stress.

As he drove her back to her house, Logan racked his brains to think what might have set her off this time.

Then he realised – Violet.

He suspected his mother *was* feeling threatened by her and his growing feelings for her.

But as long as he continued to make his mum feel she was important to him, she'd accept it. Eventually.

She'd have to, because he had no intention of letting Violet go.

CHAPTER 19

VIOLET

Being unable to concentrate had never been an issue for Violet. Until now.

She hadn't been able to stop thinking about Logan since she'd dropped his van off yesterday morning. Having a strange man in her house overnight had been disconcerting enough, but having such a sexy man and one who she found irresistible, had taken being disconcerted to a whole new level. How she'd managed to keep her hands off him was beyond her.

At least she was seeing him this evening, and she was on her way to Ticklemore now.

She'd spent more time than she should have done over her appearance, but she still felt nervous. Her hands were clammy and her pulse was slightly erratic. She had the uncomfortable sensation of her heart skipping a beat now and again, which wasn't doing her composure any good. Unsettled was how she was feeling, and she wasn't used to it. Violet had always been in control, both of the situation and her emotions. But once again, she found she was facing another first as she felt more out of control than a truck careering downhill without any breaks. On an icy road. With the driver asleep at the wheel.

It was rather exhilarating. And frightening. Violet had never had her heart broken and she prayed she never would.

She mightn't be head over heels yet, but it was only a matter of time if things carried on the way they were. The only alternative was to knock this whole thing on the head and allow life to return to the comforting steady pace pre-Logan. However, she didn't want to do that either. The thought of not seeing him again gave her an unpleasant feeling in her tummy.

She may as well add *#confused* to her social media profiles and be done with it, because she didn't know what to think or how to behave. All she knew was that she wanted him as much as he seemed to want her – and not just physically either (although the physical bit sent shivers of delight down her back). It wasn't all about the kissing: she enjoyed his company.

She pulled up in the Tavern's car park and sat for a moment, gathering herself before she went inside. And when she did, she was instantly rewarded by Logan's wide-eyed reaction to her barely-there makeup, artfully messy hair, and strappy dress, which was probably too strappy for the time of year but she was too flushed to notice the September chill. Anyway, common sense hadn't totally deserted her, because she was carrying a cardi slung over her handbag.

Wobbling slightly on the unaccustomed heels, she made her way to a free table, then squeaked when she realised Logan was immediately behind her.

'You look gorgeous,' he whispered in her ear, his warm breath tickling the back of her neck and sending a delicious shudder through her. He pulled out a chair for her and she almost dropped into it as her legs gave way, then he pulled out one for himself.

'Are you OK to join me?' she asked.

'I'm here if I'm needed.' He sent a daggers glance at his staff, who were huddled behind the bar, gawking at them.

Violet wished she could hear what was being said out of the sides of mouths and behind hands. And that went for some of the Tavern's customers, too, as she gradually became aware that several of them were staring with undisguised interest.

'I feel like an exhibit in a cage,' she murmured, smiling vaguely at the surrounding tables.

'That's Ticklemore for you – you'll soon get used to it.'

'Will I?'

'Assuming you want to stay around long enough…?'

'I'd like to.'

'I was hoping you'd say that.'

They beamed at each other, lost in their own world, Violet feeling the dance and spin of the butterflies which had taken up residence in her tummy. She desperately wanted to fast forward to when the Tavern's doors closed on the last member of staff and she and Logan were able to be alone.

'Wine?' he asked when their food arrived, delivered to the table by a smirking Yasmine.

'Sparkling water, please,' she said. 'I want to keep a clear head.'

'Because you're driving?'

'That's one reason – the other is that I don't trust myself around you.'

Yasmine sniggered, almost dropping a plate, and it landed on the table a tad heavily.

'How *is* Sam?' Violet asked her innocently, and took great delight in the girl's blushes as she hastily scuttled away.

The tension eased somewhat after that, and Violet was able to settle down to enjoy her meal, although she didn't eat as much as she normally would have done. Her stomach was in knots as she thought about kissing Logan later and excitement had diminished her appetite.

She'd seriously considered doing more than kissing and she desperately wanted to, but not yet. Soon, though…

Eventually the last customer had gone and the staff had nothing further to do. Logan had left Violet perched on a stool at the bar whilst he helped clean up, and from the looks on their faces his staff had cleared up in record time.

'I take it you don't want me in early tomorrow?' Scarlet hinted and Logan swatted her with a towel.

'Go!' He ushered her out of the door, before locking it behind him and sinking against it, embarrassment written all over his face. 'I'm sorry.'

'It's OK. It's quite funny the way everyone is taking such an interest.'

'Believe me, it's not. My mother was quite put out when Barbara in the post office told her that she'd seen us having breakfast together. Mum jumped to the wrong conclusion, of course, and she was in the middle of telling me how unhappy she was when you brought the van back. Fancy a coffee?'

'Could I have tea, please? Herbal if you've got it.'

'I can do you an Earl Grey?'

'That'll do. Sorry if I came in at a bad moment this morning. Is your Mum feeling better? She didn't look too good yesterday.'

'Do you mind if we go upstairs to the flat? It's more comfortable up there.' He winced. 'I didn't mean it the way it sounded. We'll only be having coffee. Or tea. You said you wanted tea. Nothing else. I don't want you to think…' He trailed off.

Violet giggled. She found it endearing how solicitous he was, making sure she didn't think he was propositioning her.

To be honest, she was beginning to hope he would; but she was also grateful that he wasn't the sort of guy who expected to get into her knickers on the first date. Or the second. She wanted to get to know him better first.

'About your mum?' Violet reminded him when they were seated on his comfortable sofa with cups of tea in front of them.

'She thought she was getting over her headache, but when I told her I stayed the night at yours she had a bit of a relapse. I'm sure the doctor is right and they are caused by stress. They certainly seem to get worse when she's upset or cross. Anyway, enough of my mum: I want to talk about you.'

'What do you want to know?'

'Everything.'

'Blimey. Are you sure? Some of it is pretty unsavoury.'

'Such as…?'

'Head lice in Year 2 and I cheated on a spelling test in Year 4 and got caught. The upside is that I can now spell a whole load of difficult words because my teacher made me memorise them and spell them in front of the whole class.'

'I'm sure there must be nicer things you can tell me?'

'I can play the flute.'

'That's good.' He moved closer, the space between them dwindling. 'Anything else?'

'I can wire a plug.'

'Handy.' He slipped an arm along the back of the sofa and leant towards her, his lips brushing her ear. 'Tell me more.'

'I like octopus. Octopi. Octopuses. Whatever the plural is. They're cute.'

'*You're* cute.' He nibbled her ear lobe and she squirmed in delight.

Oh, man, that was exquisite. Her toes curled and she almost melted. Violet turned her head so his lips hovered above her mouth. 'As cute as an octopus?'

'Way cuter.'

'Kiss me.'

He didn't need asking twice. As his mouth claimed hers, she buried a hand in his hair as though she never wanted him to stop.

But stop they had to, unless Violet intended ending up in his bed.

Which she did, very much. But not tonight.

When she eventually pulled away from him to compose herself, they were both breathless, and Violet could barely hear herself think for the drumming of her pulse in her ears.

Vowing to take it slower, she scooted out of kissing distance and picked up her cup of tea, which had gone cold.

'Ew,' she said tasting it.

'Would you like me to make you another?'

'No thanks, I'd better be off. It's getting late.' Besides, the only thing she wanted him to make was love to her, so it would be best if she left whilst she still could. If she stayed any longer, if he kissed her again, she was in danger of never leaving.

And no matter how sexy he was, or how much she was falling for him, she wanted to make doubly certain of her feelings and his before she gave herself to him totally.

CHAPTER 20

LOGAN

Logan did a double-take when Marie strolled into the Tavern the following day. He'd been restocking the artisan ales, his mind full of Violet, and was surprised to see his mother.

'What are you doing here?'

'I still work here, don't I – unless you're giving me the push?'

He tried not to sigh: she was becoming more difficult by the day, and he had a feeling today wasn't going to be any better. 'I thought you'd be resting.'

'I can't sit around feeling sorry for myself. I need to keep busy.'

'Don't overdo it, yeah?'

His mother bustled through to the office, shrugging her coat off as she did so, and came back minus coat and bag, with her sleeves rolled up. He was pleased to see she looked a little happier than she had yesterday, and not so drawn and peaky.

Lunchtime was Logan's favourite time in the Tavern.

People were there mainly for the food and that was what he wanted the pub to be known for. The clientele was different during the day than in the evenings; there weren't as many locals, for a start. People passing through Ticklemore on their way to and from the Brecon Beacons, often spotted the pub and decided to give it a go. But more and more of them were making the Tavern their destination as a decent place for a spot of lunch, and it was all down to Franklin's wonderful cooking. The pub was slowly but surely gaining a good reputation.

As soon as the doors opened, hungry customers began to arrive and Logan was kept busy taking orders, serving food, clearing tables, and sharing banter with those who wanted a chat, or who had questions about the local area. It helped enormously that Ticklemore was a pretty village with a little river running through it, a quaint stone bridge and several lovely shops.

It wasn't until the last of the food orders had been served, that he and his staff were able to take a breather.

'I'll be off home in a minute,' Yasmine said, 'unless you need me for anything else?'

'We'll be fine,' Logan said. 'Why don't you get off, too, Mum? You've done enough for today. Scarlet and I can manage until Wayne comes in later.' Logan didn't expect his staff to work in the quieter time between the end of the lunchtime service and the start of the evening one, and shifts were usually split to reflect this.

'Should I come in later?' Yasmine asked. 'I know I'm not scheduled to work, but I thought you might like me to.'

'Why would Logan want you to come in if you're not on the rota?' Marie asked. She rolled her eyes and gave a derisive shake of her head.

'If Violet—' Yasmine halted abruptly as Logan widened his eyes at her and pulled a face.

'What about Violet?' his mother demanded.

'Ah, Violet…' Franklin emerged from the kitchen, saying, 'I need some more ale for the steak and ale pie. Did she enjoy the wild boar? And I put a splash of her rosehip gin in the raspberry coulis. It was divine – lifted it to a whole new level.' Franklin kissed his fingers.

'When did she have wild boar?' Marie looked from Logan to Franklin and back again.

'Last night,' Franklin said.

'Violet was *here*?' Marie's hands were on her hips. Her eyes bored into Logan. 'You didn't say.'

'I didn't think I needed to. Mum, we've been over this.' Logan hoped she wouldn't cause a fuss, especially not in front of his staff. He might have known that their little chat on Tuesday wouldn't be the end of it.

Marie's face darkened. 'I'll be out the back if anyone needs me,' she said. 'I want to check on the crisps.'

The crisps were fully stocked, Logan saw, glancing behind the bar at the rack where they were nicely displayed. They didn't need replenishing, but he let Marie go, concluding that she probably needed a minute to herself, and if counting their stock of crisps gave her a chance to get over the news of Violet being here last night, then he was happy for her to count away.

'Sorry, I didn't—' Yasmine began.

Before she could finish her sentence, Logan jumped in. 'It's fine. I expect Mum thought we'd be too busy for me to take a couple of hours off,' Logan said, but he could tell by the way Yasmine looked at him that she didn't believe him.

He watched her leave and heaved a sigh. His mum would

be even more cheesed off when she found out he was taking Monday off again and that he'd planned to spend it with Violet. But maybe he'd not mention it just now, eh?

A loud crash from the direction of the stockroom made him jump.

'Are you OK, Mum?' he called, walking swiftly toward the back. Those damned crisp boxes had a habit of toppling over, but the room was so small that they had to be stacked high out of necessity. At least they were light—

'Mum!' he cried, seeing her. She was lying on the floor, half in and half out of the stockroom. 'What happened? Are you OK?' All the boxes were in their place and he couldn't work out what had happened.

Logan dropped to his knees. She was on her side, her cheek pressed against the floor, and for an awful moment he thought she was dead.

She opened an eye and blinked.

Thank God! 'Speak to me, Mum.'

'I fell.' Marie began to push herself upright, but Logan held her down.

'Let's see if there's anything broken first, before you try to move. Did you pass out? Wiggle your toes for me.'

Marie's feet twitched.

'Now your hands.'

She waggled her fingers.

'Does anywhere hurt?'

'I don't think so. Ooh, come to think of it, my back isn't the best.'

Logan helped her into a sitting position, taking it slowly just in case she'd done herself some real damage. 'How did you come to fall?'

'I don't know.' She rubbed her back, just above her hip,

and winced. 'I felt a bit dizzy, then bam, I was on the floor. My head hurts.' She grimaced.

'Did you bang it?

'I don't think so.

'Maybe I should take you to the hospital, just in case.'

'Don't be daft. I'll be all right – there's no need to fuss. Just take me home.'

'Let's get you on your feet, then we'll see,' he said. If she could walk and nothing seemed to be damaged, he'd take her home. If not, it was the hospital for her.

'Is everything OK?' Franklin was standing in the corridor. He'd removed his chef's whites and was about to leave.

'I think so,' Logan said. 'Mum had a fall, but nothing appears to be broken. If she can walk without too much difficulty, I'll take her home.'

'Here, let me help.'

Handling her with care, the two men helped Marie get to her feet and they slowly walked her into the bar. Franklin pulled out a chair for her and they lowered her into it.

'Ow,' she moaned.

'Hospital?'

'No. I'm fine stop fussing. I'm just a bit sore, that's all.'

'Will she be OK?' Franklin asked and Logan straightened up.

'I think so. Do you mind hanging on for a bit? I might need some help to get her into the van.'

'Sure. No problem.'

'If you wait here, I'll get my keys.' Logan dashed up to the flat, grabbed his keys and was back in the bar in less than a minute. 'Ready?' he asked.

Franklin was frowning.

'What?' Logan asked. Franklin gave a tiny shake of his head.

'Help me up,' his mother instructed.

Franklin hesitated for a second, then gave Marie his arm. Logan took her other one and between them they hoisted her up and walked her slowly outside.

After they'd helped her into it, Logan said, 'Thanks, Franklin.' He patted the chef on the shoulder and took a step towards the driver's side.

'Er, boss, can I have a quick word?' Franklin looked perturbed and he shot a glance at Marie.

'Of course.'

Franklin led Logan to the rear of the van, where he halted and took a deep breath. 'Your mum said something to me, in confidence. She doesn't want you to know, but I feel you should. I don't like breaking her trust but… While you were looking for your keys, she told me she's scared that she has a tumour. She asked me not to tell you because she doesn't want to worry you, but how could I not? If she was my mum, I'd want to know.'

'Oh, blast.' Logan scratched his head, a lump catching in his throat. Dear God, no…

'I know. Sorry, mate. She also said she's struggling to cope at home.'

'Is she?' He'd not seen any evidence of that, but it didn't mean to say she wasn't. 'Thanks for telling me. Can you do me a favour and hold the fort for half an hour, while I take her home?'

Franklin readily agreed, and Logan hurried off. He needed to get her settled and come back.

But to Logan's dismay, what Franklin had told him was confirmed when he opened his mum's front door and guided her inside.

There was an unpleasant whiff in the air and he saw why as he entered the kitchen after settling her in her favourite chair. Dirty dishes were piled in the sink and more were on the worktop next to it. The bin was overflowing and a bottle of milk had spilt, its contents leaking across the counter and dripping onto the floor, where it was starting to congeal.

Yuck.

Without saying anything to his mum, Logan switched the kettle on and while it was coming to a boil he swiftly emptied the bin, wiped up the milky mess, and ran some hot water into the sink.

When he took her tea into the living room, Marie was lying half on her side and rubbing her back.

'Lovely, a nice cuppa,' she said, straightening up with a grunt and taking the mug from him. He noticed she used both hands and they were trembling slightly. 'What are you doing out there?' she asked.

'I'm about to do the washing up.'

She pulled a face. 'I haven't had a chance to do it yet. I was going to sort the kitchen out after work.'

To Logan, it looked as though she'd had some kind of a party – considering she lived on her own, she appeared to have used most of the plates, bowls, and saucepans she owned. What was even more concerning was that Logan had popped in to see his mum yesterday and the house had been as spick and span as usual.

How had she managed to create such a mess in such a short space of time?

What if the headaches *were* caused by a tumour, or by early-onset dementia, and this mess was another symptom. His mother didn't seem to be suffering with her memory, but…

'Where are you going?' she asked when he made to return to the kitchen.

'I'm going to have a bit of a clear up, so you don't have to, then I'm going to pack an overnight bag for you. You're coming back to the Tavern with me.'

'I can manage.' Her protest was feeble and not at all convincing.

'I know you can,' he replied diplomatically. 'But humour me, eh? I want to look after you, but I can't do that when I'm at the pub and you're here. I've got to get back because I've left Franklin in charge and you know what he's like – he'll be nicking all my best wine to put in his casseroles.'

Logan tried to keep the conversation light, but inside a feeling of dread was stealing over him.

He'd take her back to the Tavern, settle her in, then try to make another appointment for her to see her GP. This time, though, he was determined to go in with her.

***

For what felt like the fiftieth time that afternoon, Logan popped upstairs to check on his mother. And for the fiftieth time, she was perfectly fine. He'd kept her supplied with tea, had given her some ibuprofen gel to rub into her back and hip, and had handed her the remote control. This time when he checked on her, she was watching Eggheads.

He also noticed that she'd polished off the soup he'd warmed up for her, and had eaten three bread rolls with butter to go with it.

'If you're still hungry, I can bring you something else,' he offered.

'I fancy ham and chips,' she said, twisting around on the sofa to speak to him, then baring her teeth as she sucked in a breath. 'Ow, that hurt.'

'Are you still in pain?'

'A bit,' she admitted.

'Where does it hurt the worst?'

'Here and here.' She touched her lower back and her hip.

'At least your headache has gone.' He smiled gently at her.

'It's not. It's still there.'

'Oh, I thought—'

'Just assume I've got a headache unless I tell you any different,' she said.

'Right…' She did seem better though, and he was sure if her headache was as severe as it had been recently, she would have mentioned it. At least she'd made herself at home, he thought, when he saw her dressing gown and nightie laid out on the bed in one of the spare rooms, and a magazine and her glasses on the bedside cabinet. She'd unpacked a few toiletries too, so she must be feeling a little perkier.

Better or not, Logan was still extremely worried about her. People don't simply fall over for no reason. His mother was only sixty-seven, so she could hardly be described as frail or old, so that wasn't the reason. Which left him wondering what it could be.

Whatever it was, she seemed back to her normal self now, he decided, as he went to make her yet another cup of tea and saw that she'd rinsed out the one she'd used earlier; it was sitting upside down on the draining board. His mum hated mess about the place, and the state her kitchen had been in had shocked him.

Logan continued to stick his head around the door as the evening wore on, glad to see she'd eaten every morsel of the ham and chips she'd requested (Franklin made the best chips ever!) and had demolished half a packet of biscuits to boot.

***

It was now nearly midnight and Marie was in bed, snoring softly. Logan had locked up and all the nightly chores had been done. But before he collapsed into his own soft bed, he simply had to speak to Violet. He'd messaged her earlier, giving her the bare bones about his mum's fall, but what with running the pub and looking after his mum, he hadn't had the opportunity to speak with her until now.

Hoping it wasn't too late, he dialled Violet's number and let out a slow breath of satisfaction when she answered.

'Hi, you,' she said.

'Hi, yourself.'

'How is your mum?'

'Better, I think. Sleeping in the spare room.' Logan glanced towards the hall leading to the three bedrooms. He was in the lounge, sprawled across a chair, exhausted. 'I'm taking her to the doctors again tomorrow.' He'd called the surgery earlier, and was thankful they'd managed to fit his mum in. 'Are we still on for Monday?'

'I am if you are.'

'Hell, yes. Try stopping me. '

'Are you sure you want to go for a walk in the woods?' Violet asked.

'I'm sure. It'll be romantic. Anyway, didn't you say you wanted to make leaf garlands?'

'I did, but you bought fabric ones off the internet instead. Is that all you want me for, my gin and my garland-making abilities?'

'Not at all. I want you for your body. And your mind,' he added hastily. 'And your sense of humour.'

'Keep going, I'm enjoying this.' Her laugh was soft and rather wicked.

'I'm missing you. I can't stop thinking about you.'

'Anything else?'

'I can't wait to see you again.'

'I'd suggest driving over, but with your mum there…'

'Goodness, no. I can't kiss you the way I want to with her in the flat.'

'What way do you want to kiss me?'

'All over.'

'Down, boy!' She paused. 'How about if I drop in tomorrow morning? I'm going to Abergavenny.'

'That's out of your way.'

'I don't care.'

He could feel the smile spreading across his face –it would give the Cheshire Cat a run for its money. 'Not here, not at the Tavern. Meet you at the little bridge over the river?' He didn't want to risk his mum spotting her and getting even more upset.

'OK.'

'See you then,' he murmured, his mind full of her as he rang off. He sat there for a short while, staring at her number on his phone, like a teenage boy with a crush. But then the squeak of a floorboard made him worry he'd disturbed his mother, and he crept into the hall to check. To his relief, she was fast asleep, and he retired to his own bed wishing with all his heart that Violet was sharing it with him.

CHAPTER 21

VIOLET

The bridge spanning the river at Ticklemore was a narrow stone-built one, only wide enough for people on foot or horseback. Mindful of where she parked her rather distinctive van, Violet pulled up outside Bookylicious and left it there whilst she strolled across the green. Despite her outwardly casual air, inside she was bubbling with excitement at seeing Logan again, and she had to give herself a shake. This was becoming ridiculous. She'd only just seen him on Wednesday evening, barely thirty-six hours ago, and here she was with a soaring pulse and butterflies in her tummy.

He was already there, leaning against the stonework and as soon as he saw her a smile spread across his face. A slow, sexy smile. One that turned her insides to jelly and made her breathe faster.

How was it possible for her reaction to him to be so intense? They'd not known each other long, but she was already unable to consider her life without him in it.

Abruptly she knew what she wanted – Logan. And what

Violet wanted, Violet got. She'd wanted to make gin, so she'd opened a distillery. She'd wanted a home of her own, so she'd moved out of her parent's house and into the run-down farmhouse. She'd wanted her independence and she'd got it.

And lately, whenever she thought about her future, Logan was in it. She didn't know how it would work or what shape it would take, but she couldn't imagine never seeing him again, not hearing his voice and not seeing his handsome face. Or feeling his lips on hers, his arms around her.

She cleared her throat and pushed her wayward thoughts to the back of her mind. A Friday morning in the middle of Ticklemore wasn't the place to be having such lascivious thoughts.

Logan, on the other hand, didn't seem at all bothered, He waited for her to get closer, then he stepped forward and gathered her to him, his mouth on hers as he kissed her soundly.

Several minutes later the sound of tutting infiltrated her mind, and Violet opened her eyes to see Hattie and an elderly gentleman staring at them.

'Sorry.' Violet aimed for contrite, but she wasn't certain she'd achieved it.

'I'm not,' Logan said.

'I don't blame you, son,' the elderly man said. 'I'd do the same if I was you.'

Hattie glared at him.

'In fact, I think I will.' And with that, he scooped Hattie into his arms and planted a kiss on her lips.

'Get off, you daft bugger,' Hattie protested, but Violet saw the pleased look on her face and the hint of pink on her cheeks.

Hattie turned to Violet and hissed, 'Do you think Logan would let me have a go? He looks like he's a decent kisser.'

Violet giggled. 'He certainly is. He might, if you ask him nicely.'

'What?' Logan looked puzzled.

'I'll do you a swap – you can have Alfred,' Hattie said to her.

'You don't mean it.'

Hattie screwed up her face. 'You're right, I don't. I wouldn't swap him for the world, no matter how handsome your fella is.'

Her fella… it was nice to hear. He *was* her fella, and the thought made her all gooey. It was a new experience for Violet – she had never been a gooey person – and she quite liked it.

She also quite liked having a boyfriend.

'Fancy joining me for a coffee in Bookylicious after you've finished snogging the face off Ticklemore's favourite publican?' Hattie suggested.

Logan said to Violet, 'In case you hadn't noticed, the Tavern is the only pub in Ticklemore so I don't think Hattie is paying me much of a complement.'

'I'll pop in before I leave,' Violet promised, chuckling.

Hattie elbowed Alfred. 'Come on, I've got to get to work, and you'd better see if the butcher has got any of those sausages you like so much, before he sells out. They go like hot cakes, do those sausages.' Hattie gave him a gentle shove in the direction of Ticklemore's main street.

Violet and Logan watched them go. 'They're so sweet,' Violet said. 'I hope I'm as much in love when I'm their age.'

'I think I'm already there.'

Violet gazed at her boyfriend wondering if she'd heard him correctly. 'Pardon?'

'It might be premature and I'm sorry if I'm scaring you off—' his expression was serious '—but…'

'But what?'

'I think I'm in love with you.'

Violet was speechless.

'Say something,' he urged after several seconds went by.

'Did you just say you think you're in love with me?'

'Er… yeah.'

'Gosh. I wasn't expecting that.'

'I completely understand if you don't feel the same way. We haven't known each other long and—'

'Shh.' Violet put a finger on his lips. 'I think I love you, too.'

'Don't you know?' She felt his mouth move under her finger as he smiled.

'Not sure yet,' she retorted, 'but when I am, you'll be the first to know. Actually, that's a lie – I'll probably run it by Beth first.'

'You'd tell your best friend before you tell me?'

'Of course.' She pulled a face. 'I suppose you'd better meet her, hadn't you. And Rory, although to be honest, he's a pain in the backside. How about we all go out to lunch on Monday after our walk, if the others are free?'

'That sounds good.'

Things were moving fast, but Violet didn't care. What was the point in procrastinating?

Hattie's advice swam into her mind… as did the words of the famous Edith Piaf song – *je ne regrette rien*. Did Violet want to get to Hattie's age and have a lifetime of regrets? Would Violet regret not seizing the day?

Definitely.

So seize it she shall.

***

Bookylicious was busy, which was always a good sign when it came to places to eat, and Violet had to wait for a few minutes until a table became free.

She used the time to peruse the books, whilst keeping an eye out for anyone leaving.

Hattie hurried over as soon as Violet sat down, her pad in her hand and her pencil poised.

'I think I'll have a cooked breakfast,' Violet said, her tummy rumbling; being in love was giving her an appetite. As was being up and out too early to face eating anything before she left home. She'd managed a cup of tea, but that had been it.

Hattie scribbled down her order. 'I'll be back in a minute,' she said, and as soon as Violet's breakfast was ready, Hattie brought it over and took a seat, popping a plateful of pancakes on the table for herself and diving right in.

'I heard Marie had a fall yesterday,' Hattie said around a mouthful of food. 'How is she?'

'From what Logan said she's a bit sore but there isn't any lasting damage. He's very worried about her, though.' In between forkfuls, Violet told her what Marie had said to Franklin.

Hattie put her cutlery down and took a drink of coffee. 'You had a meal in the Tavern on Wednesday evening, didn't you?'

'I did.' Violet blinked at the change of subject.

183

'Did you spend the night?'

'No, I didn't.' Flipping heck, Hattie was nosey.

'Hmm.' Hattie had another bite of her pancakes and chewed, a frown creasing her already wrinkled brow. 'As I said before, it's strange how Marie is ill whenever Logan does something she doesn't like. I can't prove it, mind you, but it happens too often to be a coincidence.'

'Logan told me Hattie's GP thinks it's caused by stress.'

'She's definitely stressed, all right: stressed about Logan having a girlfriend. He was going out with this girl from Abergavenny once, and I think he quite liked her. Marie didn't. She soon saw her off – was horrid to her, if I remember rightly. Marie was ill then, too. Funny how she got better pretty damned quick when Logan stopped seeing her. And that wasn't the only time. He was courting Mrs Hamilton's granddaughter not long after he finished school, and Marie played her face then. She's done it with every girl he's gone out with.' Hattie studied her. 'She's done it with you, too, I'll warrant.'

Violet shrugged, not wanting to say anything negative about Logan's mum to someone who lived in the same village and who clearly didn't like Marie very much.

Hattie pulled a face. 'I used to think she was a hypochondriac, but now…? I think she's just plain mean. Or scared.'

'Scared?'

'Of losing Logan. You know that old saying, "a son is a son until he takes a wife, but a daughter is a daughter all her life"? Marie has taken it to heart. I reckon she thinks he won't have any time or love for her if he gets wed. Silly woman!' Hattie snorted. 'She thought the same when he bought the Tavern.'

Violet continued to plough her way through her breakfast, her appetite waning with each word Hattie uttered.

'Marie wasn't pleased when he took over the pub,' Hattie continued. 'She was ill for weeks. Months, even. But she couldn't change his mind.' Hattie continued to study Violet, and Violet felt heat steal into her face at the woman's scrutiny.

'It looks like she won't change it this time either,' Hattie said. 'Although I suspect she'll have a good try. I don't know how she expects to get away with it. The last time she was ill the doctors weren't able to find anything wrong with her, but that was most likely because there wasn't anything *to* find. She needs to be careful what she wishes for. Karma is a bitch as they say, and she might get it into her head to show Marie what for.'

'In what way?' Despite herself, Violet was curious. She didn't like what Hattie was saying, but she thought she needed to hear it regardless.

The old lady sighed. 'Logan might just decide he's had enough of her ways. You know what they say about not being able to choose your family, but you do get to choose the person you want to spend the rest of your life with.'

'They also say that blood is thicker than water,' Violet pointed out.

'Let's hope Logan isn't forced to choose, for his sake as much as yours. Whatever decision he'd make would tear him apart.'

Violet watched Hattie get to her feet and collect up the dirty plates.

The situation was clear as far as Violet saw it: she had three choices. She could either end it now, and take the decision out of Logan's hands before he even realised a decision had to be made. She could fight his mother for him (not literally, obviously), or she could try to win Marie over.

The first one, walking away, wasn't something she wanted to contemplate. The second would cause everyone grief. Which left the last option as the only viable one. But even that might lead to heartache for her and for Logan if she wasn't able to make Marie see that she wasn't a threat and that there was room enough in Logan's life for both his mother and his wife.

It was then that Violet realised she wanted to be Logan's wife more than she'd ever wanted anything in her life before.

CHAPTER 22

LOGAN

Logan couldn't believe that he was a grown man, yet he was sneaking out to meet a girl and hoping his mum didn't catch him. Is this what his life had become?

Nevertheless, he slipped back into the flat after saying goodbye to Violet at the bridge and crept up the stairs, praying his mother hadn't noticed his absence. It was only half-past eight, so it was still rather early and she might not have woken yet.

Both the living room and kitchen was empty he saw, when he returned from his clandestine rendezvous, and there was no sound from the spare room. He breathed a sigh of relief.

The surgery opened at eight, so whilst he waited for the kettle to boil, he phoned and made an appointment for later that morning. His mother, however, wasn't pleased when he told her.

'Mum?' He knocked on her bedroom door and heard a muffled response. 'I've brought you a cup of tea.' He pushed the door open and placed the mug on the bedside cabinet. 'I've made an appointment for you to see the doctor at ten fifty,' he said.

'Why?' She pushed herself into a sitting position and reached for the drink. 'I don't need a doctor. I'm a bit achy, that's all.'

'Because of what you said to Franklin. I'm worried about you.'

She looked away.

Logan continued, 'You didn't honestly expect him not to tell me?'

'I don't need to see a doctor,' she repeated.

'I think you do.'

'I just…' She ground to a halt, and waved a hand in the air. 'Can't I stay here for a bit?'

'You don't need to ask.'

'I don't want to intrude.'

'You aren't.' He perched on the end of her bed. 'You can stay here for as long as you want.'

'But you've got enough to be going on with,' his mother said. 'You're doing too much.'

'I'm not doing any more than I usually do.' Logan patted her hand. Bless her, she always worried about him, and he guessed it was a cross all mums bore, no matter how old their kids were.

'You look tired,' she insisted.

Did he? He didn't feel it. He felt exhilarated. He was still zinging from the kiss on the bridge. He'd be quite happy to begin every day like that, and the thought of waking up next to Violet made his heart constrict with longing.

'How's your head?' he asked, trying to deflect the conversation back to his mum.

'Still on my shoulders.'

'You know what I mean.'

'So do you. You're burning the candle at both ends, and something has got to give. I'd hate to see everything you've worked so hard for suffer.'

'I'm fine,' he insisted. He was more than fine. He was in love, and it felt darned good. His mum had a point, though – he couldn't be in two places at once. And he knew which one he preferred to be in.

'Take your time,' he said to her. 'Come downstairs when you're ready and I'll make you some breakfast.'

'I expect you've had yours already.'

'I haven't actually.'

'Oh? I thought… never mind.'

Logan didn't ask what she thought, but he was left with the impression he hadn't been as sneaky as he'd hoped.

***

Logan and Wayne were helping the chap from the brewery unload the barrels when Scarlet came in. Checking that Wayne was OK to carry on by himself, Logan told Scarlet he wanted to talk to her.

'That sounds ominous,' she said, as he took her into the office.

'Do you like working here?' he asked.

'What an odd question? Yes, I do. I would have left ages ago if I didn't.'

'Good. How would you like to be the Tavern's manager?'

'Me?'

'Yes, you.' He grinned at her.

'What are you going to do?'

'Enjoy life.'

'Ah.'

'What do you mean *ah*?'

'Violet.'

Scarlet didn't need to say anything further. It was fairly obvious he had more on his mind lately than the pub. He could sense his priorities shifting; he was distancing himself emotionally from the Tavern at the corresponding rate he was getting closer to Violet. It was both exciting and scary, but he knew he should follow his heart. If he didn't, it might become one of his biggest regrets.

'I'm going to need more staff,' Scarlet said.

'OK.' He was pleased to see her take up the reins so quickly.

'Will you put an advert in the paper?' she asked.

'No. *You* will. You are the Tavern's manager, starting from today. I'll have overall responsibility and the final say, but the day-to-day running of the pub is down to you. Are you happy with that?'

'You bet!'

'As soon as you take someone on, you can phase me out of the rota, although I'll still be around a fair amount, especially on the weekends when it's busiest. Just think of it as an added bonus when I'm here. But even when I am, you'll be the one running the Tavern, not me.'

'Thank you. I appreciate this and I won't let you down.'

'I know you won't.'

Scarlet hesitated. 'What about Marie?'

'Mum won't be working here any more.' Logan wasn't looking forward to telling his mother that, but it was for her own good.

If he *was* looking tired (and after examining himself in the mirror, he didn't think he did) it was because he was worried about her.

He wasn't the one doing too much; it was his mum who was. By taking on Yasmine he'd hoped Marie wouldn't feel obliged to help out in the Tavern, that she'd begin to take things a little easier. But, if anything, she appeared even more stressed. Logan didn't know whether that was because she wasn't feeling well, or, as the doctor had suggested, her physical problems were caused *because* she was stressed,

Either way, he was determined to find out.

* * *

Deja vu. Logan and Marie were in more or less the same seats in the waiting room as the last time they'd visited the surgery.

But this time, Logan wasn't going to let her see the doctor by herself.

'Hello, I'm Dr Osman, and I'm standing in for Dr Rayner today. What can I do for you?' Dr Osman was young, about Logan's age and she was new to the practice as far as he could tell. Perhaps a fresh pair of eyes would be able to give another diagnosis or opinion.

He let his mother explain what was wrong, only adding the occasional comment when he thought she wasn't being specific enough, and afterwards the doctor gave his mother a thorough physical examination as far as she was able, even giving her an ECG, which thankfully was normal. She also arranged for Marie to have some blood tests.

'Your notes say that you had a barrage of tests done a few years ago, but there's no harm in repeating them as things have a habit of changing. The results should be back within a few days, and we can go from there. Let's see what they tell us first, shall we?'

'Thank you, doctor.' Marie was smiling as she left and Logan felt as though they were getting somewhere.

However, he was curious about the tests she'd had previously. 'You didn't tell me they've investigated this before,' he said as he drove back to the Tavern.

Marie waved a hand in the air dismissively. 'I didn't want to worry you.'

'When was this?'

'A few years back.'

'When you were getting the really bad headaches the last time?'

'Around about then. I don't remember.'

'I thought they went away all by themselves?'

'They did.' Marie's lips were tight and she was staring straight ahead.

'And the doctor didn't find anything wrong?'

'Clearly not.'

'That's good, isn't it? Maybe they won't find anything this time.'

'Hmm.'

She was looking utterly fed up, and he decided to drop the subject. He'd try to push his worries about his mother's health to the back of his mind for now, and only think about it when the results were in.

But there was something else he couldn't put off, and he had to do it soon before any of his staff mentioned it – and that was to tell his mother that he'd made Scarlet manager.

Oh, dear, he had a feeling his mum wouldn't take the news well.

CHAPTER 23

VIOLET

The trees were busy preparing for winter, withdrawing the chlorophyll from their leaves, turning them brilliant shades of yellow, red, orange, and brown, and as Violet and Logan strolled through the woods, those leaves drifted slowly down from the branches above like huge velvety flakes of colourful snow to land with a patter on their cousins which had already fallen and lay in drifts on the ground.

They kicked through the leaves, holding hands, stopping to kiss now and again. The air was cool under the canopy, sunlight sending shafts of light to illuminate the woodland floor, making the leaves gleam like jewels.

At this time of year few birds sang, although plenty could be seen darting about in search of food. They were joined by grey squirrels who chattered crossly amongst themselves, chasing each other along branches, or bouncing along the ground, fleeing up the nearest tree when they caught sight of the humans invading their territory.

As she and Logan strolled, neither of them made any move to collect the leaves – they were too busy concentrating on each other. Despite their glorious surroundings, all Violet could focus on was Logan. Although to be fair, the location was rather romantic.

Once or twice she noticed a hazelnut tree or blackthorn berries, but she didn't feel the urge to pick any. Gin-making could wait. Violet had love-making on her mind.

Curiously, despite devising the loganberry flavour, she'd not felt inclined to create any other new flavours, content to leave the nuts and bolts of gin production to Rory, and fleetingly she worried she'd lost her gin-making mojo to the first heady flush of love.

Then she decided she didn't care. It would come back, and the distillery had plenty of flavours to be getting on with. They'd built up a substantial stock ready for the festive season, and she always had the old spring and summer favourites to fall back on in the New Year.

For the time being she was content to simply be with Logan, revelling in the feel of his hand in hers, the taste of him, his scent. Just being with him was enough.

'We're meeting Rory and Beth at a little place on the outskirts of Hay in an hour,' she said, after a particularly long embrace when the rest of the world faded away leaving only the two of them and their feelings for each other. 'So we'd better get going.'

'I'm perfectly happy where I am,' Logan said, tightening his grip on her waist.

'Me, too, but we've made arrangements now and they're dying to meet you.' Violet hoped Rory wouldn't embarrass her too much, and she was seriously regretting making the suggestion Logan should meet him. It could have waited. A few months wouldn't have mattered. Or years. Or never. 'Maybe we *could* stay here,' she decided. 'They'd never find us.'

'We've got to go home at some point.'

'Let's not bother.'

'My mother would soon send out a search party. She wasn't happy about me going out today in the first place. I promised her I'd be back by six. Honestly, it's like being a teenager all over again, having her stay in the flat.'

'At least you can keep an eye on her.'

'Not when I'm in the middle of the woods, I can't,' he replied, his expression rueful. 'I've arranged for Scarlet to check on her while I'm gone, because Mum is still in some pain with her back after she had the fall, but she's not happy about that either. Although that undoubtedly has as much to do with me promoting Scarlet to manager, as it has with me taking a day off. She went ballistic when I told her.' He flinched. 'Between you and me, I think Mum is scared of change of any kind. She wants things to stay the same; but nothing ever does, does it?'

'Thank goodness for that, because I never would have met you.' Violet stretched on tiptoe to kiss him.

'I'm so glad you decided to try to flog me some gin that day.'

'Is that the only reason you bought it?' By this time they'd reached Logan's van and she climbed into it.

'Yeah...'

She slapped him on the arm. 'Cheeky! My gin speaks for itself.'

'I can't argue with that,' he admitted, and started the engine. 'That reminds me, I need to place another order. I can't believe how well it's selling.'

'I can,' Violet retorted, having total confidence in her flavours and her skill in mixing them.

'How did you get into gin making in the first place?' Logan asked as he drove to the restaurant.

'By drinking it. It was just starting to become popular with the younger crowd. Before then it was more of a "G & T before lunch middle-class" kind of drink, and most of my friends were into vodka shots. But flavoured gins put in an appearance and suddenly it became *the* drink to have. So I tried it and liked it, and was scrolling the internet one day, as you do, wondering how it was made, and I ended up buying a still.' She saw his expression. 'It was only a small one. The kind I use to experiment with botanicals. I've bought a few more of these for when we start our tours, so people can have a go at making their own flavours.'

'Buying a still for personal use is a bit different to buying a distillery,' Logan pointed out.

'It wasn't a distillery when we bought it – it was an old farmhouse with some outbuildings. When the old gent who owned it died, his family decided to sell up rather than renovate. I talked Rory into coming into business with me, and that was the ideal place. So we bought it. As you've seen, we've done huge amounts of work on the business side, but my little house leaves a lot to be desired.'

'It's rustic,' Logan said gallantly.

'Dilapidated,' Violet said, as they pulled into the restaurant's car park. 'I see Beth's car is already here, but there's no sign of Rory. Typical.'

They went inside and Violet introduced Logan to her best friend.

'So, you're the man responsible for making Violet all starry-eyed,' Beth said, and Violet shot her a look.

'Are you starry-eyed?' Logan asked Violet, and she shook her head in despair.

'Thanks, Beth,' she hissed. 'I'm trying to make an impression here.'

'You needn't bother, I'm already impressed,' Logan said, giving her a hug and she nestled into him.

'Impressed with what?' Rory asked, coming up behind them.

'With me,' Violet replied haughtily.

'You're kidding, right?' Rory was staring at Logan. He stuck out his hand. 'I'm Rory, and I have the misfortune to be this one's brother. What's your excuse?'

'I love her?'

Rory's brows rose, then he said slowly, 'That's a good enough reason. Just don't hurt her OK, else you'll have me to answer to.'

'And me,' Beth piped up.

In desperation and feeling utterly embarrassed, Violet said, 'Shall we look at the menu? I'm starving. I hear the fish here is particularly good.'

Logan chuckled at her discomfort, and she thumped him playfully on the arm as they were shown to a table. 'You're not helping. I'm sorry about Rory and Beth,' she said in his ear.

'I'm not sorry; I think it's wonderful the way they're looking out for you.'

To her surprise, the pair of them behaved themselves for the rest of the meal, only making the occasional embarrassing comment, to which Violet responded that as they were both still single, she was looking forward to getting her own back on them one day.

'You'll have to come to the Tavern next time,' Logan said, as they lingered over coffee. 'No doubt Violet has told you there's an autumn theme going on, with *oriGINal Gin* featuring rather heavily on the drinks front. My chef has concocted a nice seasonal menu.'

'I must say, the food there is rather good,' Violet said, keeping her voice down. The meal here had been lovely, but the food in the Tavern was even better. 'And I helped decorate the place.'

Rory groaned. 'Not with skeletons and cobwebs?'

'You're thinking of Halloween – although I did carve some pumpkin lanterns. I meant to show them to you, but I got distracted.'

'Yeah, we know who by,' Beth said, nudging her.

Violet had been referring to her worry over her date with Sam (which had thankfully turned out to be a non-date), but she let it go. If this was the sole extent of their ribbing, she'd take it; it could have been much worse.

'Now you come to mention it, skeletons and cobwebs might be a good idea,' Logan said thoughtfully.

'That's taking your autumn theme too far,' Violet objected.

'Not if it's for a Halloween party. What do you think? We could hold it on the Saturday before, and people could wear fancy dress.'

'I think it's a great idea,' Rory said. 'Violet could make a special gin for the occasion.' He lowered his voice and said in a dramatic tone, 'All Hallows Gin – the flavour of the grave.'

'Ew, I don't think that will sell.'

'It will,' Rory insisted. 'People will be curious.'

'They'll be repulsed. It sounds dreadful. This is why I do the marketing,' Violet told him. She paused. 'I quite like the idea of a special one-off gin, though, so how about All Hallows Gin – the spirit of the dead?'

'And you laughed at *my* idea?' Rory was astounded.

'It'll have to have a unique flavour,' Beth pointed out.

'I agree and I think it should be black,' Violet said.

'Black?'

She nodded. 'That'll be the selling point, that and the fact it's only available at this one event and on this one night.'

'That's an awful lot of trouble to go to,' Logan said, a frown creasing his brow.

'Nah, it'll be great fun. I enjoy a challenge.' Suddenly Violet felt all fired up again. There were already a couple of black gins on the market, but there was always room for one more, and her gin would have a totally different taste. She couldn't wait to get started.

'What will you go as?' Beth asked her.

'A witch,' Violet replied instantly. 'It's apt considering I mix potions. What about you?'

'Am I invited?' Beth wanted to know.

'You both are,' Logan said. 'The more the merrier.'

Violet hesitated, then plunged right in. 'It might be a perfect opportunity for you to meet my parents.'

She was aware of Rory's surprise, but she ignored him: this would be the first time a boyfriend of hers met their mother and father.

And it told her more about her own feelings for Logan than anything else she could possibly say.

CHAPTER 24

LOGAN

'You're back then.' Marie was sitting in what was fast becoming her usual spot – the armchair nearest the TV. She had a plate of biscuits and a cup of tea on the lamp table next to her, and the remote control in her hand.

Logan didn't reply to her slightly snarky comment. Instead, he asked, 'How are you feeling?'

'I've felt better.'

'Has Scarlet been looking after you?'

'She's stuck her head around the door once or twice, if that's what you mean. Did you enjoy yourself?'

'Yes, thanks.'

'I had soup for lunch,' Marie stated. 'Out of a tin.'

'You could have had something off the menu.'

Marie wrinkled her nose. 'I wasn't very hungry. It's not the same when you have to eat by yourself.'

Logan wanted to point out that even if he hadn't gone out today, he would have been downstairs, working, so she would have eaten alone anyway.

When he'd informed her he was taking today off, he'd

only done so at the last minute, not wanting her to fret. Or, if he was honest, he hadn't wanted to have to listen to her repeatedly tell him he was *needed* at the Tavern. When she'd asked him where he was going, he'd told her the truth. Now, though, he was beginning to regret it.

'What was *your* meal like?' she asked.

'The food was good, but not as good as ours. Rory had pork chops with peppercorn sauce, and I swear the sauce had come out of a packet.'

'Rory?'

'Violet's brother.'

'You had lunch with Violet's brother?'

'And her friend, Beth.'

'That's cosy.' His mother stared stonily at the TV.

'You can meet them yourself when they come to the Halloween party.'

'What party?'

'I thought we'd have a Halloween party at the Tavern.'

'Did *you* think of it, or did *she*?' Marie spat out the word.

'Does it matter?' He sighed. '*I* did, if you really want to know. I thought a party would be a good conclusion to the autumn theme. Then we'd have a break for a few days until Bonfire Night was out of the way, before we started promoting the Christmas menu.'

'I think it's all a load of rubbish.'

'Halloween is becoming more popular,' Logan said.

'Halloween is for kids.'

'It can be for adults, too. And it's just a bit of fun. We'd sell tickets and people could come in fancy dress, and instead of table service for the food, we'd have a buffet. Violet is making a special gin for the occasion—'

'I might have known *she'd* have a hand in it. Can't you

see she's taking you for a ride? All she wants you for is to sell her bloody gin.'

'That's not true,' Logan objected. 'Violet doesn't need my help to sell her gin; her business is doing well.'

'So why is she going out of her way to make a special gin for you?'

'Because——' He'd been about to say that's the sort of thing people do when they love each other, but he didn't want to upset his mother.

Who was he kidding? She'd be upset, regardless of when he told her how he felt about Violet. She'd always made it obvious that she didn't consider any woman good enough for him; which was touching, but she had to learn to get on with his girlfriends. Especially this one, because although Violet had only just become his girlfriend, Logan dearly hoped she would one day be much, much more than that. He wished the two most important women in his life would get on; he wanted that more than he wanted anything – apart from Violet herself.

He was sick and tired of sneaking around, of trying to play down the growing importance Violet had in his life, of trying to keep his mother happy whilst not deliberately lying to her.

Maybe if she got to know Violet a bit better Marie would realise Violet wasn't the ogre she was making her out to be, that Violet wasn't using him; that they were good together and that she was here to stay.

He'd have a think and see if he could come up with a solution.

Leaving Marie to it, Logan retreated to the calmer waters of the bar and the less fraught conversation with Father Todd, who had popped in for a pint and a moan about the leak in the church roof.

'How's your mum?' Father Todd asked, after he'd ordered a second pint. 'I haven't seen her around for a couple of days.'

'She had a fall on Thursday – nothing serious,' he hastened to add, seeing the vicar's concerned expression. 'So she's staying with me for a while.'

'She looked as right as rain earlier, so thankfully it couldn't have been a bad one,' Benny interjected. The chairman of the Allotment Association was propping up the bar alongside the vicar. He held up his empty glass. 'Another one of these, please,' he said to Wayne, before turning back to Logan. 'Marie wants to be careful – I know she's not as old as me, but even at her age she could do herself a bit of damage.'

'How old are you, Benny?' Father Todd asked.

'Seventy-five.'

'I must say, you don't look it.'

'It's all that fresh air. I'm up the allotment every day.'

'I didn't realise growing your own veg needed that much work.'

'It doesn't.' Benny chortled. 'But the wife doesn't know that. What do you say, Logan?'

'Our Logan isn't married, so he can't appreciate a bit of time away from the wife,' Father Todd joked.

Logan was listening with half an ear. The rest of him was trying to work out when Benny could have seen his mother, and where. 'I didn't realise Mum had been out today,' Logan said. 'Where did you see her?'

'She was going into her house. Around lunchtime, it was. She was picking the post up off the mat.'

'And she seemed OK to you?'

'Let's put it this way, I can't remember the last time I was able to touch my toes, and your mum made me feel quite envious. I wish I was as flexible as her. Mind you, as I said, she's a bit younger than me, so what do I expect?' Benny drained a third of his pint. 'I can't stay long; the wife will have my guts for garters if I'm late for supper. She's had one of those recipe boxes delivered, and we're having something called halloumi. No idea what it is, but it sounds like you should be able to get ointment for it from the chemist.'

Father Todd laughed, but Logan was still mulling over what Benny had said.

His mother hadn't mentioned going out. He hadn't thought she was well enough, but it seemed that spending a few days with him had done her the world of good. He was glad she was feeling better. Strange for her not to have mentioned it, though, because when he'd asked her how she was this morning, she'd said her back was still paining her and she was finding it hard to get around.

If that was no longer the case, maybe she'd want to return to her own house soon…?

Whether she did or didn't, Logan decided to cook Sunday lunch for his mum and invite Violet. It was about time his mother got to know his girlfriend properly, and once she did, he was certain she'd like her, because there wasn't anything about Violet *not* to like. Marie would see that he and Violet had feelings for one another and that this wasn't a casual fling for either of them. When she understood Violet was now a part of his life, his mother would welcome her with open arms.

OK, maybe he was being optimistic, but he was convinced that at the very least she'd accept Violet.

Despite his optimism, though, Logan made the decision

not to tell his mother he was inviting Violet to lunch, too.
There was no point in her getting all het up beforehand.
He'd tell her on the day. That would be soon enough.

CHAPTER 25

VIOLET

It was one thing Logan meeting her brother and her best friend for a bite to eat, Violet thought: it was quite another being invited to Logan's to have lunch with him and his mum. This was more akin to "meeting the parents", because even though she'd met Marie several times now, she hadn't really *met her*, met her.

If she was honest, she was surprised Marie had agreed to have lunch with her at all. Hattie's comments lurked in the back of her mind like a lingering smell, and Violet was in two minds about the whole thing. There wasn't any question of her not going, though: she owed it to Logan. Anyway, she was curious. How would Marie behave? Maybe Logan had talked his mother round, made her realise they were an item and she may as well get used to it. However, it was with a degree of trepidation that Violet entered the Tavern on Sunday lunchtime.

Logan was waiting for her.

He looked as nervous as she felt, and she realised this was a big deal for him. It was a big deal for both of them, and its significance wasn't lost on her.

Scarlet smiled at them and Violet could have sworn the woman mouthed 'Good luck.'

'You look beautiful,' he said, ushering her through the bar

Logan was pretty handsome himself, Violet thought and she marvelled at the way her heart skipped a beat every time she saw him.

He paused at the bottom of the stairs, drawing her to him, and smoothed a strand of hair away from her face. 'I mean it, you're beautiful.' The love in his eyes melted her insides as he drew her closer, his lips brushing hers.

Her lids fluttered closed and she deepened the kiss, her body pressed against his, feeling the heat of him through her dress.

'Stop,' he groaned, breaking their connection. 'You're killing me.'

'You started it,' she retorted.

'And I want to finish it, but my mother is upstairs.'

Violet wondered what would have happened if Marie hadn't been, and the knowledge made her tremble. Logan gazed into her eyes, and she felt herself drowning. She was in far too deep to return to the shallows. No more paddling about on the edge of a relationship – she was in over her head. But she wasn't drowning, she was floating, and it was the most wonderful feeling in the world.

'By the way,' Logan said, as she placed a foot on the first step. 'Mum doesn't know you're coming to lunch. I thought we'd surprise her.'

Violet almost turned tail and ran. Oh boy, she had an awful feeling this wasn't going to go well. She looked back at him and raised her eyebrows.

'Do you think I should have told her?' he asked.

'Um... yeah?'

'Should I go on ahead and tell her?'

'It might be a good idea.' Violet moved to the side to let him pass.

'Wait here. I'll just...' He gestured upwards. 'I'll be back for you in a tick.'

She caught the nervous expression on his face as he walked past, and she watched him climb the stairs.

She'd been expecting to eat lunch in the bar with plenty of other people around, but it suddenly struck her that the three of them would be lunching in private, and her apprehension grew.

The Tavern was quite busy, noise filtering through into the corridor, and Violet strained to catch any sound from upstairs.

After a short while, Logan returned. 'Sorry about that,' he said. 'You were right, I should have told her. Never mind—' his voice was bright '—she knows now.'

'She doesn't mind me gatecrashing her lunch?'

'You're not gate crashing. I invited you.' He took her hand and gave it a squeeze, then motioned for her to go ahead of him. 'I hope you like beef,' he said as they climbed the stairs.

'I assumed we'd be eating off the menu.'

'Do you want to?' She heard the sudden doubt in his voice.

'It depends how good a cook you are,' she replied, deadpan.

'I get by,' he said. 'Besides, it didn't feel right inviting you to mine for lunch, then ordering from the kitchen. It would be cheating.'

'I'm sure it'll be lovely,' she said, then she ground to a halt when she saw Marie waiting for them.

'Hello, Mrs Cassidy,' Violet said, forcing her lips into a smile. Logan's mother had her hands on her hips and a face like thunder.

'Call her Marie,' Logan said. 'You don't mind, do you, Mum?'

Violet got the impression the woman minded very much indeed,

'Can I get you anything to drink?' he continued. 'Take a seat and I'll lay the table. Oh, you've already done it: thanks, Mum.'

Violet saw that the dining room table located at one end of the spacious lounge had been laid with place settings for two.

'I didn't realise we were having company,' Marie said, following Logan's gaze. She stalked into the kitchen, presumably to fetch more cutlery.

Logan turned his attention back to Violet. 'Drink?' Logan reminded her.

'Just water, please.'

'Sparkling? Ice and lemon?'

'You can take the barman out of the bar, but...' she joked feebly.

'Sorry, force of habit.'

When his mother returned to the open plan living-dining area to find them laughing, she scowled. The loud clatter as she dropped the silverware on the table made Violet jump.

'Drink, Mum?'

'Not for me. It's too early.'

'It doesn't have to be alcoholic,' Logan pointed out. 'Violet is having water.'

'I thought she'd be having gin.'

'It's too early for me, too, Mrs— Marie,' Violet said. 'Anyway, I'm driving.'

'I'd better check on the beef,' Logan said.

Violet wished he didn't have to; she didn't fancy being alone with his mum. Her relief when he returned with a glass of chilled water, was short-lived as he went back to the kitchen immediately, leaving Violet and his mother together without him as a buffer.

'How are you feeling?' Violet asked. 'Logan told me you'd had a fall.'

'I'll live.' Marie winced as she sat down and rubbed her lower back. 'Logan tried to insist I stay with him for a few more days, but I wanted to go home.'

'There's nothing like your own house is there?' Violet agreed.

'Have you got your own place?' Marie asked.

Finally, they were beginning to have a proper conversation, and some of the tension eased out of Violet's shoulders. 'Yes. When Rory and I set up *oriGINal Gin*, we bought a farmhouse and some outbuildings. I live in the farmhouse.'

'On your own?'

'That's right. My brother prefers to live in Hay.'

'How convenient.'

'It works for us,'

'I bet it does.'

Violet had no idea what Marie meant by that, and she had no intention of asking. An uncomfortable silence stretched between them, only broken by the clatter of pans from the kitchen.

'Need any help in there?' Violet called desperately.

'If there's any help needed, I'll be the one to give it to him,' Marie said, rising to her feet.

Violet didn't know how she was supposed to respond to that.

'I'm fine,' Logan shouted back.

Violet wished *she* was. She felt anything but. The hostility was coming off Marie in waves so hot Violet was surprised the woman didn't spontaneously combust.

His mother sank back into her seat and glared at her. Violet looked away.

Should she make an excuse and leave? Marie was most definitely not happy with Violet being there and the last thing she wanted to do was to cause any problems between Logan and his mother.

But the issue was that Marie may always see her as a problem…

Violet decided she'd stay, even if it was because she simply couldn't think of a reasonable excuse to leave that wouldn't alert Logan to the fact that his mother was being a bit of a cow. Anyway, it wasn't as though Violet couldn't stand up for herself – she'd dealt with worse than Marie in her time.

Also, there was the hope that if she kept her cool and didn't bite back, Marie's behaviour might improve.

Determined the woman wouldn't get a rise out of her, Violet smiled sweetly, and at that exact moment Logan came back into the living room and she saw the relieved look on Logan's face. It served to renew her resolve. His happiness was more important to her than her own, and the realisation amazed her. Apart from her family, Violet could truthfully say she'd never felt this way about anyone else before, and certainly not a man.

'If you'd like to take your seats, I'm about ready to dish up,' Logan said. 'Mum, if you sit there, Violet, you can sit here.' He pulled out two seats facing each other either side of the six-seater table, then he darted back into the kitchen.

Violet sat down and so did his mother. Marie didn't look at her, so Violet concentrated on the salt and pepper grinders and wondered what the hell she could talk about.

'Did Logan tell you about the Halloween party?' she asked, after a dig around in her mind for common ground.

'It's a ridiculous notion,' Marie said. 'Did you put it in his head?'

'He came up with it all by himself.'

'Was this before or after you promised him a special gin?'

'Before. It did give me the idea, though. I'm hoping it'll draw people in.'

'The Tavern doesn't need anything to draw people in, and certainly not gimmicks like a Halloween party.'

Violet tried again. 'It's just a bit of fun. My parents will probably come to it – they can't wait to meet Logan.'

'Does Logan know?'

'Of course, I wouldn't just spring it on him. Oops.' Violet put a hand to her mouth – that was exactly what Logan had done today. She'd fallen neatly into Marie's trap, and she could have kicked herself.

Marie's mouth twisted and her expression hardened. She was about to say something, then her demeanour changed abruptly as Logan walked into the room.

'Here you go.' He placed a tureen of vegetables and another of potatoes on the table. 'I'll just bring the meat and the gravy, and then we should be good to go.'

'Plates?' his mother asked.

Logan slapped a hand to his forehead. 'They're in the

oven, warming.'

As soon as he left the room, Marie said in a low voice. 'See what you're doing to him? You're stressing him out. He should be downstairs dealing with the customers he's already got, not faffing about planning parties for new ones, and certainly not wasting Sunday cooking for you. I don't know what's got into him since he met you.'

'Mind your backs,' Logan said, hurrying through the door with three plates clasped in oven-mittened hands. He carefully put them down on the placemats. 'Don't touch them, they're hotter than the centre of the sun,' he warned. 'And don't wait on ceremony – start serving yourselves, and I'll be back in a sec.'

Violet didn't move. Marie grabbed a serving spoon and began piling carrots onto her plate.

'Aren't you having any, after the trouble Logan has gone to?' his mother asked.

'Er, yes, of course.' Violet's appetite had disappeared. However, she picked up another spoon and scooped up a couple of potatoes.

Logan came back with the meat and gravy, and sat down with a sigh. He looked from Violet to his mother and back again. 'This is nice,' he said.

'Hmm.' Marie stabbed her fork into a slice of beef and dumped it on her plate.

Violet didn't comment.

The three of them ate in silence for a few minutes before Logan said, 'It's busy downstairs.' He turned to Violet. 'Sunday lunch is always popular.'

'Yes,' Marie said quickly. 'I was just telling Violet that your time would be better spent in the pub, rather than entertaining *her*.'

Logan's face tightened. 'This isn't entertaining; this is you and Violet having an opportunity to get to know one another properly. If Violet is going to be a part of my life, it would be nice if you two could be friends.'

'I don't think we have much in common, do you?' his mother retorted.

'You have me,' Logan joked, but Violet noticed a tick on the one side of his jaw. He seemed to be finding this as excruciating as she was.

His mother's eyes narrowed. She put her knife and fork down and pushed her plate away. 'I think one of us should be downstairs, and as *you* don't intend to be, *I'd* better go. Enjoy your lunch.'

Logan watched Marie leave, his expression unreadable. Then he slowly shook his head. 'I'm so sorry; I don't know what's got into her. I can't believe she was so rude.'

'Look, I'd best be off. Maybe this wasn't such a good idea.' Violet sent him a sympathetic smile. 'Perhaps she's not feeling too good…?'

'I think you're being very generous, considering her behaviour.' Logan had gone pale and he was chewing at the inside of his lip. 'I can't apologise enough.'

'No need to apologise. It's not your fault.' Violet got up, put a hand on his shoulder and bent down to kiss him on the cheek.

'Why is she being like this?' he said, his voice full of bafflement and hurt.

Violet recalled the conversation she'd had with Hattie, but felt it wasn't her place to say anything. Besides, Hattie may well be wrong, and there might be an altogether different explanation for Marie's behaviour – but for the life of her, Violet couldn't imagine what that could be.

'I don't want you to go,' Logan said.

'I know, and I don't want to go, either, but it's for the best. Make your peace with your mum, and I'll speak to you later. Have you got tomorrow off?'

He nodded.

Violet stroked his cheek. 'I'll see you tomorrow then, if you want?'

'Try stopping me.' Some colour had come back into his face, and he pulled her down onto his lap and hugged her fiercely. 'I can't wait.'

'Neither can I.'

'Are you sure you won't stay?' he murmured into her hair.

'I'm sure. Go see to your mum – she needs you.'

'Does she?' His voice was serious. 'I'm not so sure.'

'It's not worth falling out with her.'

'Oh, it is,' he insisted. 'It most definitely is; because nothing and no one is going to stop me from being with you.'

Violet had an awful feeling that Logan just might be tempting fate.

CHAPTER 26

LOGAN

Logan rarely lost his temper, but right now it was so lost he didn't think he'd ever find it again. How dare his mother treat a guest of his so disrespectfully!

As he watched Violet pick up her bag and leave, he was so furious he didn't trust himself not to march into the bar and give his mother what for. Violet had been so understanding, it made him feel ashamed, and he remained in the flat for a while, not daring to go downstairs, fearful of what he might say.

Eventually, though, he calmed down: however, it was time he and his mother had a few words. He found Marie leaning against the bar, her face like thunder. Her attitude was enough to put his customers off their food.

'Everything OK?' Scarlet murmured to him as she walked by with a handful of dirty plates and dishes.

'No.'

'Didn't think so.' She gave him a sympathetic look.

He inhaled deeply and let the breath out slowly. 'Mum, can I see you in my office, please.' He tried to keep his tone neutral, not wanting anyone to realise how angry he was.

'Now?'

'Please.'

'What's it about?'

Logan blew out his cheeks – as if she didn't know. How could she not realise how obnoxious she'd been? Or maybe she knew, and she simply didn't care. 'We'll talk in my office.'

Marie pursed her lips, then pushed herself away from the bar. Logan studied his mother's gait as she walked ahead of him, noting that she didn't appear to be in any discomfort whatsoever. Her back must be fully recovered.

'Your girlfriend left, I see,' she said as soon as he'd closed the door.

'Are you surprised, after the way you spoke to her?'

'I don't know what you mean. All I did was tell the truth – you were needed in the pub.'

'They were managing perfectly fine without me. And even if they weren't, it's not for you to step in.'

'Someone had to. You were too busy trying to impress Violet.'

'I'll say it again, it wasn't up to you to make that decision. Let me ask you something – if Violet hadn't arrived, would you still have walked out halfway through the meal?'

His mother steadfastly stared over his shoulder at the pin board behind him.

'I thought not,' he said. 'You were happy enough to let my staff get on with it when it was just the two of us for lunch.'

'I realised it wasn't a good idea both of us being AWOL,' she said, still not meeting his eyes.

'OK, let's assume you're right. Did you have to be so

nasty about it? I was ashamed and embarrassed, and so was Violet.'

'She'll get over it.'

Logan leant forwards and put his hands on the desk. '*She* might – and I must say, she was very understanding – but *I* won't. You treated her inexcusably, and I won't put up with it. I love Violet—'

Marie gasped.

'You might as well know how I feel about her,' he carried on, ignoring his mother's stricken face. 'And you might as well get used to her being in my life. She's going to be around whether you like it or not, and if you can't accept that, then I'm sorry.'

'What are you saying?'

'Don't force me to choose, Mum… just, *don't*, OK?'

'I can't believe you're saying this.'

Logan blinked hard. Bloody hell, this was the most difficult conversation he'd ever had in his life. 'You'll always be my mother and I'll always love you. Nothing will change that. But I also love Violet. She's my future.'

'And I'm your past, am I? I can't believe you're putting me out to pasture after everything I've done for you.'

'As I said, you're my mum. But Violet is going to be my wife.'

Marie clutched a hand to her bosom. '*You've asked her to marry you?*' Her incredulous voice was little louder than a whisper.

'Not yet. But when I do, I hope she'll say yes.'

'What if she doesn't? You'll have cast me aside for nothing.'

'I'm not casting you aside. It's not a question of you or her. Not unless you make it that way. There's room in my life for both of you.'

'Is there?' She didn't sound convinced. 'I don't think so.'

Disbelief washed over him. How could she think that? She was acting more like a supplanted wife than a mother whose son had fallen in love. OK, she mightn't approve of, or even like the woman he'd chosen, but it was his choice to make, not hers.

'That's up to you,' he said. 'I won't stop calling in to see you. I'll pop in every day if you want, but you're not welcome here until you change your attitude. I can't let you be so disrespectful to Violet.'

Her eyes were wide and glistened with tears, and he almost faltered, her distress stabbing him in the gut. But he knew if he backed down now, she'd continue to behave despicably, and he simply wouldn't put Violet through that.

'What about the Tavern?' she asked.

'What about it?'

'You've worked so hard to make it a success. Don't throw it all away.'

His smile was sad. 'I seem to recall your extremely strenuous objections to me taking over the Tavern in the first place. It's nice to see you've changed your mind.'

'I was wrong, I admit it.'

'And you're wrong about Violet, too. Get to know her, please… for my sake.'

But all his mother did was stare at him.

She didn't need to say anything – her face told him everything he needed to know.

CHAPTER 27

LOGAN

Logan pressed his mobile to his ear and walked into his office, away from the noise of empty barrels being loaded onto the lorry, but he still couldn't work out what his mother was saying. He hadn't spoken to her since yesterday afternoon after she'd stormed out of the pub in tears. He'd thought it best for both of them if they had some time to cool off and think about what had been said.

'Slow down, Mum. What's happened, what is it?' She was saying something over and over. He wasn't sure, but it sounded like, 'I can't stand it.'

'My head,' she shrieked the word tailing off into a moan that had the hairs on his neck standing on end and his heart thudding loudly in his ears.

'Ambulance,' she said distinctly, and he was out of the Tavern door and tearing down the road before his brain caught up with his feet. Please God don't tell me she's had another fall, he prayed, pounding along the pavement, his own breath coming in jerky gasps.

'What's happened, Mum. Talk to me.' He was yelling into the phone as he ran, trying to make sense of what was happening.

'It hurts; oh God, it hurts.'

'What does? Don't move, I'll call an ambulance now.'

'Done it. On way.' She was crying so hard he had trouble understanding her.

'You've already called an ambulance?' he gasped, trying to catch his breath as he ran.

'Yes.' Another sob. 'Please make it stop.'

When he flew in through her front door, his mother was slumped forward in her favourite chair, her head in her hands, her breathing coming in shallow gasps punctuated by moans.

'What is it? What's happened?' He dropped to his knees in front of her, and tried to prise her hands from her head. She was clutching her temples and crying.

'My head, my head. Please make it stop.'

Oh God, she was having a stroke, or an aneurism. Logan felt cold all over, as though his body was immersed in ice. Please no, not this, he prayed, his stomach clenching with each new cry. He'd never seen her in so much pain…

'How long ago did you ring for an ambulance? How long have you been like this? *Mum*, speak to me.'

Marie didn't say anything, but her cries tore his heart to shreds.

'Hurry up,' he muttered into the air, at a loss to know what to do. She could take the tablets the doctor had prescribed, but he was reluctant to give them to her in case it made things worse.

Relief made his knees go weak when he heard the distant sound of a siren and he was glad he was already sitting on the floor. 'I can hear the ambulance,' he told her. 'Not long now. Hold on, Mum, hold on.'

He scrambled to his feet and rushed outside, wanting to

make it easy for the paramedics to identify the correct house. The front door was standing wide open as he'd forgotten to close it behind him in his haste to reach his mother, and it was only when he saw it he realised it hadn't been locked. Had his mother been out earlier this morning, or had she had the sense to unlock it after she'd phoned the ambulance?

Whatever, it didn't matter. They were here.

Two paramedics got out and hurried over to him and he waved frantically at them.

'She's in the living room,' he said, standing aside to let them go ahead of him, anxious not to get in their way.

'What's her name?'

'Marie Cassidy. She's my mother.'

'And she's suffering from head pains? How long has this been going on? Hello, love, I'm Sandra and this is Blake. Let's take a look at you, shall we?'

'She's had headaches on and off for years,' he said, 'but I've never seen her like this.'

He watched Sandra ease his mother's hands from her head as they began examining her. Thankfully she seemed to have calmed a little, and although she was still in pain, the awful crying and wailing had ceased. Her breathing was shallow and fast though, and he scanned her anxiously searching for signs that she'd suffered a stroke. Although her face was screwed up, both sides of it looked equal, so he was none the wiser.

'All right, my lovely, let's get you secured and into the ambulance,' Blake said after what seemed like an impossibly long time.

'What's wrong with her, do you know?'

'Her blood pressure is a little raised and so is her heart

rate. We've given her some pain medication, but we can't give her too much. We need to take her to hospital where a doctor can assess her.'

'Is it… do you think…?' He didn't like to ask.

'We'll know more when she's been assessed and they've run some tests,' Blake told him firmly, and Logan realised this was the best answer he was going to get.

No matter how desperate he was to know what was wrong, the paramedics weren't the best people to tell him. And, as Blake said, they needed to run some tests before they'd know anything for certain.

'Can I travel in the ambulance with her? Oh, hang on, it might be best if I follow behind.' He was thinking fast – as much as he wanted to be by her side for the journey (and not just to reassure her either, because he was thinking "what if…"), he was also trying to think logically. He might need to come back to her house to fetch some things for her if they decided to keep her in. Or, if they told her she could go home, he'd be able to take her home there and then, and not have to phone someone for a lift.

'Mum, listen to me; I'm popping back to the Tavern to fetch the van. I'll be as quick as I can,' he said.

After checking which hospital she was being taken to, he waited for his mother to be loaded into the back of the ambulance, locked her front door, then raced up the road to get his van.

The ambulance had already left by the time he drove through Ticklemore but he wasn't too far behind and he was tempted to put his foot down to catch it up. However, common sense prevailed as he realised speeding might get him into more trouble than he could handle, and the last thing his mum needed was for him to be taken to hospital by ambulance himself. The one consolation was that she wasn't being blue-lighted, so the paramedics didn't think whatever was wrong with her was life-threatening or time-critical. Or, and the thought made him feel sick, maybe they didn't think there was any point in rushing because the worst had happened and his mother was lying de—

'Stop it!' he muttered. He couldn't think like that. Of course the worst hadn't happened. Even if she was suffering a stroke or something equally serious, they'd given her some medication.

She'd be all right.

She had to be.

***

It took Logan a while to find somewhere to park at the hospital, and when he eventually did and went into the reception area, he was told to take a seat, and that he'd be called shortly.

Hoping he wouldn't be kept waiting long, he took the opportunity to give Violet a quick ring.

'Sorry, I'm not going to be able to see you today – I'm at the hospital.' He swallowed convulsively, forcing down the worry threatening to spill over.

'What's happened? Are you all right?'

'It's Mum. She's in terrible pain. I've never seen her this bad. I'm scared she's had a stroke, or a bleed on the brain. Or—' He bit down on the word.

'Let's hope you're wrong,' Violet said. 'Let me know as soon as you hear anything. I love you.'

After telling her he loved her too, he said goodbye quickly, not trusting himself to be able to keep it together and he was also scared he might miss being called.

"Shortly" morphed into a half an hour however, then an hour, and he had begun to pace nervously, imaging the worst whilst praying for the best, before a nurse's head peered around the door and she called his name.

'How is she?' he asked, following her inside.

'Comfortable.'

'Do they know what it is?'

'The doctor will be along to talk to you soon. She's in here.' The nurse pulled aside a curtain to reveal his mother lying on a bed in a cubicle.

She was connected to a drip, had a cannula in the back of her hand, and what looked like a small grey peg on her finger. A monitor next to the bed bleeped and flashed, and he gave it a cursory glance, not sure what the readings indicated.

His mum, despite being hooked up to what appeared to be the National Grid, looked far better than he'd anticipated. He'd expected her to be comatose, or not far off it, grey-skinned and dull-eyed, and maybe appearing to have aged significantly since he last saw her. Instead, she was sitting up and looking far perkier than he'd thought she'd look. She continued to wear a pained expression on her face, and he guessed she must still be in some discomfort, but she was better than he'd thought she'd be.

He leant over to kiss her cheek, then slumped exhausted into a plastic chair next to the bed. 'How are you feeling?' he asked.

'I've been better.'

'You gave me a nasty scare, there.'

'You and me both.'

'Have they told you what's wrong?'

'Not yet. They're sending me for a scan and some other bits and bobs. I'm not sure I understand.' She reached for his hand, and he took it, feeling it tremble.

'It'll be OK,' he said. 'You're in the best place.'

'You'll stay with me, won't you?'

'Of course I will!' What did she think he was going to do – leave her on her own? 'Do you know if they're going to keep you in?'

'They've not said.'

'OK.'

After that, all they could do was to settle down and wait. The waiting was interspersed by visits from the doctor (who was non-committal at this stage), nurses taking readings, and orderlies taking Marie away for various reasons, and bringing her back again.

Finally, someone came to talk with them.

'We know what it isn't,' the doctor said. 'There's no evidence of a tumour, a bleed, or a stroke.'

'Thank God!' Logan was clammy with relief. Those were the three things he'd been dreading.

'We're going to admit her for observation and run a couple more tests, if that's all right?'

'Thank you, Doctor,' Marie said. She seemed to be more or less pain-free at the moment, apart from the odd grimace.

'I'd better pop back and fetch you some things,' Logan told her, thankful that he'd had the presence of mind to bring the van. Reluctant to leave her, but knowing she was in safe hands, Logan promised her he'd be back as quickly as he could. There was no way he was leaving his mother on her own unless he absolutely had to.

***

Logan briefly considered popping into the Tavern to check they were managing without him, but he decided against it; he was eager to return to the hospital and he ran the risk of getting caught up in something.

He did, however, phone the pub once he was safely on his way back to the hospital.

'We heard about your mum,' Scarlet said before he had a chance to say anything.

He guessed she probably had. Word spread through Ticklemore faster than fleas on a dog. 'I've just popped to her house to pick up a few things; they're keeping her in.'

'Did they say what it was? Hattie was in earlier and she said she heard lots of noise coming from Marie's house this morning, and then an ambulance showed up. She says if there's anything she can do… And that goes for all of us.'

Thanks. Just keep the Tavern ticking over, will you? I know it's a big ask, but would you mind locking up for me? I'm aware it's going to be a very long day for you.'

'Of course I will.'

'Thank you so much – I'll make it up to you. As for a diagnosis, she hasn't had one yet, although the doctor on duty didn't seem to think it was a stroke or a tumour. When I got to her, she was crying in pain and holding her head – as you can imagine I feared the worst.'

'That's a relief. With any luck they'll sort her out and she'll be home in no time.'

'At least her pain seems to be more manageable. I don't know what they gave her but she was far more settled when I left. I'm on my way back there now.'

'Don't worry about the Tavern. Everything's fine. Look after Marie and we'll see you when we see you. Be sure to call me as soon as you know anything though, please?'

'Absolutely. Thanks, Scarlet.'

'Take care, and give my love to your mum.'

Logan ended the call, thinking that he'd try but he wasn't sure his mother would appreciate the sentiment.

He was right, he discovered, when he was shown into Marie's cubicle some time later and told her that the Tavern staff sent their love.

She pulled a face, so he knew she must be feeling better. He didn't mention Hattie's name, as he didn't see the point. Sitting on the plastic chair beside his mother's bed, he treacherously wondered if his mum was jealous of the older woman. Hattie was so full of beans, so thoroughly immersed in her job at Bookylicious, and so at the centre of the Ticklemore community, that she put women half her age to shame. Not only that, there was her late-in-life romance with Alfred, which he knew his mother didn't approve of but which he thought was wonderful.

'You'd think she'd know better at her age,' was what his mother had said, but Logan didn't consider age had anything to do with love. More than once he'd wished his mother had a love interest, and not only because it would give him some respite from her undivided attention. She'd been on her own for almost as long as he could remember – surely she deserved to have romance in her life? It might make her less bitter—

Oh dear, had he really thought that?

When she was finally taken to a ward, Logan sloped off to the hospital canteen for a quick coffee whilst she was settled into her new accommodation. Even though he hadn't eaten since breakfast, the smell of food made his stomach churn, so he took the drink outside and sat on a bench until he thought it was OK to go back in.

By the time he'd found the ward Marie had been admitted to, visiting hours had begun so he was able to sit with his mum on the ward for a while. He even took her a magazine, a bottle of squash, and a pathetic-looking bunch of grapes that he'd bought in the hospital shop.

'It's traditional, isn't it,' he said, popping the grapes on the table beside her bed.

Bless her, she looked tired and washed-out, which wasn't surprising considering what she'd been through. One good thing might come of all this, though: they might finally get to the bottom of what was causing these terrible headaches of hers. Guilt that he'd thought it might have been stress made him cringe, because it was obviously more than that.

He stayed with her until visiting time ended and he was ushered off the ward. 'I'll give you a call first thing in the morning,' he said before he left, 'to see what sort of a night you've had.' Logan checked her mobile was plugged in and charging. 'Maybe you'll have some news by then.' He brightened. 'Maybe you'll be allowed home?'

'I doubt it.'

'But let's hope so, eh? I don't like you being in hospital.'

'I'm not too keen, either. But I daresay it's the best place for me, considering I'm on my own.'

'You're not on your own, Mum. You've got me.'

'Have I?'

'Mum!' Logan was exasperated. 'I'll look after you for as long as you need.'

'You're busy. You've got the pub—' she hesitated '—and other things.'

'I'll never be so busy that I can't look after you. Anyway, once they find out what's causing these headaches of yours, they can treat it, and you won't need looking after.'

For some reason his mother didn't look as pleased with that as he'd expected.

'I've got to go before Sister throws me out,' he said, kissing her on the forehead. 'Try to get some sleep.'

'Hmph.'

Logan felt awful leaving his mother in hospital but he had no choice, and he knew she was in the best place.

Outside he took a deep breath of fresh autumn air. The sun had set, but it wasn't dark yet, although it would be soon. He supposed he'd better get back to the Tavern, but for once he didn't feel like it. The pub could manage without him.

Impulsively he took his phone out of his pocket…

CHAPTER 28

VIOLET

'It's my fault,' Logan said as soon as he saw Violet waiting for him on her farmhouse doorstep, and her heart went out to him.

'I'm sure it isn't,' she replied, pulling him close and hugging him tight. He smelt of antiseptic and exhaustion.

'You don't understand. I was going to tell you all about it when I saw you today – Mum and I had a bit of a falling out after you left yesterday.'

'Because of me?'

'Because of the way she treated you and her attitude. I was appalled – I still am. We had words and I told her not to make me have to choose between you.'

Violet froze – that was exactly what Hattie had predicted might happen.

'I think the stress of it all has put her in hospital,' he added.

Violet drew him inside and into the living room, where she pushed him down onto the sofa and sat next to him, taking his hand in hers. 'You can't blame yourself.'

'But I do. They know it's not a tumour or a stroke, but what if it's some kind of neurological problem? What if it's serious and I've just made it worse? And now she's fretting about being sent home and having no one to look after her.'

'She's got you,' Violet said, diplomatically.

'That's what I told her, but she was going on about me being too busy, and I knew she was referring to you.'

Violet didn't know how to respond.

'I'm taking care of that,' he continued. 'Scarlet is hiring more staff specifically to free up my time. I was hoping to spend some of it with you, but....'

'Your mum needs you more,' Violet said, but Hattie's words circled in her mind like vultures over a carcass. Did this signify the death of their relationship? Violet hated the suspicion that Marie might be exaggerating or even completely fabricating her illness in order to garner Logan's sympathy and attention, but if that was the case it was certainly working. On the other hand, if she wasn't then it meant Marie was ill, and Violet felt guilty for even thinking she mightn't be.

Either way, she felt sympathy for Logan. If his mum was ill and needed caring for, then he wouldn't have a minute to himself, and would also be emotionally strung out and constantly worried about her. If, on the other hand, Marie was feigning illness for reasons of her own, Logan would still have a lot to deal with.

The only thing Violet could do for the moment was to sit tight and see what the doctors diagnosed. If Marie was genuinely unwell, the last thing Violet wanted to do was to upset the woman more than she already was. Logan's mum had taken against her, and it wouldn't be fair to give Marie anything further to worry about. If she was ill (and Violet hoped she wasn't) then Violet would butt out gracefully. Logan would have his hands full caring for Marie anyway, without the added complication of a romance.

But if she wasn't…?

'When was the last time you ate anything?' she asked, hearing his tummy rumble.

He shrugged. 'I don't know… breakfast?'

'I'll go make us something. I haven't eaten dinner yet. I was planning on having cannelloni. I've got to warn you, it's a frozen one – I usually cook but I didn't feel like it this evening. Care to join me?'

'Yeah, thanks. I better had; I'm not all that hungry, though.'

He might think so now, but she hoped when the food was put in front of him he'd recover his appetite.

'How about a glass of wine while you wait?' she suggested.

'No thanks; I might get a call from the hospital.'

Violet squeezed his hand. 'I doubt you will, not from what you've told me.'

He considered what she'd said. 'Go on then, just the one.'

She fetched him a glass, then retreated to the kitchen to make dinner. She didn't have much of an appetite herself, but both of them had to eat something, so she took a couple of cannelloni out of the freezer and popped them in the oven. Then she prepared a salad and put it in the fridge while they waited for their meals to heat through.

***

'Would you like a coffee or a tea, or something stronger?' she asked after they'd picked at their food and she'd cleared the plates away. Logan was staring into space, his mind clearly still on his mum.

'No, thanks.' He continued to gaze at a spot in the distance.

'Do you think you should be here?' He might feel better if he was at the Tavern keeping himself busy, rather than being here, brooding.

'It's as good a place as any,' he replied, and Violet flinched, wondering whether he was regretting being with her when his mother was in hospital.

'I'm sorry,' he said, 'that came out wrong. What I meant was, I don't care where I am as long as you're with me.' He moved towards her. 'Come here.'

Violet scooted closer and sank into his embrace, her face buried in his neck. She felt the tension in him, the stiffness in the way he held her, the hitching of his breath. He was coiled so tight she thought he might explode. So she did the only thing she could think of – she kissed him.

He was hesitant at first, when her lips sought out his, but quickly he was kissing her with an ardour that stole her breath, and when he ran his fingers up and down her back and let out a small gasp, she realised the only thing on his mind right now was her.

It was a heady thought and one which made her senses swim.

His hand moved lower, pulling her hips into him and she knew if she didn't stop this right now that she wouldn't be able to stop it at all. His desire for her was obvious and arousing, but Violet didn't care. She felt desirable and reckless, as though she was on the cusp of something momentous, irreversible, and inescapable. If she went ahead and slept with him, there would be no turning back.

Was she ready for that?

Oh, yes… She was more than ready.

'Let's go upstairs,' she breathed, and with a groan Logan took her hand, took her to bed, and took possession of her heart.

And afterwards Violet discovered she had no regrets.

None whatsoever.

CHAPTER 29

LOGAN

'She's had a comfortable night,' a nurse said when Logan rang the hospital early next morning to see how his mum was, but was unable to tell him anything more.

'I'll have to wait until visiting time,' he said to Violet, taking her in his arms. It had been wonderful waking up next to her, and he'd slept surprisingly well last night, too. Or perhaps he shouldn't have been so surprised, considering it was very late by the time he'd finally drifted off to sleep. He glowed when he thought about what they'd done – and how often they'd done it. He also felt rather guilty because his mum was languishing in hospital while he'd been enjoying himself. But guilty or not, he wouldn't have changed things. Last night had been the most magical night of his life.

'I love you.' He breathed in the heady scent of her, wishing he didn't have to leave. He could quite happily stay here and pretend the rest of the world didn't exist.

'I love you, too.'

His heart sang. To think this beautiful, sassy, vibrant

woman loved *him*.

The exact shape of their future together was hazy, as yet unformed and undecided, and there were so many considerations, but as long as they *were* together that was all that mattered. They had plenty of time to work it out.

Talk about a whirlwind romance! He couldn't believe how much his life had changed in just over a month. But when you knew, you knew. And he *knew*. Violet was the woman he wanted to spend the rest of his life with, the woman he wanted to have a family with, to grow old with. But there was no rush. They had their whole lives ahead of them, and several obstacles to overcome first – the chief one for him right now being his mother's health. So, despite his reluctance to let Violet go, after yet another passionate kiss, that's exactly what he did.

'I've got to make tracks,' he said. 'I wish I didn't have to, but…'

'Me, too. I've got work to do as well, and Rory will be here soon. Let me know how your mum gets on.'

Back to reality, Logan thought as he drove to Ticklemore, his mind brimming with Violet. He was finding it difficult to concentrate on anything else, and once more he felt a stab of guilt for having had such a wonderful night while his mum only had a comfortable one – whatever that meant. He shouldn't feel happy, but he couldn't help it, and that was yet another thing to beat himself over the head with.

When he pulled into the Tavern's car park, he headed for his usual parking space, switched off the engine and slumped in his seat, despair replacing his earlier euphoria as he thought about his mother. He'd managed to push his worry about her to the back of his mind last night, but it returned in spades now he was back in Ticklemore, and it threatened to overwhelm him. Logan would like nothing more than to turn the van around and head back to Violet, where he could lose himself in her and forget about the real world.

Sighing, he reached for his phone. He'd better call his mother and let her tell him how she was in person.

***

Reluctantly Logan got out of his vehicle and let himself into the pub; that hadn't been fun. Marie had done nothing but complain, and to his shame he wasn't looking forward to visiting her later. On the plus side though, at least she was back to her usual self, which meant she must be feeling better.

The sound of bottles clinking together had him heading for the bar, and he saw Scarlet already there, stocking the fridge.

'How's your mum?' she asked as soon as she saw him.

'Comfortable, the nurse told me, although my mother didn't think she'd had a comfortable night at all when I spoke to her just now. She did nothing but complain about the food, the woman opposite who was shouting all night, the nurses who woke her up to take her vitals… You name it, she whinged about it.'

'She must be feeling better. Do you think she'll be home today?'

'I've no idea, but I hope they find out what caused her headache before they discharge her. I'm scared it'll happen again.'

'Quite a few people came in to ask about her.' Scarlet's

gaze went to the nearest window. 'There's one of them now – Hattie is outside.'

Logan turned around to see the old lady peering at him, her nose pressed against the glass, her hands cupped around her eyes, and he smiled. 'I'll let her in.'

'I saw the ambulance and was going to ask if I could do anything to help,' Hattie said, hurrying through the door as soon as he opened it and enveloping him in a hug. 'But I thought better of it – I didn't want to make Marie any worse. How is she?'

'She's OK, I think. I rang the hospital this morning and they said she'd had a comfortable night, although when I spoke to her she didn't think it had been all that comfortable,' he repeated.

'I called in the Tavern yesterday evening. Scarlet said you were still at the hospital and they didn't know what was wrong other than it wasn't a stroke,' Hattie said. 'That's what I feared.'

'Me, too.' Logan rubbed a hand across his chin.

'Have you been there all night, only your van wasn't here half an hour ago,' Hattie asked, her eyes boring into him.

He was conscious of Scarlet's curious gaze, too. 'Er, no, I, um, went to see Violet after visiting time, and, um…'

'OK, boy, there's no need to spell it out. Good for you.'

Scarlet sniggered and Logan could feel the colour rising in his cheeks. Dear God, by lunchtime the whole village would know he'd spent the night with Violet.

Suddenly he felt like a right heel. How could he have done such a thing when his mother was in hospital?

His dismay and self-disgust must have shown on his face because Hattie's thin arm came around him and she gave him a cuddle. 'Don't beat yourself up. Your mum will be

OK.'

'But—'

'There was nothing more you could have done last night, and no one will blame you for seeking comfort where you could find it.'

Logan could think of someone who might…

'Anyway, it's not as though your mother is seriously ill, is it?' Hattie continued bluntly. 'Scarlet said they were only keeping her in for observation. Isn't that right?'

Scarlet nodded. 'That's what Logan told me.'

'There you go! Keeping her in was just a precaution, and I know they have to run all the tests and whatnot, but they're not going to find anything serious; if there was anything worrying they'd have found it by now. Mark my words, it'll all be down to stress.'

Logan wished he was as certain as Hattie.

***

'Her over there, the one stuffing her face with Liquorice Allsorts, has gallstones. That one there—' Logan's mother pointed to the lady in the next bed up '—is in for heart problems. She's going home in the morning.'

'How about you? What did the doctor say?' It was late afternoon and visiting time had not long started.

'Another day, they said. I'm baffling them.'

'Have they given you a hint what it might be?'

'Nothing. If you ask me, they don't know.' She dipped her hand into the box of Maltesers he'd brought her and popped a couple in her mouth.

'You seem much brighter,' he said. 'You must be feeling better.'

'It comes and goes. I was awful earlier on.'

'Would it help if I spoke to the doctor myself?'

'I wouldn't bother, if I was you. When they know something they'll tell me. Anyway, they do their rounds in the morning. Mrs Bacon, her name is. Nice woman. She said I might be able to go home tomorrow, but I'm not holding my breath.'

Marie did look a lot perkier. Maybe the enforced rest was doing her good?

'I'll keep my fingers crossed,' he said.

'How's the Tavern? Did they manage without you yesterday? At least you were there for some of it. What time did you get back?'

'Early enough.' Yeah, early *this morning*, so he wasn't technically lying. It briefly crossed his mind that he should simply tell her the truth, but he didn't want to vex her unnecessarily.

'I bet you're rushed off your feet without me there,' his mother said, helping herself to more Maltesers.

'We miss you,' he said diplomatically, 'but Yasmine is a great help, so don't worry about the Tavern. It can function perfectly well for a day without either of us being there.'

'You've been there today, though, haven't you?' Marie suddenly looked anxious.

'Where else would I be?' He knew where he'd *like* to have been and that was anywhere Violet was. Despite the uncertainty and worry about his mum, Logan's future was looking considerably rosier. Or should he say, *violet*-ier?

As soon as Marie had a diagnosis and they knew what they were dealing with, Logan vowed to make a concerted effort to get her to accept Violet. They were never going to be best friends, but as long as his mother could be civil to the woman he loved, that would have to do. It was a shame she'd taken such a dislike to Violet, but she'd just have to get over it and learn to accept her.

Logan thought back to what he'd said to his mum about making him choose, and he cringed. He didn't want to have to choose. His mother was being unfair and unrealistic. He knew she only wanted what was best for him, but she had to learn to step back. Maybe he'd been too indulgent with her in the past, allowing her to have more influence over him than was reasonable for a mother to have over her grown-up son, but it had simply been easier to let her get away with it than butting heads with her all the time.

He'd only stood his ground with her once, and that was when he'd bought the Tavern. She'd argued and wept, and had alternately showed off or had a tantrum, and it had even made her ill, but she had eventually come to terms with it: she'd had no choice. He had been determined to buy the pub, so buy it he had. He was equally determined regarding Violet. More so.

The Tavern meant a great deal to him, but Violet meant more. If he hadn't been prepared to walk away from his dream of owning the pub because of how his mother felt about it, then he was doubly certain he wasn't going to walk away from the woman he hoped would be his wife.

He'd meant it when he'd told his mum that one day he'd ask Violet to marry him. And that he wasn't going to let her come between them.

Marie would just have to learn to live with it.

CHAPTER 30

LOGAN

Logan wanted to be at the Tavern this morning, but *wanting* to do something didn't mean that he *should* do it. These interviews were Scarlet's show and he had to step away. After all, he'd told her that the employment of more staff was down to her, so it was only fair he stepped aside and allowed her to get on with it, no matter how hard it was for him to let go.

This was the reason he'd made her the Tavern's manager, so she could deal with the day-to-day running of the place, giving him more free time.

But taking on an additional member of staff wasn't a day-to-day thing, was it? At least, that's what he told himself until Franklin, noticing him hovering around as Scarlet tidied the office, dragged him into the kitchen.

'What are you doing, man?' Franklin asked.

'Nothing…'

'You've got to let her do this by herself.'

'I know.'

'Can't you, I don't know… go for a walk, or something?'

'On my own?'

'Give Violet a call.'

'She's busy.' He knew for a fact that Violet was conducting interviews of her own. Even though she and Rory were still squabbling over the role they wanted their new person to play, they'd gone ahead and set up some interviews anyway. He hoped they'd find what they were looking for; if the business was to expand into tours and gin-making experiences, they'd definitely need more help.

He was also being selfish, because with him taking more time for himself, he wanted Violet to be able to do the same. It seemed ages since he'd seen her, but it was only twenty-four hours. Maybe he'd get over there today? Or she could come to him?

'Well?' Franklin had his arms folded. 'You need to leave Scarlet to it.'

Logan knew his chef was right.

He checked the time. 'I could go to the hospital, I suppose. I'd like to have a chat with the doctor, if they'll let me.'

Franklin's expression immediately softened. 'How is Marie? Do they know why she's getting the headaches?'

'She's OK, I think. I spoke to one of the nurses on the ward this morning who said they should know more later when the doctor does her rounds. If I hurry, I might be in time for a quick chat. Mind you, they probably won't tell me anything, but at least I can say I tried.'

Which was why, a short while later, Logan was pacing up and down outside the ward his mother was on, hoping he'd be allowed to speak to the doctor responsible for her care. So when a nurse came to fetch him and showed him into a family room, he was extremely grateful.

He had been waiting for over half an hour and was wondering whether another cup of coffee from the vending machine in the corner was a good idea knowing how awful the last one had tasted yet wanting something to do with his hands, when the doctor came into the room.

'Are you Mrs Cassidy's son?' she asked.

'That's me.'

'My name is Wendy Bacon and I've been treating your mother. Please, take a seat.' The doctor sat down and Logan studied her. About ten years older than him, short-haired, bespectacled and slim, she had an air of authority and an expectant look on her face.

Logan sat.

'This is what we *do* know,' she began. 'There isn't a mass in the brain, so it's not a tumour. There doesn't appear to be inflammation or any other issue with any of the blood vessels. Her intracranial pressure is within an acceptable range. She doesn't have an infection such as meningitis.' She paused as if to gather her thoughts. 'The cause of headaches can be difficult to pinpoint. Age, stress, posture, overuse of caffeine, poor sleep, not drinking enough fluids… the list goes on. Very often we don't find a cause. Your mother's blood pressure is a little on the high side, her cholesterol could do with being a point or two lower, but neither of these things is necessarily headache inducing.'

Logan inhaled deeply as some of the tension drained out of him.

'We've performed an MRI scan and given her an ECG. We've done a lumbar puncture. We've tested her blood for liver, kidney, and thyroid function, plus we've checked her for diabetes and looked at her vitamin B12 and folate levels. We've also tested her urine and found nothing untoward.'

Another pause. 'Mrs Cassidy is in good health.'

'Apart from the headaches.'

'Apart from the headaches,' the doctor agreed.

'I'm worried it might be dementia,' Logan blurted.

'An MRI scan gives us certain information about the structure of the brain, including detailed information about any blood vessel damage which occurs in vascular dementia, and the scan would also show any shrinkage in specific areas of the brain which causes other forms of dementia. There was no evidence of either in your mother's case. Of course, it is still something to be aware of going forward, and if you have any future concerns her GP can perform some cognitive tests in the first instance.'

'So, you're saying you can't find anything wrong with her?'

'Let me be frank: I doubt if we will find a cause. The best we can do is to help her manage them when they occur. I've recommended some lifestyle changes such as cutting out caffeine – at least in the short term, to see if there's any improvement – structured exercise such as swimming, and meditation to reduce her stress levels. Yoga also might prove to be effective.'

'When can she go home?'

'Now. I've already signed her discharge.'

Relief was the overall emotion Logan was experiencing when he walked onto the ward a few minutes later to collect his mother and take her home, and there was a bounce in his step and a smile on his face.

Seeing his mother soon wiped it off.

He took one look at her pinched face as she sat in the chair next to her bed, and he wanted to run after the doctor and ask her to check those tests again, because something was most definitely not right.

They must have missed something. Headaches like the ones she suffered from must have a root cause. They *must*!

She couldn't go on like this; she was clearly still in pain, and when he picked up her overnight bag she held out her arm for him to help her get to her feet. Shuffling slowly, she leant on him until they got to the van.

'You're staying with me,' he said to her after he'd helped strap her in because her fumbling fingers were shaking so much.

'I'm fine. Take me home.' She slumped back wearily.

'You're not fine.'

'I *am*.' She turned anguish-filled eyes to him. 'I want my own bed, my own things.'

He stared at her, marshalling his thoughts. 'OK, but only if I stay with you.'

'What about the Tavern? You're needed there.'

'They'll cope.' They would have to, because he couldn't leave her alone like this, but neither could he force her to stay at the pub. Besides, look what had happened the last time she'd stayed – he'd spent most of his time downstairs, working. Or going out and enjoying himself. At least if he was in her house, he wouldn't be serving customers and neither would he be with Violet.

Despite the hospital being unable to find the root cause of Marie's headaches, Logan still felt inordinately guilty that he'd swanned off that day when he and Violet had gone for a walk and had lunch out. Only a week later his mum had been rushed into hospital…

As he drove back to Ticklemore in silence, his thoughts swirled.

A desperate longing to be with Violet swept over him,

but how could he now that he had his mother to look after? Despair joined the longing as he wondered just how long he would have to look after her for, because he knew he'd take care of her as long as she needed him to.

Marie's dislike of Violet and her obvious animosity to her was the main issue. If the two women got on, there wouldn't be a problem. But they didn't. Or, to be more accurate, Violet would happily get on with his mum, but his mum wouldn't let her. And him seeing Violet was causing his mother considerable distress.

The fact that his mother was so unwell altered things considerably.

How could he walk away from her? He wouldn't be able to live with himself if something happened to her because of what he said or did. Therefore, he had no choice other than to put his relationship on hold for the time being.

Violet would understand and hopefully it wouldn't be for too long. His mother's headaches would ease, as they'd done in the past (they'd never been as severe as this, though) and he and Violet could pick up where they'd left off.

But what if they *didn't* ease? What then? Or if things did improve and his life began to return to normal, only for them to return in the future?

Maybe it would be better all round if he ended it with Violet now, before it went any further? He loved her and he believed she loved him, but their relationship was still relatively new. It wasn't too late to walk away. He had to think of his mother's health first and foremost.

But as he drove, the only thing he could think about was not seeing Violet again, and the pain in his heart was more than he could bear.

CHAPTER 31

VIOLET

We need to talk. That's what Logan had said when he'd phoned her earlier. Never in a million years had that phrase been a precursor to anything good, and dread coiled its way through her stomach. He'd told her his mum was home from the hospital and that he was staying at hers for the time being, and Violet prayed he hadn't been given bad news. But that was exactly what she feared, because she'd heard the defeat and the pain in his voice, and she selfishly couldn't help wondering what that would mean for them.

If Marie was as ill as Violet guessed she might be from the tone of his voice, then Logan would be torn. He already felt bad about falling out with his mother, and she knew he blamed himself for her collapse. With Marie disliking her so much, Violet didn't know where they could go from here. If the woman had been more like Gretchen, the situation would be vastly different. Sam's mother would have welcomed any help Violet could give her. Marie…? Not so much. The woman's open animosity would make things extremely difficult. Not only would she shun all Violet's efforts, it would also put an incredible strain on her relationship with Logan. And on him.

It was the last thing he needed right now.

He needed to concentrate on his mother.

Violet sank onto the stool and rested her elbows on the workbench, the fruity scent of the loganberry gin she was making filling her nose. She was tempted to have a glass. Or three. But she was about to drive to Ticklemore, so gin-drinking would have to wait. There'd be plenty of time later. More time than she was going to know what to do with, soon. Because she'd made a decision. It hurt like hell and she didn't know how she was going to live with it, but it was the right thing to do.

***

Logan's face spoke volumes and Violet knew she'd made the right decision, no matter how much it hurt. He was tearing himself apart and she couldn't stand to see him like this.

The Tavern was hardly the ideal place to tell the man you loved that you were ending your relationship with him, but it was as good a place as any. This wasn't going to be easy, so she might as well just say what she had to say and be done with it.

When she walked into his office, and saw the tiredness in his eyes and the hurt in their depths, her heart twisted with love for him. The poor, poor man.

'Logan, I love you, but I don't think we should be together right now. You need to concentrate on your mum.' She blurted it out, biting down on the sob that threatened to accompany it.

Logan staggered back a step. He looked as though he'd been shot.

'Sorry, I'm so sorry,' Violet stuttered. 'Maybe when things are—' she hesitated, searching for the right words '— resolved, we can try again, but for now, you should be with her. She needs you.'

'She does,' he nodded. 'She really does, but—'

'This is the right thing to do. I love you with all my heart, Logan – I want you to know that – and some day we *will* be together. Just not right now.'

That was it; she'd said what she'd come to say.

Her heart breaking, Violet fled, leaving the best thing that had ever happened to her staring after her with tears streaming down his face, her own spilling down her cheeks.

It might be the best thing for both Logan and his desperately ill mother, but all Violet could think of as she drove erratically back to the sanctuary of her distillery was how hard it was going to be to live without him.

CHAPTER 32

LOGAN

'The interviews went well,' Scarlet said when Logan finally emerged from the office and staggered into the corridor, his head reeling from his encounter with Violet. Scarlet was coming up from the cellar and it was impossible to avoid her. He'd have preferred to hide away for the rest of the day, week, month, and not speak to anyone, but he had to get back to his mother. He'd left her alone for long enough.

When they'd arrived home from the hospital, he'd unpacked her overnight bag, had put a load of washing on, had made her some lunch, and had then pottered around for a while, trying to keep busy so he didn't have to think about Violet and what he was about to say to her.

To his immense disbelief and incredulity, he hadn't had to say anything. Violet had said it for him.

It was the last thing he'd expected, and the shock had rendered him speechless. She was so understanding and thoughtful, that it made his soul ache, along with his heart, which was shattered into a million pieces, each one of them grinding against the other until the pain of it made him gasp.

How was it possible to fall in love with someone so hard and so fast, in such a short space of time?

If he'd known what was ahead of him the day Violet had danced into his pub, he might well have run for the hills. Whoever said it was better to have loved and lost than never to have loved at all, was a fool. Logan had never felt pain like this, and he wouldn't wish it on his worst enemy. But even now, with all the hurt it was causing him, he didn't regret meeting her.

'Yeah, she's got two heads and her skin is the most amazing shade of green. You'll like her.'

'That's nice.' Logan wasn't listening to Scarlet. He was too busy trying to keep himself together and not fall apart.

'The other one is a llama. A black and white one, with these huge long ears—'

'What?'

'You haven't heard a word I've said, have you?' Scarlet peered at him. 'I was telling you about the two new members of staff I've taken on.' She paused and peered at him. 'Where's Violet? I thought I saw her a few minutes ago? What's happened?'

Logan closed his eyes slowly, took a deep breath, before opening them again. 'We're taking a break.'

'Ooh, anywhere nice?'

'Not that kind of break.'

'Ah.' Scarlet grimaced. 'I see. I'm sorry.'

Not half as sorry as I am, Logan thought. 'What were you saying about new staff?'

'Um… are you sure about this? Now that you're not going to need as much free time…?'

'I'm sure. I don't know how long Mum will be out of action.' That was the immediate future taken care of when it came to having spare time – looking after his mother. What he'd do with it once she was back on his feet was anyone's guess.

'I've taken two people on, if that's OK.' Scarlet broke into his thoughts. 'Wait here, I want to show you something.' She darted out the back and returned with a couple of sheets of paper. 'I've made a graph showing the busiest times and the busiest days.' She jabbed a finger at it. 'From this, it's easy to see that employing two part-timers is a better use of resources than employing one full-timer. I had a play around with the staff rota and pencilled the two new ones in to see what it looked like, and I think it's going to work. Is that OK?'

Logan looked at the pieces of paper she was holding up. 'It looks fine.' Then added, 'Really good; I'm impressed,' when he saw her crestfallen expression.

Logan left her to it, grateful he had someone competent and reliable to run the Tavern for him. His mind wasn't in the right place to think about staffing, or anything else to do with the pub for that matter. He should start planning the Halloween party, but he couldn't be bothered, even though it was less than four weeks away. He should be handing out flyers and selling tickets by now, but what with everything that had been going on, he hadn't given it much thought apart from to ask Juliette to advertise the event in the Tattler.

Oh, damn. The advert would have already gone out but he hadn't sorted any tickets out yet.

'Scarlet, have we had anyone asking for tickets for the Halloween party yet?'

'Quite a few. I've gone ahead and printed some. Is that OK?'

'Thank goodness you did. It completely slipped my mind.'

'I'm not surprised, what with Marie being rushed into hospital like that. I bet you're relieved they didn't find anything.'

'I certainly am.' Logan's reply was fervent.

'I'd better get back out there,' Scarlet said. The pub was starting to fill up with people wanting an early dinner. 'Are you staying for a while?'

'No. I'll go back to Mum's. She's still not well. Can you manage?'

'Of course. I'll be putting in an overtime form, though,' she joked. Then she sobered. 'I'm sorry you and Violet didn't work out. You looked good together.'

'I thought so too, but these things happen.' He ran his fingers through his hair. 'Violet understands.'

'Understands what?'

'Why it won't work. Not with my mum the way she is.'

'But I thought you said they didn't find anything serious, that the headaches were just headaches?'

'Yes, but she's still in so much pain. It doesn't seem to want to go away.'

Scarlet rubbed his upper arm. 'Now that Marie knows it's nothing to worry about, maybe it'll ease off. Have you told her about you and Violet?'

'Not yet.' He'd only just told Violet. Or, rather, *she'd* told *him* they were breaking up.

Scarlet gave him a long look. 'I think you should.'

She was right. He didn't want his mother fretting that he was about to disappear off at any moment to see Violet when he was supposed to be caring for her. She had enough to contend with. Hopefully if he removed as much stress from her life as he could, made sure she ate proper meals at regular intervals, and encouraged her to relax a bit more, she'd soon get better.

Until the next time – but he didn't want to think about that. One hurdle at a time, eh?

Thinking about regular meals took him into the kitchen before he left, and he asked Franklin to plate up two portions of barbeque chicken melt to take to his mum's, then he had another idea and popped into Bookylicious on the way.

The café-cum-bookshop was just about to close, but he persuaded Maddison to let him pick out a book or two for his mum. She didn't read much, claiming she was too busy, but when she did she liked light-hearted stuff.

Hattie pointed him in the right direction. 'Would this be for Violet?'

'No.'

'Marie?'

'Yes.' He picked up a book with a cheerful cover.

'She's already got that one. It's been out ages.'

Logan put the book back on the shelf. 'Can you recommend anything?'

'How about this?' She chose another by the same author and handed it to him. 'It's a sequel, so she mightn't have read it. If she has, you can always bring it back tomorrow and I'll swap it for you. I heard she's out of hospital and back home.'

'She is, thank God.'

'What did they say?'

'They gave her a thorough check-up and she's got a clean bill of health.'

'That's good news. But if that's the case, why have you got a face like a slapped arse?'

Logan shook his head. Hattie was being her usual

forthright self. 'Her headache is still there, and they still don't know what's causing it.'

Hattie muttered something, which sounded like 'I do,' but when he said 'Sorry, I didn't catch that,' she replied, 'Just clearing my throat. Got a frog in it.'

'I'll take this one,' he said, hefting the book in his hand, conscious of Maddison waiting to lock up. 'This will keep her going for a couple of days. The doctor suggested she tried to relax a bit more. You don't know of any yoga classes around here, do you?'

'You could ask Father Todd. He lets out the church hall for all kinds of activities and groups.'

'Good idea.' He handed over a ten-pound note and waited for his change.

Hattie sniffed. 'What's that smell?'

Logan held up the bag containing tonight's dinner. 'Barbeque chicken; I'm trying to make sure Mum eats properly.'

Hattie sniffed again, but Logan didn't think it was because of the mouth-watering aroma.

'She doesn't look as though she goes short of a decent meal. Your mum is sturdy enough,' she said.

'She's not *well*, though,' he argued.

'Isn't she?'

'The doctor said she's to eat healthily. It might help with the headaches.'

Hattie raised her eyebrows. 'You still haven't told me why you look so bloody miserable.'

'It's nothing.'

'Don't you play that game with me, Logan Cassidy. I've known you since you were a baby. There's something wrong and you might as well tell me now, because I'll find out anyway. So save me the hassle and spill the beans.'

Logan rolled his eyes, knowing she'd keep on until she got to the bottom of it. 'Violet and I have split up.'

'Why doesn't that surprise me.'

'Didn't you think we were good together?' Logan thought they'd been very good together indeed, and his chest clenched in pain.

'I thought you made a lovely couple. Who split up with whom?'

'Does it matter?'

Hattie waited for an answer, and Logan sighed. 'It was a mutual decision,' he said. 'I've got my hands full with my mum.'

'And it's less hassle if Violet isn't around?'

That wasn't quite what he meant. 'The doctors think Mum's headaches could be caused by stress—'

'And Violet stresses her out?' Hattie leapt in.

'Put it this way, my being in lo— in a relationship with Violet doesn't help matters.'

'I see.'

Why did people keep saying "I see" when it came to his mum, Logan wondered before pushing the thought aside. It was just a turn of phrase.

Hattie shook her head solemnly. 'Take my advice, you'll regret it if you let this one slip through your fingers. You and Violet are made for each other.'

Logan had thought that, too. 'Too late, she already has.'

Once again Hattie muttered under her breath. This time it sounded like, 'We'll see about that.'

But there was nothing Hattie could do, no matter how well-intentioned.

He'd been forced to choose his mother's health over his

own happiness, and he knew he wouldn't have been able to live with himself if he'd made any other decision.

CHAPTER 33

VIOLET

Violet's heart wasn't in making gin today. Violet's heart wasn't in anything at all. The last two weeks had been the most difficult two weeks of her life and she didn't see the next two being much better. Recovering from a broken heart was going to take time.

However, today was the first tour day, when o*riGINal Gin* opened its doors to the general public, so she had to at least try to put a good face on things. She and Rory had agreed they should start small and see how it went, so they'd invested in ten small copper infusers, as part of the tour would involve people making their own flavour of gin. Only two people had booked, but it was a start. Violet hadn't expected a stampede, but she knew this side of the business would grow as word got around. She should be excited and looking forward to her first tour, but she wasn't. All she wanted to do was to hide away and cry.

'You'll be fine,' Beth said. She was here for moral support, and because Violet had asked if she wouldn't mind taking some photos for the website. Besides, she didn't want to do this on her own. Rory was too busy to help, and he was also showing their new employee, an enthusiastic young man by the name of Tyler, the ropes. Violet called him "young" even though Tyler was only five years younger than her, but Violet felt as though she'd aged a decade or two in the past few weeks.

'Will I?' Violet didn't think she'd feel fine ever again. Who knew that being in love could be so damned agonising.

Beth slung an arm around her shoulders and gave her a hug. 'You will. You'll do a brilliant job today. And as for the other, you'll get over that, too.'

'When?'

'I don't know, my lovely, but this will pass.'

'What if I don't want it to pass?'

'Then you'll have to do something about it. Have you had any contact with Logan?'

Violet shook her head. 'I thought we should have a clean break. I do feel rather bad that I haven't called to ask how his mother is, though. I didn't even hang around long enough for him to tell me what was wrong with her. I hope he's coping OK.'

'Even if he isn't, there's nothing you can do,' Beth pointed out. 'His mother made it clear she doesn't like you and she won't appreciate your help.'

'Didn't she just. I can't believe how rude she was that Sunday when I went to Logan's for lunch. But then again, her illness might well have affected her personality. You do hear of such things happening.'

'Didn't you say the old lady – Hattie was it? – seemed to think she'd always been like that.'

'True... But whatever Marie has, she could have had it for some time.'

'Why don't you phone him? You're driving yourself nuts with all this speculation and conjecture.'

'There's no point. It won't make any difference, will it? Nothing is going to change. While his mother is so unwell, he's got to put her first.'

Violet checked the time. The tour was about to start, so she should pull herself together. Customers didn't want to see a mopey, miserable face when they were shown around the distillery. They were here to enjoy themselves, and it was down to her to make sure they did.

'Can you greet them by the door, Beth? I want to get a couple of drinks ready.' She was aware that one of the party might be driving, so she wanted to make sure she had some non-alcoholic options on offer. And although the designated driver mightn't be able to sample the gin today, she'd ordered tiny weeny bottles for them to take away to try at home.

Violet could hear voices as she hastily checked the selection of cordials and soft drinks, and she forced a smile to her lips as she turned around. To her surprise there was only one person with Beth, and Violet raised her eyebrows.

'The other lady has just popped to the loo,' Beth told her, and Violet had a mild panic that she'd forgotten to put out a fresh towel and some of the nice hand-soap she'd bought. No, she'd done that yesterday evening; she distinctly remembered because the soap had a lovely vanilla scent and—

'This is Juliette Seymour.' Beth broke into her thoughts. Her eyes were wide as though she was trying to tell her something. 'She owns the Ticklemore Tattler.'

'Oh, right, well… lovely to meet you.' Violet walked towards her and held out her hand. 'I'm Violet Archer.

Welcome to *oriGINal Gin*. We'll just wait for your companion to join us, then we'll make a start.' Violet's heart was thudding. Not only was the woman from Ticklemore but she ran the newspaper to boot. Could the first tour get any worse? Violet had planned on contacting the local press at some point to try to gain some publicity (she would offer them a free gin-making experience to make it worth their while) but she'd hoped to have had several tours under her belt by then so she could iron out the wrinkles. This unexpected development had the potential to go horribly wrong.

But when Violet saw who had just come in, she realised it already had.

'I hope you haven't started without me,' Hattie said, sailing into the reception area like a galleon with a following wind. She was wearing an orange and yellow patterned kaftan which billowed around her, and a pair of bright red Wellington boots. Her long grey hair was loose and flowed around her shoulders. 'I need a gin before I start,' she chortled.

'Hattie,' Violet said weakly. 'What are you doing here?'

'Tasting gin, I hope!'

'You're with…?' Violet gestured towards the journalist.

'I wasn't going to come on my own, was I? I had to have someone to drive me. Besides, I thought you could do with the publicity. It's not easy when you're starting out.'

'Did Logan—?'

'Send me? Nah, he doesn't know I'm here.'

'Oh, OK. Shall we get started?'

'I thought you'd never ask. I'm parched. No gin for this one, mind.' She pointed to Juliette. 'I want to get home in one piece. I said I'd buy her a bottle to take home with her.'

Hattie leant closer and whispered, 'Or do you think I should make it two, as been as she's driven me all this way.'

'She can take some samples home with her,' Violet said, 'and a bottle of the gin she makes. It's included in the price.'

'Good-o. Fetch me a drink, then we'll have a nice little chat.'

'I thought you wanted a tour?' Violet was confused. Hattie wasn't here to chat, she was supposed to be here to see how gin was made. What on earth was going on?

'Maybe later. This nice young lady can show Juliette around, while me and you talk.'

'Don't you want to look around yourself?' This wasn't going as Violet had planned. In fact, the tour was in danger of not happening at all.

'No. I told you, I want to have a chat. Just me and you.' Hattie turned to Juliette and made flapping motions with her hands. 'Off you go. I'll sit here and wait. Violet, get me a drink.'

Violet did as she was told with the feeling that she'd totally lost control of the situation. 'What would you like, Juliette?'

As soon as Juliette had a glass of something cold and non-alcoholic in her hand, Hattie told them to go away, and Beth led the journalist into the depths of the distillery, glancing anxiously over her shoulder as she went.

'You'll be fine,' Violet mouthed. Beth knew the mechanics of gin making almost as well as Violet did. In the very early days, Violet used to use her as a sounding board and had subjected her long-suffering friend to hours of her going on and on about it.

Hattie waited until they were alone and she'd taken a deep gulp of her G & T (Violet had decided to start the tour with basic, unflavoured gin and go from there) before she said anything.

'I expect you're wondering why I'm here,' the old lady began.

'You could say that…'

'I was hoping the pair of you would have sorted yourselves out by now, but no such luck. So I thought I'd better step in. Did *she* do it?'

'Did who do what?' Violet was confused.

'Marie. Was she responsible for you and Logan splitting up?'

Violet was careful how she answered. 'In a way, I suppose she was.'

'I knew it! The nasty, spiteful baggage.'

Gosh, that was a bit harsh: but remembering the warnings Hattie had given her previously, Violet was able to put her straight. 'It's not what you think,' she said. 'I broke it off with Logan because of Marie's health. He needs to focus on her, not me.'

'Rubbish!'

'It's true – haven't you heard how ill she is?' Violet was surprised – according to Logan Hattie usually knew everything that went on in Ticklemore. And what she didn't know, she guessed.

'Marie isn't ill,' Hattie declared.

'Yes, she is. I saw Logan the same day he brought her home from the hospital.'

Hattie polished off her drink and held out her empty glass. 'I'll try one of the flavoured ones this time.'

Violet got up and poured her a full measure of the Earl Grey Tea. She poured one for herself, too – she got the feeling she was going to need it.

'What did he say, exactly? Ta.' Hattie took the glass and sniffed it. 'What's this?'

'Earl Grey Tea.'

Hattie sipped at it. 'Mmm, not bad. Go on, you was about to tell me what Logan said.'

Had she been? She didn't think it was any of Hattie's business. 'He said…' Violet paused. What *had* he said? 'Um, I'm not sure, exactly.'

'Can't you remember?'

'It's not that – I didn't give him a chance to say anything. Let me see… He said they'd checked her for signs of a stroke or a bleed on the brain when she first went to hospital, and I think Logan said they'd ruled that out. But they kept her in to do some more tests, so something must have shown up. He phoned me after she'd been discharged and said we needed to talk. But in all honesty, I didn't give him the chance to tell me anything further. You should have seen him – he looked dreadful, as though he had the weight of the world on his shoulders.' Violet drank a mouthful of gin, then she had another. 'I didn't think it fair me adding to that. He has enough to do with looking after his mum. She needs him.'

'And you don't?'

'Not in the same way. I'm not the one who's ill.'

'Neither is she.'

'Excuse me?'

'Marie isn't ill.' Hattie emptied her glass again. 'That was nice, but I think I'll try a sweeter one next time. Do you have chocolate flavour?'

'Um, how about bubblegum?'

'That'll do nicely.'

Violet was glad of an excuse to get out of her seat, even

if it was only for a minute or two, so she had her back to Hattie as she asked, 'What do you mean "she's not ill"?'

'She isn't. They didn't find a single thing wrong with her. She had a clean bill of health.'

'But I thought…' Violet didn't know what to think. She sat down again, dropping heavily into her chair and slopping some of Hattie's drink in the process.

'Careful.'

'There's plenty more where that came from,' Violet replied absently, handing her the fresh drink. She put her own glass down, suddenly feeling rather sick. 'Are you sure they didn't find anything?'

'Quite sure. It's stress. Or sheer nastiness.'

'I'm sorry, I don't understand.'

'Remember what I said about Marie always being ill when she felt threatened? Guess what? I think she was more than threatened when he met you – she was bloody terrified.'

'Of *me*?' Violet was astounded. How could anyone be scared of her? She was the least scary person she knew.

'As I said to you before, if his mother kept up with her antics Logan would be forced to choose between her and his woman. He chose you.'

'Did Logan tell you that?'

'He didn't have to. Marie got herself taken to hospital, didn't she.'

'That doesn't mean anything.' But it did, though. Logan had told her he'd fallen out with his mother after Violet left in the middle of the disastrous Sunday lunch – and on the Monday, Marie had been rushed into hospital.

'She's better now,' Hattie said. 'Her headache has gone.'

'But it could come back?'

'It probably will, the next time Logan gets involved with a girl. Or falls in love with one,' Hattie added wryly.

The thought of Logan being in love with someone else made Violet's chest ache and her stomach clench. She didn't think she could face it. But what choice did she have? Marie's headaches were real and tangible, and no matter what the cause, they gave the woman considerable distress. Violet didn't want to be responsible for her having another one.

Hattie said, 'He needs to sort her out, else he won't have a life of his own. He's got a face like an undertaker and as much get up and go as one of Alfred's wooden toys. Your Logan is moping around and it's enough to curdle his beer.'

'Beer doesn't curdle.'

'You get my drift, so stop being obtuse. The man is pining after you, and by the look of you, you're missing him just as much. Stop being a pair of numpties and get your act together. Logan's going to have this same problem with his mother no matter who his girlfriend is, so it might as well be you. If you love him enough to put up with her, that is.'

'Let me check I understand what you're saying.' Violet spread her hand out and counted the points off on her fingers. 'One, Marie doesn't have anything physically wrong with her, and her headaches are caused by stress. Two, she gets stressed when Logan does something she doesn't approve of, like buying the Tavern.'

'Or courting a girl.'

'Three, she'll continue to suffer from these headaches no matter who he dates.'

'Yes, and four, she'll carry on doing it until Logan puts a stop to it.'

'But what if he can't? You can't magic stress and anxiety

away – it's a recognised medical condition.'

'There's a number five.' Hattie held up her thumb. 'What if she's making all this up?'

'Marie wouldn't have made it up, would she? How could she do such a thing? No one would be that desperate. Or mean.' Violet was reeling.

'People do surprising things when they're desperate, and Marie is desperately clinging on to Logan.'

'But she wouldn't pretend to be ill,' Violet insisted. 'That's cruel.'

'It's been known to happen.'

'I don't know what to say.'

'And you don't know whether you believe me or not,' Hattie observed. 'I don't blame you. It does sound far-fetched, but I know I'm right. Can I make a suggestion?'

Violet eyed the old lady warily. 'I'm listening.'

'Go and speak to Marie. Tell her the reason you finished with Logan was because you want what's best for him and for her. Tell her his heart is broken and ask her if she wants him to be miserable for the rest of his life – because that's what he will be if she carries on.'

'That's a bit blunt.' And Violet didn't think confronting Marie in such a manner was going to make things any better.

'You also need to convince her you can be an ally and an asset to her, and not a rival for his affections.'

'I don't think it would work.'

'It's up to you, but if you love Logan as much as I think you do, then you need to fight for him.'

'What about *him* fighting for *me*?'

'Logan is a good man, a decent man, and he's trying to do his best for his mother. You wouldn't want him any other way.' Hattie pursed her lips. 'Not only that, even if he did have an inkling of the truth, he's not going to admit it to himself. He wouldn't want to believe his mother was capable of being so manipulative.'

'To be honest, I'm not sure she's capable of that either.'

'What harm would it do to have a chat with her?'

'It might make things worse.'

'Hattie snorted. 'How much worse can they get? You and Logan have split up – you can't be any more split up than you already are.'

Violet couldn't fault Hattie's logic, but she still didn't think it was a good idea.

'Look, my girl, you love Logan and Logan loves you. His mother is the only thing standing between you and both your happiness, and the sole reason for that is she's scared of being alone. If you can show her she won't be on her own, she might get over herself.' Then Hattie played her trump card. 'If you don't, you'll only regret it, and who wants to live a life full of regrets?'

'OK,' Violet sighed, 'I'll speak to her.'

'When?'

'You don't give up, do you?'

'No, I don't. When?'

'Tomorrow.'

'What time?'

'I don't know… when Logan is busy in the Tavern?' If Violet was going to have this talk with his mother, it was probably best done without him around. She'd speak to Marie woman to woman.

'He'll definitely be in the pub at eleven-thirty and will stay there until they finish serving lunches. Although Scarlet is running the place – and she's doing a brilliant job of it – he likes to be on hand to help if he's needed. He spends most of his time hiding away in his office, though. Scarlet says it's because he's planning the Halloween party, but how much planning does it take? I think it's an excuse to get away from his mum for a bit. You know he's moved back in with her for the time being?'

'I didn't know.' How would she? She'd not spoken to him for a fortnight.

'Get there at about noon. Logan will be at the Tavern, and Marie should be at home.'

'What if she isn't?'

'Then you wait for her. She won't have gone far. The woman doesn't know what to do with herself now she's no longer needed in the pub. If you ask me, she should take up a hobby. Or find herself a man.' Hattie's expression softened. 'You're never too old for love, but some people are just too damned stubborn to realise it.'

The two of them sat in silence for a moment, then Hattie suddenly sprang into life. She rubbed her hands together and said, 'I think I'd like to see your distillery now, and make some gin.'

Violet smiled, relieved the conversation was over. 'That's why you're here.'

'As for what we've talked about, you can thank me later. Now, top up my glass and let's get going!'

CHAPTER 34

VIOLET

Whose stupid idea was this, Violet asked herself as she pulled up outside Marie's house in her conspicuous purple van. Oh, yes – Hattie's. But it was Violet's stupid choice to allow herself to be talked into it, so she had no one else to blame.

She briefly considered turning around and running back to Hay, but a figure at the window and a twitch of the curtain indicated she'd been seen. She had considered asking to borrow Beth's car but had decided against it: she wished she had now. She'd have been far less conspicuous.

Oh well, she was here, so she should say what she'd come to say, and see if it made any difference. Frankly, she doubted it would, but she had to try. Being apart from Logan was killing her and, as Hattie had pointed out, Violet knew she'd regret it later if she didn't give it a go.

'What do you want? I thought we'd seen the last of you,' was Marie's greeting.

'I thought you had, too, but for Logan's sake I had to speak with you. Can I come in?' Violet didn't want to do this on the doorstep.

'If you must. But I don't see the point in you being here.'

'You might, once I explain.'

Marie led her into the kitchen at the rear of the house, where she leant against a cupboard and folded her arms. 'Well?'

'I'm glad you're feeling better,' Violet began.

'Who told you I was better?'

'Um, the lady who runs the Tattler was at the distillery yesterday.' Violet thought it mightn't be a good idea to mention Hattie's name. And technically Violet wasn't lying: Juliette had been very complimentary and had been delighted with the herb and olive flavoured gin she'd made, which she said she was going to present to Oliver, her partner. She'd also said she was going to give the distillery a decent write-up in the paper.

'What does Juliette Seymour know? Nothing that's what,' Marie scoffed.

'So you're still not well?'

Marie narrowed her eyes. 'Why are you here?'

'Because Logan is unhappy and it breaks my heart to know that.'

'Logan is fine. Or he will be if you stay away from him.'

'I thought that, too, but now I'm not so sure. He loves me, Marie, and I love him, and the only reason we aren't together is because of your health, but surely it doesn't have to be like this?' Violet was trying to be diplomatic and not come straight out with it.

Marie grunted. 'You only want him for his pub, so you can sell your bloody gin. You're using him.'

Violet gasped. 'That is so untrue! What have I ever done to you? You don't know anything about me.'

'I know enough. He was fine until you came along, and he doesn't need you messing up his life.'

'I'm not messing it up,' Violet said through gritted teeth. 'I can enhance his life – if you'll let me.'

'Not a chance. My son is too good for the likes of you.'

'The likes of me?' What the hell was that supposed to mean? This conversation wasn't doing either of them any good: Marie hated her and Violet realised nothing she could say or do was going to change her mind. But she had to give it one final shot before she quit.

'Let's be honest,' Violet said. 'No woman is going to be good enough for Logan in your opinion, and I get that, I really do. But you've got to let him decide who he wants to be with.'

'He doesn't want to be with *you*, I can tell you that for nothing.'

'Has he said that?' Violet's heart was in her mouth. Maybe he didn't love her…?

'He finished with you, didn't he?' Marie looked incredibly smug.

'I was the one who called it off, because I thought you were seriously ill. He had enough to deal with, and you were so hostile to me, I didn't think he needed the aggro. But I can help, if you'll let me. Logan and I can look after you together.'

Marie barked out a laugh, making Violet jump. 'I don't need "looking after". I'm perfectly capable of looking after myself. It's Logan who needs looking after so the likes of you can't get their claws into him.'

The realisation that Hattie was right slowly dawned on her. There *was* nothing wrong with Marie. 'You're not actually ill, are you?'

'It doesn't matter whether I am or not.'

'You don't suffer from headaches at all. *You're making it up.*' Disgust and disbelief filled Violet's mind. She hadn't believed Hattie, not really.

'So what if I am? If you say anything I'll deny it. I'm his mother – he'll believe *me*, not you. Get out of his life and stay out. We were getting on fine before you turned his head.'

'Were we, Mum?' Logan said.

Violet gasped and Marie let out a small cry. Logan was standing in the shadows of the hall, his face terribly pale.

'Son, I didn't see you there. I was just telling Violet—'

'I heard.'

'She's accusing me of lying about being unwell.' Marie put a hand to her head. It was shaking, Violet saw.

'That's because you are.' Logan's expression was grim and his eyes, which were sunk into the dark circles surrounding them, were filled with despair.

'I'm not, I swear I'm not. Oh dear, all this upset is making me feel very unwell. Logan, help me into the living room. I need to sit down. I need my tablets. Logan? *Logan!*'

Logan stared at his mother, an unreadable expression on his face, as he slowly shook his head and backed away. Then he disappeared, his footsteps sounding in the hall and Violet heard the front door slam.

There was a horrified silence for several seconds, as Violet tried to gather her thoughts and control her whirling emotions. She felt like crying – the pain in Logan's eyes was more than she could stand, and she wanted to run after him and comfort him, but she was scared he'd push her away.

Marie snarled, and Violet shot her a frightened glance.

Gone was the ill and tearful woman of a moment ago.

In her place was a woman who was consumed with hatred and fury.

'Look what you've done! You've broken my son's heart. I hope you're proud of yourself! Get out of my house, before I throw you out.' Marie took a step towards her, tears streaming down her face, and Violet ran.

The last she heard as she fled out of the door was the sound of Marie's hysterical sobbing.

CHAPTER 35

LOGAN

'Logan—' Hattie put out a hand as he dashed past, but Logan brushed her off. He didn't know how, but he had a feeling she'd had a hand in what had just happened. He should have guessed something was afoot when he saw the old lady lingering around outside the pub earlier. She'd been there for nearly half an hour, and when she'd finally entered the Tavern it was to tell him that Violet's van had just pulled up outside his mother's house.

He'd been out of the door as fast as a rat up a drainpipe, his heart full of hope and fear in equal measure.

Violet had come looking for him, but what she had found was his mother, he realised, when he pushed the door open and padded into the hall. What he heard had turned his blood to ice.

His mother had made the whole illness thing up.

She'd made it up.

She'd lied to him and to everyone else. She'd made him worry until he felt physically sick with it, and his head and heart were in pieces. She'd wasted the valuable time of numerous medical professionals, as well as taking up a bed someone else might have needed. And last, but not least, she'd been responsible for the ending of his relationship with Violet.

How could she have done such a thing? How could she live with herself, knowing the heartache and anxiety she'd caused?

He didn't think he'd ever forgive her.

Suddenly the odd comments and strange looks of the likes of Hattie and Scarlet, and numerous other residents of Ticklemore began to make sense. Had they suspected all along that his mother wasn't as ill as she'd been making out? That she was putting it on?

She'd made a total fool of him, and of herself.

But worse than that, he'd been prepared to give up the only woman he'd ever loved in order to care for her. He'd put her needs before his own: but what had *she* done? She'd trampled all over his feelings, and had crushed his emotions to serve her own selfish purpose.

He never wanted to see her again.

Ever.

Which wasn't going to be easy considering they lived in the same small village, but he'd try. It would hurt him, but he'd have to do it for his own sanity, and if he wanted to repair his relationship with Violet.

Oh, my God… *Violet*. What on earth was she making of all this?

He'd reached the end of the road, the Tavern ahead of him, when he realised he'd left Violet standing there in his mother's kitchen with a stricken look on her face. He slowed to a walk his mouth dry and his eyes damp.

He'd have to go back for her. He had to talk to her, to

beg her to start again and to put all this behind them. When Hattie had told him Violet was in Ticklemore, his heart had soared with gladness. There was only one reason he could think of for her to be in the village, and that was because she wanted to see him, and he'd hoped and prayed she wanted to get back with him.

Would she still want to after hearing the awful and inexcusable things his mother had said?

He wouldn't blame her if she didn't.

Coming to a halt, he whirled on his heel and ran back the way he'd come. But he didn't have to go far to see that her van had gone.

Logan slowed, staggering slightly, blowing hard. And as he came to a stop he put his hands on his head and felt like howling.

'Go after her, son,' Hattie said. She too was puffing as she hurried along the pavement after him. 'You see to Violet, I'll see to your mother.'

'Don't bother. She's… she's…' He'd been about to say she wasn't worth it, but whatever she'd done she was still his mother. He had to make sure she was OK. Instead, he said, 'She won't thank you for it.'

'I don't expect her to. But it's the neighbourly thing to do. Go, I'll sort your mother out.'

Good luck, he thought: Hattie was going to need it.

But he had the feeling he was going to need it more.

CHAPTER 36

VIOLET

Violet hadn't gone far. She hadn't been able to because she was crying too much to see the road properly. She'd driven a short distance, then had pulled over on the main street to try to calm down before she carried on home. Now she was sandwiched between a flashy four-by-four and a refrigerated lorry unloading its cargo, so she couldn't move if she wanted to.

Which was probably a good thing, as tears were pouring down her face and her breath was coming in hitching, hiccupping sobs. She was also trembling as she remembered Logan's face and the terrible expression on it. Violet wished with all her heart that he hadn't heard Marie say what she'd said. What must be going through his mind? He was bound to be devastated. To think his mother had been making everything up! Violet had experienced his worry and strain first-hand, his terrible dread that Marie's diagnosis would be life-changing, or worse. And to think the woman had allowed her son to go through all that heartache just because she didn't want him to be with Violet.

Violet put her head in her hands and sobbed. If she hadn't gone to speak to Marie none of this would have happened. And although it wasn't her fault, Violet couldn't help feeling responsible.

A knock on the window of the van roused her slightly, and she held up a finger to indicate that she'd only be a minute.

The knock came again, and she felt like screaming. She'd move her van in a minute. Couldn't they see she was upset? Not only that, there was the sound of horns beeping impatiently.

Violet gathered herself together and looked up, ready to tell the person to get lost, but when she saw who was banging on her window, she crumpled.

Logan had abandoned his vehicle in the middle of the street and was standing by the driver's door, his hand raised to knock again.

'Shift your arse, mate, you're blocking the road.' The driver of one of the cars behind Logan's van had stuck his head out of his window and was yelling out of it.

Logan, his eyes not leaving hers, shook his head.

The beeping intensified and a crowd began to gather.

Violet swiped her fingers across her face, dashing her tears away, and wound her window down. 'Hi.' Her voice was small and uncertain. Was he there to have a go at her?

'Hi, you.' He gave her a tiny smile, more a quirk of the lips.

'You're blocking the road.'

'I know.'

'Don't you think you should move your van?'

'Not unless you come with me.'

'Where?'

'Away from here, the pub, my mother, Ticklemore…'
He waved a hand in the air, then let it fall to his side.

'Why?'

'Because I love you.'

'Oh.' She hesitated. 'OK.'

He opened the door for her and she slid out, and hopped up into his. When Logan got into the driver's seat a cheer went up, but he didn't react as he pulled away.

'Where are we going?' she asked.

'Somewhere we can talk in private.'

After that they travelled in silence, Logan manoeuvring the van out of the village and along narrowing country lanes. The gradient was increasing as they headed into the Black Mountains, the terrain becoming wilder and more rugged, and oh so beautiful. It was going to be private, that's for certain, she thought as they drove into a rough parking area on the side of a mountain and Logan switched the engine off.

'Fancy going for a walk?' he asked.

'Up there?' Violet stared up at the mountain looming above them. It was quite a hike to the top, steep and demanding. Thank goodness she was wearing trainers, although hiking boots would have been better.

'There's a stream over there.' He pointed. 'I thought we could find a spot to sit down. And chat.'

A steep rocky path led them upwards and Violet was breathless by the time they reached the gurgling water and chose a place to sit. The stream tumbled down the mountain, cutting a small valley into the bedrock which was lined with ferns and low-growing bushes. Every so often the water met a sturdier band of rock and a little waterfall was the result.

It was peaceful and the view was breathtaking even though the summit was still some way above.

'We'll have to hike to the top one day,' Logan said, his eyes roaming over the patchwork farmland below.

'Will we?' Her heart leapt – he was talking as though they would have more days together than just this one.

'If you want to,' he added.

'I'd like that, very much.'

'We'll bring a picnic and watch the sunset.'

'That would be lovely.'

Logan shifted so he was facing her, his expression unreadable. 'I'm sorry.'

'You have nothing to be sorry for.'

'I believed her.'

'Who wouldn't?'

'Quite a few people had their doubts, I understand.'

'Hattie?'

He sighed and pulled a face. 'You know she orchestrated today's fiasco?'

'I guessed as much,' Violet admitted. 'She came to the distillery yesterday. The lady who owns the Tattler brought her. She told me your mum had been given a clean bill of health.'

Logan studied her. 'You didn't know?'

'That day when I broke up with you, I thought she had been diagnosed with something awful. You looked terrible.'

He exhaled sharply. 'That was because I was about to break up with *you*. You beat me to it.'

'Oh.'

He reached for her hand. It was the first time they'd touched since the morning after they'd made love, and it raised goosebumps on her skin. 'The hospital said it was stress. My mother was convinced it was something more, but even if it wasn't I couldn't stand to see her suffering. I thought she needed me.'

'She does.'

'Yeah, right.'

'That's why she behaved the way she did.'

'It's inexcusable, and I'm sorry.'

'As I said, you don't need to be. You thought you were doing the right thing.'

He puffed out his cheeks. 'I let her get away with it. If I hadn't given in every time she'd had one of her episodes then this would never have happened.'

'You weren't to know. Hindsight is a wonderful thing.'

'I do love you, you know.'

Violet felt her world tilting – this sounded suspiciously like goodbye. And once again, she didn't blame him. Resuming their relationship was fraught with obstacles, the main one being his mum. Building bridges with Marie and setting boundaries he and his mother could live with should be his priority now, not romance.

When she didn't say anything, he gave her hand a squeeze, then let go of her.

Violet raised her face to the sky and blinked back tears.

This was it – this was the end. The brief flame of hope she'd carried with her from the moment she'd seen him standing next to her van a mere hour ago, was extinguished.

'I understand,' he said, sadly. 'I don't think I'd like a mother-in-law like her in my life, either. But please don't give up on us, Violet.'

Violet froze, hope flaring once more. 'I thought you were about to tell me that you never want to see me again.'

'Why would I do that? I love you and I want to spend

the rest of my life with you.'

The despair that had been weighing her down suddenly lifted, and she thought she might float away with the relief of it. 'I love you too.'

'But…?'

'There is no "but".' She hesitated. 'Actually, there is. You should make your peace with your mum.'

Logan's jaw tightened. 'I'm not sure I can.'

'She's hurting and she's scared. She still needs you.'

'I can't forgive her.'

'You will,' Violet said confidently. 'You're a good man, Logan. She's your mum and you love her. You'll tear yourself apart if you don't.' She knew she was right. Logan wasn't the sort of person who could walk away from family or responsibility.

'What if she still doesn't accept you? I won't have her treating you badly.'

'If she doesn't, it'll be her loss – I really want to be friends with her and I'm sure we would get on like a house on fire. But whether she does or doesn't, you can't cut her out of your life. We'll just have to work around her, and if that means me and her having to stay out of each other's way, then so be it. It's a shame, but if that's how it has to be…'

'Thank you for being so understanding.'

'I'm not at all understanding,' Violet confessed. 'I want to give her a good shake.'

Logan laughed softly. 'So do I.' He stared into her eyes, and the love she saw in their depths made her heart soar. 'There's something I want to do more, though.' He gently pulled her closer and slipped his arms around her.

Violet tipped her head back, offering him her mouth,

and when his lips fluttered against hers, a wave of happiness engulfed her. This is where she belonged, in the arms of the man she loved, and she vowed that never again would she allow anyone to come between them.

CHAPTER 37

LOGAN

'Do you have to go home just yet?' Logan asked later that evening as they drove into Ticklemore. He was reluctant to let her out of his sight. 'Are you hungry?'

'I am, but I'm not sure whether it is food I'm hungry for.' She let out a wickedly sexy laugh, and Logan's stomach did a slow somersault.

How had he ever thought he'd be able to live without her? She was incredible.

'I suppose we'd better eat, though,' she added. 'We need to keep our strength up.' She twinkled at him, leaving him in no doubt as to what they needed their strength for.

He'd been hard pushed not to make love to her in the grass next to the tumbling stream, but had contented himself with kissing her senseless instead. Eventually though, the chill seeped into them and they were forced off the mountain to make their way back to Ticklemore.

Sobering, Violet said quietly, 'I think you'd better check on your mum, before we eat.'

She was right. He might be annoyed with his mother, but

he supposed he should make sure she was OK.

'I'll phone her as soon as we get to the pub,' he said, but the second he pulled into the car park, Hattie was flagging him down.

'There you are!' she cried. 'Where have you been? Oh, hello, Violet.' She peered into the van. 'Hurry up, we've been waiting for you for ages, and we do have other things we could be going on with.'

'We?' Logan was mystified. 'You and Mum?'

Hattie gave him a look.

'No, of course not. Silly me,' he said. His mother wouldn't come within a mile of Hattie unless she had to.

'The gang,' Hattie said.

'What gang?' Logan was confused.

'I was going to call it Team Make Marie See Sense, but it's too long. Got any suggestions?'

Logan rolled his eyes, as her meaning became clear. He was aware of Violet's confusion and he tried to explain. 'Hattie loves lost causes. It all began with her fiancé, Alfred, when she saved his handmade toys from being thrown away and helped him to set up the Toy Shop. She called a handful of people together and formed a committee to get the shop off the ground. She's been forming committees for one thing or another ever since. Looks like it's my turn.'

'It's not really a committee,' Hattie said. 'It's a few friends meeting to discuss how to help someone who needs it. And you must admit, no one needs help more than Marie. Hurry up, they're waiting.'

'Do you want me to scoot off?' Violet asked as Hattie darted ahead of them.

'No way! If I've got to sit through this, so have you. We're together now, remember?' He grabbed her hand in case she did a runner.

Four tables had been pushed together and about fifteen people were seated around them. Logan felt Violet hesitate, and his fingers tightened around hers. These were friends, they were here to help – although what help they could possibly give when it came to his mother, Logan had yet to discover. He had a feeling Marie wasn't going to take kindly to them interfering.

'Sorry to keep you waiting,' Hattie said. 'You all know Logan, obviously, but for those of you who have yet to meet her, this is Violet. She makes the gin you're drinking.' Hattie turned to him. 'I hope you don't mind, but the only way I could get everyone here tonight was to bribe them with free drinks. They are busy people, you know.'

Logan didn't know what to say. He was utterly nonplussed by the whole thing.

'I'll introduce you,' Hattie said to Violet. 'This is my Alfred – he makes the toys you see in the Toy Shop. The girl next to him is his apprentice, Zoe. On his other side is his daughter, Sara – she's a retired headmistress but she was bored, so she manages the Toy Shop now – and next to her is her husband, David. He's got a sound head on his shoulders. Then there's Nell, who owns the Treasure Trove, and her – what would you call him?' This last was said to Nell.

'Boyfriend?' Nell suggested with a grin.

'Hmph. Boyfriend, it is, although you're both a bit long in the tooth to be called boy and girl. Anyway, the bloke drooling all over her is Silas: he's an artist. Then we have Father Todd – I don't need to tell you what he does. And next to him is Juliette who you already know, and her partner, Oliver. He's a famous author. Or he would be if he didn't write under a pen name.' Hattie sucked in a breath and carried on. 'This is Marge, who's a big noise in the WI.' Hattie leant closer to Violet and hissed, 'Women's Institute,' before turning the volume up again. 'And her husband Benny is Chairman of the AA. Allotment Association, before you assume he's got a problem with alcohol. Actually, we've all got a problem with alcohol in that we could do with a top-up. Scarlet!'

Violet jumped as Hattie yelled in her ear, and Logan clutched her hand tighter. This must be overwhelming for her.

'Get us another round, will you?' Hattie called. 'Logan is paying.'

Logan's nod to Scarlet was resigned. 'Soft drinks for these two,' he said, indicating a pair of teenagers.

'I was just coming to them,' Hattie interjected. 'This is Tanesha and Max, apprentices extraordinaire: They were part of my apprentice scheme – the girl works for Nell, the boy works for Silas. You can have a sip of mine later,' she said to them, out of the corner of her mouth.

'No, you can't,' Logan said firmly. He dragged a couple of chairs across from a nearby table, indicated that Violet should sit, and collapsed onto a seat and put a protective arm around her. This lot were formidable en masse. 'What's all this about?' he asked, searching their faces.

'I told him why I've called a meeting, but he clearly didn't listen.' Hattie leant forward and spoke slowly. 'It's about your mother.'

'What about her?'

'She can't go on like this. It's making her ill.'

Logan and Violet exchanged glances.

He wished he didn't have to air his dirty laundry in

public, but the whole village would know sooner or later that he and his mother had fallen out, so they might as well hear the truth from him, and not make up what they didn't know.

He opened his mouth to speak, trying to find the right words, when Father Todd said, 'It's an illness of the soul, she's got, son, not an illness of the body.'

There were nods around the table. Logan closed his mouth. It seemed they already knew.

'She's so scared of losing you, that she's made out she's unwell,' Benny said.

His wife, Marge, said. 'We could see this coming.'

The first fluttering of anger stirred in Logan's chest.

'We all could,' Juliette added. 'Those headaches of hers were always so convenient…' She trailed off, a sympathetic smile on her face.

'I see.' The fluttering was becoming a stiff breeze. 'You all knew, yet none of you thought to share it with me?'

Glances were swapped, then people dropped their gazes. All except Hattie.

'Get off your high horse, Logan,' she said. 'You'd never have believed us. You had to find out for yourself.'

Logan closed his eyes and counted to ten before opening them again. 'You still should have told me,' he insisted.

'Maybe we should have,' Silas conceded, 'but we didn't, so we need to move on.'

'What are *we* moving on to?' Logan wanted to know. And what did this lot have to do with his relationship with his mother.

'We want to help.' This was from Sara.

'How?' He knew he was being blunt but honestly, they were taking this community spirit thing too far.

'Your mum has never – how should I put it? – been one for taking part,' Hattie said.

'She keeps herself to herself,' Marge added.

'Her sole focus is you.' That was from Father Todd. 'And we're not saying that's a bad thing—'

'Yes, we are, Father,' Hattie jumped in. 'Marie needs a hobby. Or a job.'

'She had one.' Logan rubbed a hand across his face.

'Aye, in the Tavern. Where you live and work. She needs to let go of the apron strings and live her own life.' Hattie pursed her lips.

Violet was sitting quietly next to him, and he wondered what she was making of all this. Was she regretting becoming involved with him? She must have sensed the thoughts whirling through his mind, because she said, 'I think it's wonderful you all care so much and you want to help.'

Hattie beamed at her. 'You've got a good bloke there. I've got a lot of time for Logan and I'm thrilled to bits that he's finally fallen in love. Marie should be thrilled too, but she isn't. However,' Hattie held up a hand when the others tried to speak. 'It's our mission to change that.'

'What do you propose?' Logan asked, giving in. There was no point in trying to fight Hattie.

'It's our fault,' she said. 'We knew what your mum was like, but we didn't do anything about it. We didn't try hard enough with her.'

'That's about to change,' Marge said, her eyes gleaming. 'We could always do with an extra pair of hands in the WI.'

'And I'd love some help in the Toy Shop,' Sara said. 'It would be a proper paying job.'

'I'd welcome her into the church,' Father Todd said, and

Logan was about to point out that his mother had never been religious when the vicar added, 'It could do with a good clean, and if she could arrange the flowers on a Sunday, I'd be very grateful.'

'We need to fill her time with other things besides you, Logan,' Hattie said. 'And we need to make her see that Violet isn't a threat to her relationship with you.'

'I don't know…' These were wonderful ideas in theory, but Logan wasn't sure his mother would accept their help, or would want to do any of those things they suggested.

'Let's see, shall we?' Hattie said. 'It won't be easy – your mother is a stubborn whatsit – but she'll come round. What do you say, Violet? Are you prepared to forgive, because you are the one she's hurt the most. Apart from Logan, of course, but she *is* his mum, so…'

'I just want Logan to be happy. That's why I broke up with him in the first place. I could see how much it was hurting him having to look after his mother when she was ill and she disliked me so much.'

Hattie gave her a measured look. Then she nodded. 'Despite everything that he's had to put up with when it comes to Marie, I've never seen Logan as happy as when he was with you. Make sure he stays that way, else you'll have me to answer to.'

'Yes, ma'am.' Violet grinned at her.

'And you,' Hattie turned to Logan. 'Don't let your mother come between you and Violet. Remember what I said about regrets?'

Logan nodded. 'I'm not letting her go.' His arm tightened around Violet; he meant what he said, even if his relationship with his mum couldn't be repaired. One thing had occurred to him as he sat around the table – and that was he couldn't be responsible for his mum's happiness. That was down to her. If she chose to reject Violet, then so be it. He'd love nothing more than to have the two women get on with each other, but if his mother refused then it was her decision.

Something else had also occurred to him, and this hurt deeply – if Marie didn't make an effort to accept Violet, then he'd have no option but to conclude that his happiness mattered less to his mother than her dislike of Violet.

'I think we're done talking,' Hattie said, getting to her feet. 'It's time to stage an intervention.'

This so wasn't a good idea, Logan thought in horror. His mother was going to flip. For some reason, he'd assumed the things they'd discussed this evening would be done slowly, over the course of weeks or months. He hadn't anticipated that everyone would go marching down to his mum's house.

'What are you doing?' he asked, as people finished their drinks and stood up.

'Going home,' Father Todd said. 'My supper is waiting.'

'We're off home, too.' Marge took hold of Benny's elbow. 'I've missed half of *Eastenders* as it is.'

The three teenagers looked relieved to be able to escape, and they were out of the door with their phones in their hands and thumbing their devices furiously before Alfred had managed to scramble to his feet.

'And I've got a cat to see to,' Hattie said. 'Puss will be thinking his throat has been cut if I don't get off home to feed him.'

The others muttered about having things to do, and one by one they sloped off until only Violet, Hattie, and Alfred were left.

'You thought I was going down there right now to sort your mum out, didn't you?' Hatti chortled. 'Your face was a picture. I should have asked Silas to paint it. It could have been called "horrified". I *will* speak to your mum and give her a few home truths, but not tonight. She can stew for a while. It won't do her any harm to think on how badly she's behaved and the damage her selfishness has caused.' Hattie's expression softened. 'She'll come round.'

'What if she doesn't?'

'Then she really will have lost a son.' She gave Violet a meaningful look. 'But I don't think it will come to that. Marie loves you too much to let that happen.' She patted his cheek. 'Because that's what this whole fiasco has been about – love.'

All Logan could do was pray that Hattie was right.

CHAPTER 38

VIOLET

Violet had never had much patience. If anyone ever asked her friends or family what she was like, they would never say that patience was one of her attributes. It was the opposite – her lack of patience was a distinct flaw. As was her forthright, get-up-and-go attitude. She had a lot in common with Hattie in that regard. Which was why she decided to take matters into her own hands, and have another word with Marie.

This time though, she told Logan what she intended to do before she did it.

'Do you think it's a good idea?' he asked. 'Hattie said they were going to stage an intervention – whatever that means.'

'It's been over a week,' Violet pointed out. A week of watching Logan trying to pretend he was OK when he wasn't. A week of Violet trying to compensate for his mother's love, when nothing could replace it. If Marie only knew what she was doing to him… Logan had enough love to go around – the shapes she and Violet occupied in his heart were distinct and separate. That he'd allowed Violet in, didn't mean that Marie was ousted. Why couldn't the woman see that?

'It's not long in the scheme of things,' Logan said. They were in his office finalising the plans for the Halloween party and organising a pop-up bar for Bonfire Night, which would be held in one of the fields on the outskirts of the village. Violet was planning a firework-flavoured gin, and having great fun doing it. So far she'd introduced a smoky quality and some fizz (sparkling gin was simply *the* best thing!) and was experimenting with putting gold and silver leaf in the bottles to represent the fireworks.

'The longer this feud goes on, the worse things will become,' she said.

'It's not a feud; I speak to Mum every day.'

'Have you heard yourself when you're on the phone to her? You sound like you're speaking to a stranger you met on the bus.'

'She's not making it easy.'

'Did you expect her to? She's not old by any means, but she's set in her ways and can't admit she's wrong.'

'She still doesn't like you.'

'I don't care. She's *your* mother, not mine. She doesn't have to like me.' Violet would like nothing more than for her and Marie to be friends, but it clearly wasn't going to happen, so the best she could hope for was that they'd tolerate each other for Logan's sake.

'I want her to like you.' Logan's voice was plaintive, and her heart swelled with love at the way he was hurting.

Violet stepped into his embrace. 'I know you do and I'd like that as well, but it might never happen and we have to be prepared for that.' She kissed him gently, breathing in the delicious scent of him. 'The only thing we can do is try, so let me speak to her.'

She could sense his reluctance in the way he held her. His arms were a rigid cage, as though he was scared to let her go.

'I'm a big girl. Nothing your mum says will hurt me.' Violet was lying; Marie's sharp tongue could hurt her plenty, but not as much as the stilted non-relationship he currently had with his mother was wounding Logan. If all Violet was able to manage was for Logan to see his mum again, it would be enough. Violet wasn't expecting miracles. But neither did she want Logan to have regrets either, and she knew he would should anything happen to Marie in the future. Family rifts weren't nice, and Violet was determined to heal this one.

'I'm still not happy about it,' Logan said, as she attempted to wriggle free of him.

'Let me go – I want to speak to her. If your mother doesn't want to listen or if she slams the door in my face, so be it.'

'She'll listen,' his mother said, and they sprang apart like forbidden lovers, Violet uttering a squeak of surprise.

Marie was standing just inside the open door and looking distinctly uncomfortable and not at all happy to be there. Violet guessed she wasn't finding this easy.

'Mum?' Logan looked startled, but there was hope beneath his wariness.

'I've… um… come to…' Marie ground to a halt.

'Apologise?' he suggested.

'To say I miss you,' Marie said. She let out a squeak of her own when a hand shot out and jabbed her in the ribs. 'Ow.'

'Remember what we talked about,' a voice hissed.

'Hattie, is that you?' Violet asked.

'No. I'm not here,' Hattie called back from the depths of the corridor.

Logan blinked and Marie rolled her eyes. 'For pity's sake,' she said.

'For *your* sake. Pity has got nothing to do with it.' Hattie jabbed her again. 'Get on with it.'

'OK, I've come to apologise,' Marie said to Logan, glancing at Violet as she did so, leaving Violet in no doubt as to who the apology was meant for.

Hattie came into view. 'You've got to sound as though you mean it.'

'I *do*.'

'It don't blasted sound like it.'

'I'm *sorry*, OK? Happy now?'

'I've been happy all along,' Hattie retorted sharply. 'It's you who's a miserable cow.'

'Who are you calling a cow?'

'If the cap fits—'

'Ladies!' Logan raised his voice and the two women fell silent. Violet put a hand over her mouth to stop herself from laughing.

'Mum, are you really sorry?' he asked.

His mother looked at the floor. 'Yes.' Her voice was so quiet it could barely be heard.

'Speak up, he can't hear you, and neither can Violet.' Hattie folded her arms across her chest. 'If you don't mean it, there's no point in saying it. Shall we go, and come back another day?' Hattie shook her head. 'I'm trying, Logan, I really am, but your mother is hard work. The stupid woman is in the wrong, but she won't bloody admit it. Talk about cutting off your nose to spite your face. This one has cut off her whole head. Or is it your heart that's bleeding?' This last was said to Marie, whose expression was thunderous.

Hattie sighed loudly. 'If I didn't know she loved you to the moon and back, I'd say she doesn't have one at all. Come on, you—' she grabbed hold of Marie's arm '—I'm taking you home. When you feel you can give Logan an apology – and Violet, mind, because she deserves one as well – I'll bring you back.'

'Hattie Jenkins, you're not the boss of me. Stop treating me like a child and telling me what to do.' Marie glowered at her.

'I'll stop treating you like a child when you stop behaving like one. Honestly,' she said to Logan, 'I should have taken her in hand years ago, when she started all that silly business when you were courting Mrs Hamilton's granddaughter. I could see the way the wind was blowing then, but I didn't do anything about it.'

Logan sat heavily on the edge of his desk, scattering papers. 'It wasn't your place to do anything. I should have been firmer with her.'

'You were just a boy – what did you know? And it *was* my place. Marie is part of Ticklemore, so she's *my* business, Father Todd's business, Silas's business – although he hadn't moved to the village at that point. We're all everyone else's business: that's what living in Ticklemore is all about. So Marie, get over yourself because you're not getting rid of me, or anyone else in the village. Apart from Logan – because if you carry on the way you're going you *will* lose him. What do you say to that?'

Marie swallowed several times and Violet wondered whether she was biting back anger or tears. Her cheeks were red but her head was down, so Violet couldn't tell which emotion she was feeling. Heck, Violet wasn't sure how she felt about this herself. Talk about weird…

'I am sorry,' Marie said, her voice low. There was a distinct lack of her usual belligerence. 'I was worried. I still am, if I'm honest. I don't like change – we were all right on our own, weren't we, Logan? The two of us against the world? I had you and you had me, and we didn't need anyone else.'

Logan went to say something, but Hattie intervened. 'Let her say her piece: it's been a long time coming.

Marie carried on. 'That was all well and good when you were little, but not when you got older. I can see that now. I wanted you to be my little boy forever, but little boys grow up into handsome men, and they start taking an interest in girls, and then before you know it, they've gone out into the big wide world and left you all on your own.'

'I didn't, though. I stayed in Ticklemore. And I didn't date much—'

'—because I didn't let you,' Marie finished.

'I could have if I'd wanted to,' Logan said. 'And I did, when I found someone I truly cared about.' His smile was gentle. 'Just because I love Violet doesn't mean to say I love you less.'

'I know,' Marie said.

'She took some convincing, mind,' Hattie added. 'We all had a go – me, Father Todd, Marge, Nell, Juliette, Silas…'

Violet was listening intently, but as she did so she was also studying the play of emotion across Marie's face, and Violet understood that this was only the first small step on what might prove to be a long journey. Marie might be saying all the right things, but whether she truly believed them was another matter.

But it *was* progress, and as long as Violet and Marie could rub along together and Logan was happy, Violet was content. She and Marie would probably never be the best of friends, but they didn't need to be. If Hattie came through with her promise, then Marie would have more friends than she knew what to do with, and activities aplenty to keep her occupied.

Which would leave Violet and Logan free to get on with loving each other.

Because, after all, love was the only thing that mattered.

CHAPTER 39

LOGAN

Logan stood back to admire the array of cobwebs, pumpkins, skulls, spiders, skeletons and other assorted paraphernalia that a successful Halloween party simply had to have, according to Violet. Between them, she and Scarlet had transformed the Tavern into a rather attractive dungeon, decorating anything that didn't move and some things that did.

Lucas himself was sporting a green face and bolts through his neck. He didn't think the look suited him. Even the coat stand by the door had been tampered with, and was now a swamp tree dripping with moss and cobwebs, and Logan hoped no one wanted to hang a coat on there.

He might be looking decidedly dodgy, but Violet looked delectable in her witch's outfit. With her purple hair, she looked the part, and the faint green tinge to her skin made her eyes pop, their intense navy colour stealing his breath. God, he was such a lucky, lucky man, and every day he was thankful she was in his life.

The pub was filling up, and Logan shook himself out of

his reverie to go and serve his customers. It was all hands on deck this evening as every ticket had been sold. Franklin had excelled himself with the food, which had been included in the price of the ticket, as had the first drink, and Logan had even managed to set up a dance area in the function room so customers could have a bop if they fancied it.

'They're here.' Violet scurried over, her cloak wafting out behind her. In one hand she clutched a bottle of black gin and in the other she was holding a broomstick. A cuddly toy in the form of a black cat was attached to the brush part. It didn't look happy.

Violet, however, did. She was glowing, despite the green make-up; her eyes shone and she had a big grin on her face.

Logan wished he could smile like that, but the most he could summon was a feeble twitch of his lips. It was a big deal meeting your future wife's parents for the first time (he hadn't proposed to Violet yet, but he would do – and sooner rather than later), especially when dressed as Frankenstein's monster. He'd read the book some years ago, and he felt a degree of sympathy for the poor creature. Logan just hoped he'd get a better reception from Violet's parents than Violet had got from his mother.

Speaking of which, he could see Marie lurking near the door behind the coat stand, trying to blend in with the draped moss; difficult because she'd come as Little Bo Peep and was wearing an incredibly colourful and voluminous outfit. If he was honest, she was more pantomime dame than shepherd girl, but if she was happy, then so was he.

Mr and Mrs Archer had come as Gomez and Morticia out of the Adams' Family, Rory was Cousin It and was wearing what looked like fifty mop heads sewn together which must be incredibly hot. Sam, Logan surmised, was

Pugsley, which explained why Yasmine was wearing a wig made of long black plaits, as she must be Wednesday, and Beth was… actually what *was* Beth supposed to be? Logan didn't like to ask, but her costume was quite strange and rather disturbing; she had a plastic severed hand on her head.

'She's Thing,' Violet said seeing his double-take. 'Yes, I know it looks as though she's giving everyone the finger, and knowing Beth she probably is. Mum, Dad…' Violet went in for a hug and a kiss.

Logan nodded at Rory and Sam, who both nodded back. Beth wasn't as reserved and she swooped on him, her lips puckered. He obligingly kissed her cheek, then his eyes met Violet's father's and he shuffled self-consciously from foot to foot.

'Logan, I presume?' the man said, sticking his hand out. Logan took it and they shook. He hoped his palm wasn't as damp as he thought it might be.

'Nice to meet you,' Mr Archer added, and Logan prayed he was telling the truth and not simply being polite. Crumbs, this was nerve-wracking and it scared him how much he wanted Violet's parents to like him.

'We've heard such a lot about you,' Violet's mum said, pushing her husband out of the way and linking her arm through Logan's. 'Get me a drink and tell me all about yourself. You're the first boyfriend Violet has allowed us to meet, so you must be special.'

'He's incredibly special, Mum,' Violet said, disentangling their arms. 'You can chat with him later. I've got something I want him to see.'

'Thanks for rescuing me,' Logan said, as soon as they were out of earshot. 'They seemed lovely, but I've got customers to serve.'

'I really do want you to see something,' Violet said. 'I've made you your very own gin.'

'That's very thoughtful of you. Can you show me later?' He looked at the bar, where his staff were rushed off their feet.

'There mightn't be any left.'

'It's proving popular then?'

'With a certain person…'

'Who?'

Violet pointed. To Logan's surprise, his mother had a bottle of deep red liquid in one hand and a half-full glass in the other. His mother had studiously avoided tasting any of Violet's gin – until now.

'She seems to be coming round a bit,' he said. 'What flavour is it? I'll make sure I keep a bottle on hand especially for her, if she fancies a tipple now and again.'

Violet was hanging off his arm, her face glowing with mischief. 'It's called Logan Gin. I made it especially for you. Except—' she began to laugh '—I saw her looking at it earlier and when she asked about it, I told her I'd made it for her as a gift. I thought she might appreciate it.'

From where Logan was standing, it seemed his mother certainly did.

When Marie saw them staring at her, she raised a glass and called, 'To Logan,' adding, 'And Violet,' as an afterthought. Then she smiled at her, a genuine smile.

It wasn't much, and it might only be the gin talking, but it was a start, and everything had to start somewhere.

VIOLET

Violet knew that this was the start of her and Logan's journey through life, with their respective families and friends by their sides. She also knew that one day soon, not yet, but not too far in the future, Logan was going to ask her to marry him and she would say yes.

She'd already started to make a wedding day gin…

THE END

Acknowledgements

Husband, of course, because he sees more of the top of my laptop than he does of my face most days (mind you, he might say that's a good thing!)

Catherine Mills, as always, for her unstinting enthusiasm for my stories and her willingness to gently put me right when I've drifted off course.

Mum for reading my stuff, Daughter for promising to (and for listening to me wittering about formatting when she has no idea what I'm rabbiting on about)

And my readers. Thank you for loving my books and making all the blood, sweat and tears – OK, coffee, sleepless nights and snivelling – worth it.

Liz x

ABOUT THE AUTHOR

Liz Davies writes feel-good, light-hearted stories with a hefty dose of romance, a smattering of humour, and a great deal of love.

She's married to her best friend, has one grown-up daughter, and when she isn't scribbling away in the notepad she carries with her everywhere (just in case inspiration strikes), you'll find her searching for that perfect pair of shoes. She loves to cook but isn't very good at it, and loves to eat - she's much better at that! Liz also enjoys walking (preferably on the flat), cycling (also on the flat), and lots of sitting around in the garden on warm, sunny days.

She currently lives with her family in Wales, but would ideally love to buy a camper van and travel the world in it.

Social Media Links:
Twitter https://twitter.com/lizdaviesauthor
Facebook: fb.me/LizDaviesAuthor1